THE AUTHOR

HENRY KREISEL was born in Vienna in 1922, and received his elementary and secondary schooling there. Following the Nazi occupation of 1938 he escaped, with the help of relatives, and fled to England. He got work in a textile factory in Leeds. Because of his Austrian nationality he was interned in 1941 and sent to Canada. He was released after a year and entered the University of Toronto, where as an undergraduate he led his class in the field of English Language and Literature. He took his Master's degree in 1947, and in 1954 got his Ph.D from the University of London. He is now professor of English at the University of Alberta.

Since the publication of *The Rich Man* in 1948, he has published short stories in *Prism*, *Queen's Quarterly*, and in the collection *Klanak Islands*. Some of his stories have appeared in anthologies and have been translated into German and Italian. His stories have also been read on the C.B.C. program "Anthology," and in 1960 he was awarded the President's Medal of the University of Western Ontario for his story "The Travelling Nude." He has written radio plays for C.B.C. "Wednesday Night" and C.B.C. "Stage." And his critical articles have appeared in *Tamarack Review*, *Queen's Quarterly*, *Canadian Forum*, and *Dalhousie Review*. In 1960 he was elected a Fellow of the International Institute of Arts and Letters.

HENRY KREISEL

THE

RICH MAN

INTRODUCTION — JOHN STEDMOND

GENERAL EDITOR — MALCOLM ROSS

NEW CANADIAN LIBRARY NO. 24

MCCLELLAND AND STEWART LIMITED

The following dedication
appeared in the original edition:

To My Parents
Helen and David Kreisel
and to
Omama Toni Mendel

PRINTED AND BOUND BY
HAZELL WATSON AND VINEY LTD
AYLESBURY AND SLOUGH ENGLAND

INTRODUCTION

ONE of the recurring patterns in fiction is the quest, the journey to strange lands, the search for new frontiers. Jacob Grossman, the central character in Henry Kreisel's novel *The Rich Man*, had started on such a journey thirty-three years before the story begins. Canada was his destination; Toronto the place where he put down roots. The opposite curve of the quest myth is the return, the voyage home, the pilgrimage. It is with this phase of Jacob's story that the novel is mainly concerned. At one level he is a modern Ulysses of the Leopold Bloom stamp. Essentially he is a passive man who has all his life been dominated by women : his mother, his eldest sister, Manya, his wife, his daughters.

Jacob is fifty-two. He had left his native Galicia when he was nineteen. In the novel he makes his way not to the small village where he was born, but to Vienna, the capital city to which his family had fled in 1915 during the violent break-up of the Austro-Hungarian empire. In one of its aspects the novel is a tale of two cities : Toronto and Vienna. The former is sketched only briefly; it does not have much character. As a city it seems to have made surprisingly little impression on Jacob, even though he has worked there most of his adult life, has married there, raised a family, and buried a wife. But Vienna is something else again. Even before he sees it for the first time, it already figures vividly in his imagination as a city where there is music and dancing in the streets, the city of the Blue Danube, interwoven with nostalgic emotion and Hollywood sentiment. In this year of 1935 it is also, of course, a city uncomfortably close to Hitler's Germany. Part of Jacob's anxiety to visit his relatives undoubtedly springs from ominous accounts of new violence breaking out in Europe.

In a sense Jacob is the naïve citizen of the New World who goes back to the land of his forefathers and in the process loses his innocence. In many ways he is still the country boy who set foot in New York years before. Only after his return to Europe does he seem to become aware of the possible heights and depths of human experience. But when he first sets out from Toronto he is quite well satisfied with himself. Through thrift and hard work he has managed to set up his son as a doctor and to provide sufficient education and dowry to marry his two daughters to acceptable husbands. The farther he gets from Canada, though, the less satisfactory do his modest accomplishments seem. Even before he leaves, in fact, he reveals a latent urge to put on a new identity for the journey by buying for himself a white alpaca suit. Almost unconsciously he is already playing the rôle of affluent American.

His self-esteem receives its first blow in his encounter with Tassigny, the French artist, on the voyage over. At first he is much flattered to be noticed by this obviously talented man, but frustration ensues when he tries to communicate with him on any but the most superficial level. He can protect his aura of self-satisfaction only by donning the mantle of patron of the arts and buying one of Tassigny's paintings, albeit one he neither understands nor admires. He has learned in the New World the levelling power of money. But the picture he buys is like his white suit—a futile status symbol. Significantly the picture is entitled *L'Entrepreneur* and portrays a faceless man with a megaphone for a head, an empty man with a siren voice. The portrait represents both Madison Avenue and Big Brother. Jacob can neither come to terms with this image nor escape it. He is haunted by it to the very end of the story, and his last recorded act is an attempt to exorcise it.

When he meets his past—his aged mother and the sisters he has not seen for so long—he immediately wants to be important in their eyes, to be the sort of person they obviously think he is. To them, his poor relations, he symbolizes the riches of the New World. The success which they imagine he has achieved in the fabulous land across the sea somehow offsets their own dingy existence. His good fortune proves at least that such things *can* happen. Jacob is flesh and blood evidence of the reality of the seemingly legendary world where dreams come true—where aliens are not only accepted but in fact become rich and powerful.

Jacob at first enjoys to the full the rôle of rich relative. He has no qualms about participating in what seems like a harmless deception. After all, like the trip itself, it is only one more means of making his mother happy in her declining years. His own son, who will carry on the family name, he has made a professional man. His mother must be given the satisfaction of thinking that her parental efforts, too, have borne tangible fruit. And certainly, to Jacob, the impecunious presser of suits in a clothing factory, the deference with which he is treated by his relatives and their friends is sweet indeed.

At the structural centre of the novel is the scene in the "cave" in the public park, the secret hide-out to which Jacob is taken by his two young nephews, the sons of his youngest sister, Shaendl. Here they can crouch unseen and observe the world outside. But the tranquillity is rudely shattered by the intrusion of the young toughs who commit the only overt acts of anti-Semitism in the entire novel. Here in essence is the novel's theme: Jacob's desire to revisit the sheltered world of childhood, but in the rôle of protector rather than protected—a wish that can be granted only in a world of make-believe in which responsibility can be evaded, a world which must be shattered by the first impact of harsh reality.

Ironically, the only other person in the novel who has assumed a different identity is Koch, the political journalist. He too had sought shelter for a time in the cave-like room at the back of the bookshop run by Shaendl's husband, Albert. He emerges in the guise of a clown to carry on his underground activities against the dictatorial regime which he hates. But his disguise, like Jacob's, proves inadequate.

Tragic circumstance calls Jacob's bluff. The money he does not have is needed with desperate urgency. His pleasant world of make-believe is transformed into nightmare. We soon realize that Jacob lacks more than money. He lacks the ability to sacrifice. He sees the troubles of his relatives chiefly in terms of effects on his own position. He is sorrier for himself than he is for them. His main suffering stems finally from the fact that his mother will have to know that her son is not rich and successful, and it is not her disillusionment which bothers him so much as his own humiliation. His principal efforts at the end are not to ease the terrible plight of his widowed sister, but rather to delay as long as possible his own unmasking.

In the final analysis he is too concerned with his own comforts—of both body and mind—to be capable of a genuine act of self-denial. One of his great regrets is that he will not be able to put the plight of his European relatives out of his mind, will not be able to escape a feeling of guilt at his inability to help them. It requires very little imagination to visualize his contrition in later years when these same relatives are swallowed up, as they inevitably will be, by the hungry maw of the gas chamber.

By escaping to the promised land Jacob has been able to provide for himself and for his children. But those left behind in Europe look to him and his kind for succour. Yet he can come to them only as a tourist, a sight-seer, not as a saviour, or even as a fellow-sufferer. The only gesture he now knows how to make—and the one he goes through agonies at not being able to make—is a financial one. He wants to distribute largesse. And he wants to do this not only to relieve their sufferings, but also, and perhaps more immediately, to prove his own worth—to give tangible evidence of his status.

Thirteen years after its first publication, *The Rich Man* has dated remarkably little, partially because it does not stress details of historical background but concentrates on the human beings in the foreground. The members of the Grossman family are what we care about, rather than the fact that they are living in Vienna in the ominous 1930's. The violence and bitterness to come hover in the air which the characters breathe, lurk as shadows in the wings, but come on stage only fleetingly. Shaendl's husband Albert is killed accidentally. Koch is taken off to prison, but we are given only a newspaper account of his capture. The atmosphere of a world spread-eagled between wars pervades the novel and adds overtones to each of its events, but the story in a sense exists independent of its time and place.

The Rich Man is a first novel. Its author, Henry Kreisel, was himself born in Vienna, He left there for England in 1938, when he was sixteen. At the outbreak of war, being technically an enemy alien, he was interned in Canada. In 1942 he was freed and was able to enrol at the University of Toronto. He now teaches English Literature (and continues with his own writing) at the University of Alberta in Edmonton.

JOHN STEDMOND

Queen's University
Kingston, Ontario

CHAPTER

I

WHEN Jacob Grossman woke up and looked at the clock which was standing on a chair beside his bed, his first thought was that he should have been at work half an hour ago. But then he remembered that he hadn't set the alarm last night. He had a special thing to do and he wanted to do it in a special way. He would get down to the factory about eleven and go straight to Mr Duncan's office. "Mr Duncan," he would say, shaking the manager's hand, "Mr Duncan. . . ." And then what? How would he go on? It was difficult to find the right words. Ah! If he could talk to him in Yiddish, everything would be fine. But in English!

He got out of bed slowly and began to dress. If he could only ask his daughter, she would be able to tell him what to say, but she thought he was crazy and she hadn't spoken to him since their big quarrel three days ago. A silly girl! A foolish girl!

He reached mechanically for his shabby old pair of pants which, as usual, he had thrown over the back of a chair before going to bed, and put them on. No! he thought suddenly, no! How would he look coming into Duncan's office in these old pants with the patch on the left knee so clearly visible? Like a nobody, like a . . . like a . . . He couldn't think of another fitting term. No! He would have to dress up a little. Not the black suit, because that would be too formal, like going to a funeral or a wedding, but the brown one, the business suit. He took off his pants and got his brown suit from the closet. He was a short, narrow-shouldered, pot-bellied man. His face was round and of a reddish colour, a bit flabby and wrinkled, and there was a large bald spot on the pate of his head. He might be fifty or sixty. It was difficult to tell his age.

He went out into the bathroom to shave. The radio was on in the kitchen downstairs and he could hear Rosie moving about. Then his little grandson began to cry, and she said in a soothing voice, "All right, all right, all right. Just a minute, dear, just a minute. Your cereal will be ready in just a minute."

Wasn't she at all curious to know why he hadn't gone to work? Why hadn't she come up to see? Perhaps he was sick.

What if she *was* mad at him? What business was it of hers in the first place? He could do what he wanted. He was old enough to make his own decisions.

His blade pulled. He searched about in the medicine cabinet for a new packet of razor blades but couldn't find one, and went on grimly scraping his cheeks with the dull blade. The baby had stopped crying. Rosie must be feeding him now. Over the air came the record of a Negro quartet, singing "Swing Low, Sweet Chariot." Their voices were deep and infinitely sad. "Coming for to carry me home." One by one the voices fell away until only a full-throated bass voice was left, carrying the last note, and then it too ebbed away. "And here, folks, to wind up this half hour of the melodies you love to hear, is a modern arrangement of that old favourite—The Blue Danube Waltz." It was a jazz version of the old tune, hammered out very fast and loud, all brass and drums. Jacob loved the waltz, but not when it was played like that. He wanted a lot of violins, hundreds of them, the way it was always done in movies about gay Vienna. He finished shaving and went back to his room. There was a moment's silence on the radio, and then the suave voice of the announcer again, "Here is a brief news report, compiled and edited in the newsroom of CFRB." Jacob opened his door in order to hear better.

"Air Minister Herman Goering of Germany said yesterday that rearmament is Germany's greatest contribution to world peace, because it is purely defensive.

"In Britain and throughout the Commonwealth preparations are almost completed for the celebration next Tuesday, May 7, of the twenty-fifth anniversary of King George V's accession to the throne.

"The Chamber of Commerce in the United States came out in strong opposition to President Roosevelt's reform legislation. In nine out of sixteen resolutions the administration was censured for what the new president of the Chamber called going too far."

The voice on the radio droned on, but Jacob wasn't listening any more. He was dressed now, and ready to go. Rosie was busy at the stove and didn't see him immediately when he came into the kitchen. The baby was sitting in a high-chair, a large bib tied around his neck, banging away with a big spoon. Jacob beamed at the child and then bent down and kissed it. Rosie turned round and for a moment stood there, flabbergasted, staring at her father. She was a young, rather pretty girl of twenty-three.

"Well," she said, putting her palms against her hips and forgetting that she was not officially on speaking terms with him. "Well. Where on earth did you come from? I thought you'd gone to work long ago. Why—why, it's almost nine o'clock."

Jacob sat down at the table. "I em not going to vork today," he announced, and it seemed to her that there was a slight challenge in the way he said it.

"Fancy that," she said. Suddenly she noticed the suit he was wearing. "I didn't know there was a holiday on the third of May. Nobody ever told me about it."

"Who said somet'ing about a holiday?" he said naïvely. "It's a ord'nary day."

"So! Well, then, I guess they've made you general manager. It's about time, too. Con-gra-tu-lations!"

He ignored her last remark. "I'm hongry," he said.

There was a box of cornflakes on the table. She gave him a bowl and he filled it up and poured milk over it. The baby kept on banging the spoon against the chair and she was getting nervous. "Oh, stop the noise, Joey," she cried and took the spoon away. The child started to bawl in protest, and she cut off a piece of bread and gave it to him. He got busy chewing the crust and was quiet. She stood there, watching her father eat. What could he be up to? Where could he be going? She had a slight suspicion, but she couldn't be sure. Busying herself again at the stove, and with her back toward him, she asked casually, "Where are you going, all dressed up like that?"

Jacob chuckled. "Hah! I t'ought you vas not talkink to me." She bit her lip. "All right. Don't tell me. See if I care."

"You ken know," he said with a magnanimous wave of his hand. "I'm not keepink no secrets from nobody. Where am I going? Where you t'ink I'm going? I'm going to the shop— You got a cup of coffee maybe?"

She filled a cup and gave it to him. "To the shop?" she asked, looking him full in the face. "At this hour? And all dressed up? What's going on?"

"Not'ing," he said, "ebsolutely not'ing. I'm goink to speak mit Mistah Donken, an' I ken't come to him lookink like a tramp."

"Duncan? He's the general manager, isn't he?"

Jacob nodded his head.

"What—what're you going to see him about?" she asked, suspicion rising in her voice.

"Vat you t'ink? Ef a person vants to go 'vay fa six-seven viks, he got to esk the manager, no?"

She didn't answer for a few moments, but kept looking at

him. It was obvious that she was getting excited. "So you're really going to do it?" she said finally, her voice ominously low. "You're really going to take a thousand dollars and throw them away just like that, to—to satisfy a foolish notion, just because you—"

"This here is no foolish notion," he interrupted her sharply, suddenly switching to Yiddish. "You think it is a foolish notion. All right. But to me it is not a foolish notion. And in the second place I haven't got no thousand dollars, so I can't spend no thousand dollars."

"So it isn't a thousand dollars," she cried, "so it's seven hundred dollars or six hundred dollars. It's a lot of money whichever way you look at it."

"Don't shout, Rosie," he said. "Don't get excited."

"Who's shouting?" she cried. "Who's getting excited? Go ahead and do it. See if I care." She turned away abruptly, went over to the radio and switched it off. Then she sat down, trying to calm herself.

Jacob leaned his elbows on the table. "A person listening to you," he said slowly, "would think I'm taking away your money. Who earned the money, I ask you? You worked hard and saved up every nickel, or I? So I want to throw away money, like you say! All right. Whose money am I throwing away, your money or my money?"

"Sure it's your money," she replied heatedly, "sure you worked hard to earn it. Have I ever denied it? That's just why I'm against your spending it like that—all at one throw."

"Don't do me no favours," he said pointedly.

"I'm not doing you any favours," she snapped. "Times are bad, lots of people are out of work, business is slow, and you can't think of anything better to do than to take hundreds of dollars and throw them away." She was all worked up now. "My father," she cried sarcastically. "A rich man! A millionaire!"

He made no answer to that, but kept on drinking his coffee slowly. Then he leaned over and began to play with the baby, completely ignoring Rosie.

This infuriated her even more, and she went on with great bitterness. "Two months ago when Morris asked you for a loan of five hundred dollars so he could get some more stock and try to make a better go of the business, what did you say? 'Five hundred dollars!' you said, 'I can't spare no five hundred dollars. What do you think I am? President of the Bank of

Commerce?' But now—now that you want to go on a pleasure trip, now suddenly you can spare the money."

He felt the need to defend himself, and he turned his head to her. "This here is no pleasure trip, Rosie," he said, "and I couldn't give no money to Morris because I need it for myself, that's why. You think I decided last week all of a sudden?" He shook his head violently. "Ha-ha-ha. For years, Rosie, for years this has been going around and around in my head. This didn't start yesterday. But how could I ever do it? You children were small, David had to go to the university—"

"Sure," she cried, "sure. It was always David, David, David in this family. David this and David that. David had to be a doctor, no less, and so everybody else had to take a back seat. Ella and I never counted as much as that." She snapped her fingers at him. Her voice was tear-choked and suddenly she went over to the high-chair, took the baby in her arms and held him close to her. "You and Mom thought only about David."

"This is not true," he said, raising his hand as if he were swearing an oath. "David wanted to be a doctor, so your mother (may she rest in peace) and I wanted to help him. Girls get married. A son is different. He carries on the name. He brings honour."

"That's about all," she said, blowing her nose. "Honour. He hasn't made any money yet."

"What you expect? He has only had an office six—seven months. He'll earn money. Don't you worry."

"He should, after all the money that was spent on him. I bet he got a hundred times more money than Ella and me put together."

"It's a lie," he said vehemently. "Didn't you and Ella finish high school? And when you got married didn't we give you as much as we could?"

"A fat lot that was. What'd we get? A bedroom suite and a couple of hundred dollars, that's what we got."

"If I had had more, I would've given you more."

"Sure," she said derisively. "So I see. As soon as you have a bit of money, you go on pleasure trips."

He threw up his hands in despair. "Noo," he said abruptly, "what's the use talking to you? You don't understand. You're a young girl, and you don't understand." He got up and walked towards the door, but before he went out into the hall he turned and pointed his finger at the baby. "Wait," he said, "wait till Joey is grown up and maybe has been away for a long time, and then you will understand."

"I understand all right," she said, instinctively pressing the child closer to her. "I understand plenty. All I can say is what I told you three days ago. You're—you're crazy, that's all."

"Sure I'm crazy," he said, turning to go. "I'm crazy, like Einstein, that's how crazy I am."

He took his hat and coat and, somewhat agitated, stepped out of the house. The street, in one of the poorer districts of Toronto, was fairly deserted at this hour of the morning. A few women, sloppily dressed, were going home, carrying bags of groceries, and here and there small children were playing in the weedy, narrow little front yards of old, shabby-looking brick houses. Jacob felt strange, walking about all dressed up on an ordinary working day. He felt self-conscious and almost expected people to stare at him and stop him to ask where he was going and why he was not at work. Rosie's words still stung him, and he began to wonder whether he was after all doing the right thing.

He walked over to Bathurst and College to take a streetcar down to the factory. When he got to this corner early in the morning, there were always crowds of people waiting to get on, and the streetcars were always jammed, so that it was often necessary for him to let several cars go by before he could squeeze his way into one. But now there were only two or three people waiting, and when the streetcar stopped, Jacob noticed, with a certain amount of satisfaction, that it was half-empty.

The car went past the Western Hospital, past Dundas Street, past Queen Street, and Jacob decided to get off and walk the rest of the way. He grew somewhat apprehensive and fidgety as he came closer to the factory. It was not so much that he was nervous about talking with Mr Duncan. After all, he was an old employee, Duncan knew him, had often exchanged words with him when he came round, looking to see how things were going. It was rather that Jacob knew that once he had settled his business with Duncan, there could then be no going back for him. Thus much he had resolved in the last three days while he was seriously pondering the problem. No matter what Rosie might say then, it would not shake him. After all— he had to admit this—Rosie was not wholly wrong. He was going to spend a lot of money, all at one throw. There were moments when he felt uneasy, and though he was strongly determined to do finally what he had so long dreamed of doing, he could not resolve all his doubts.

The big factory building, with the words PERFECT CLOTHES

LTD spelled out in huge black letters against the sky, now rose before him. He hesitated a moment when he came to the front entrance, and then decided to go into the factory through the side door where the workers entered. He might as well talk with his own foreman first before going to see Duncan.

He swung open the door. There, against the walls, were the time clocks, and instinctively his eyes wandered to the rack where his own time card was. It was there, No. 1003, standing lonely in the left-hand rack beside one of the clocks. He walked quickly past it and up the stairs into the plant. The familiar smell of the factory, the stale smell of cloth, mingled with the steam of the Hoffman presses and the sweat of hundreds of workers, enveloped him, and a familiar noise, the steady, vibrating hum of whirring sewing machines broke against his ears.

The Hoffman presses took up the far side of the second floor. This was the hottest part of the factory. Jacob's eyes picked out his own machine, standing idle in the first row. Sydney Black, the foreman, who was making in his way slowly between the long rows of machines, saw him walking up, and, grinning broadly, shouted, "Well, well, look who's coming! Hello, Jake! Since when did you start keeping bank directors' hours, eh? What's up, Jake?"

Jacob came over to him. "Shhh,'" he said. "Don' shout, Syd. Everyt'ing is okay."

A few of the men stopped working and called to Jacob, and he answered them.

"All kidding aside," said Black, "what's going on? What're you all rigged up for, eh?"

"I'm goink in to see Donken," said Jacob. "I got to talk mit him. You t'ink he's busy?"

"How do I know? I only look after this section. Duncan is old enough to look after himself. What you got to see the big shot about, anyway?"

"I—I'm gonnaway fa a few viks," Jacob said, raising his voice imperceptibly, "so I got to see Donken."

Black looked surprised. "Where you going?"

"I'm goink to Europe," Jacob announced slowly.

Black started. One of the men close to Jacob burst into laughter. "Jake, you sure are a card, ha-ha-ha. Hey, boys, you hear this? Jake Grossman is going to Europe Ha-ha-ha. Hey, Jake, what you using for money these days?"

"Green toilet paper," said Jacob.

There was a great deal of laughter all round. Jacob was well liked. He was the oldest of the pressers, and he was known as a good sport and a great joker. But now he was embarrassed because they thought he was merely playing a game.

"Let's cut the monkey business, you guys," the foreman broke in. "It was a good joke, but it's getting stale. Come on, Jake, get to work. You've lost three hours' pay already. Break it up now."

Jacob looked quickly at Black. "Money, money," he said, sing-songing the words and swaying his body slowly from side to side. "So I lose a few cents. Noo, Syd, noo?"

A young chap who was working at a machine just behind where Jacob was standing laughed out loud and said, "Sure, what's a few bucks to a guy like Jake? You fellows keep forgetting that his full name happens to be J. Rockefeller Grossman."

There was a renewed outburst of laughter, and Jacob, a bit red in the face, turned round. "Money, money, vork, vork," he said. "Vork a little less, Hymie, you'll vork plenty in your life. Look at me. I vorked here for t'irty-t'ree years. Noo?" He raised his brows and leaned his head a little to the side. The word *Noo* was the richest and most expressive word in his vocabulary. He could play with this little word like a virtuoso. He could thunder it in a loud bass, and he could whisper it softly, drawing it out gently. He could pronounce it sharply, almost threateningly, like a stab, and he could speak it lightly and playfully, modulating his sing-song, his voice wavering and trembling until it died away like the closing notes of a sad aria. In the mouth of Jacob Grossman this little sound was capable of expressing the profoundest emotions and the most delicate shades of meaning.

Black suddenly had an idea. "I know," he cried, pointing his finger at Jacob. "I bet you're trying to get a raise. That's why you're all dressed up."

"You talk childish like. Ef a person vears a suit wit' no patches or a jacket that is the same colour of the pants, he mus' be vanting a raise. You t'ink Donken vill give me a raise because I am vell dressed up? It's a good joke." He dismissed the subject with a short laugh and a downward motion of his hands.

Black looked puzzled. "Say, what is this? Are you really on the level?"

"You don't believe me?"

Black didn't want to commit himself. "I don't know. Maybe you're on the up and up. It's always hard to tell when you're joking and when you're serious."

"Ef you don' believe me, you don' believe me." He shrugged his shoulders. "Noo," he said, "there's no percentage talkink mit you. I'm going to see Donken now."

They looked after him, puzzled and uncertain.

He went up another flight of stairs and then along a corridor that led into the administrative wing of the building. Here the air was clear and there was no noise, and the employees hurrying to and fro with papers wore their coats. The floors and the walls were of pale-green marble, cool-looking and clean. Duncan's office was at the end of the hall. There was a little anteroom with a few chairs, and a stenographer who also acted as receptionist was sitting at her typewriter.

Jacob asked to see the manager.

"Have you an appointment?"

"No."

"What name, please?"

"Jacob Grossman. I'm a presser."

"What do you want to see Mr Duncan about?"

He hesitated a moment. "It—it's a private affair," he said, lowering his voice.

"Can't your foreman or the department manager help you?"

"No," he said firmly. "I have to see Mistah Donken."

She went into the inner office.

"He'll be busy for about fifteen minutes," she said when she came out again. "You can wait if you wish."

"T'anks," he said.

He sat down and began to hum softly to himself—a slow, sad, chanting melody, and the fingers of his left hand tapped out the melancholy rhythm on the arm of the chair. After what seemed a very long fifteen minutes, the door of the inner office was opened, and Duncan beckoned him to come in.

Jacob Grossman went shyly into the office. He walked slowly to the chair which the manager offered him and sat down clumsily. Duncan asked him what he wanted, but he did not answer immediately. He was thinking hard, trying to find the right beginning. He stammered a few words and then he was quiet. He fumbled about in his pockets for nothing in particular and brought his hands out empty. Twice, without opening his lips, he began to talk with his hands, but dropped them again. At last a smile broke over his clouded face and he said, "I vished I could talk in Yiddish mit you, Mistah Donken. It is not good for me to talk in English over serious t'ings. English is all right to make a joke or kibitz wit' the boys. But over

17

serious t'ings it is good to talk in the modder language. I'm right, Mistah Donken, no?"

Duncan smiled. "I'll understand," he said. "You just go ahead."

"Mistah Donken, I come to ask you for a long holiday because I am goink to the old contry. To Austria, Mistah Donken. In six—seven viks, mit God's help, I'll be back."

Duncan sat up in his chair and looked into the tired, twinkling eyes of Jacob Grossman. "Oh!" he said. Just that one word. If the small, pudgy man sitting before him had not looked at him with such a determined, searching gaze, he would have thought that he was being fooled.

Jacob nodded his head slowly. "Yeah." He did not use his hands. They lay stretched out on the desk now, rough hands, hands tired after a lifetime of labour. And now they looked like strangers because he was expressing something in which they had no part. "I—I em gettink to be old, Mistah Donken," he said. He tried to make his voice sound impersonal, casual, cool. His hands strained to take part in the talk. Two or three fingers tapped lightly on the desk, but then he let them slide quietly down again until they lay flat and motionless. "Always, Mistah Donken, since I am in this contry, I vork here. T'irty-t'ree years. Since 1902. Meantime I often vant to go back to see my family, but I couldn't, never." A slow, nostalgic smile spread slowly around his watery eyes. "I marry here. We live quietly, we have children. T'ree children, Mistah Donken. Then, back in the old contry, my fahder, he died, an' my children, they grow up." He could no longer treat his hands as strangers. He drew them to him and they joined in the conversation. "I have a son a doctor, Mistah Donken!" The pride nearly burst him. His voice took on an almost unearthly tinge of happiness. It was a cry of joy, an expression of a supreme achievement.

He watched closely to see the response in Duncan's face. Duncan nodded his head approvingly, but he did not say anything, and after a little while Jacob went on, his voice betraying a slight irritation because it seemed to him that Duncan had not shown the proper respect and enthusiasm. He talked more rapidly now, eager to bring the interview to a close. "Last year my wife died, Mistah Donken. She was sick for a long time. It cost a lot of money. Now I have left a little money, a few hundred dollars, so I vant to go and see my family vat I left t'irty-t'ree years ago. I vant to go see my

18

modder before she is dead, and the grave of my fahder, may he rest in peace."

A quick glint of surprise slipped into Duncan's lean, tanned face. "You still have a mother, Mr Grossman?"

Jacob distorted his pudgy, wrinkled face into the semblance of a smile. "Yeah. She should only live and be healthy. She is in Vienna, my modder."

"Vienna, eh? I didn't know you came here from Vienna, Mr Grossman."

"No, no, Mistah Donken," Jacob hastened to correct him, "I don' come from there. I come from a little place in Galicia. But before the war it was all Austria. It belonged all to the Kaiser Franz Josef. In 1915 when there was big fighting there wit' the Russians, my modder an' my fahder an' my t'ree sisters fled away to Vienna, to the capital. But I don' come from there."

"I see." Duncan leaned his elbows on the desk, and it seemed to Jacob a few minutes before he went on. "As you know," he said, speaking calmly and authoritatively, "it is not the general policy of this firm to allow its employees extended holidays."

Jacob's heart sank, and he was about to begin arguing with the manager, but Duncan proceeded rapidly so that he had no chance to break in. "However, you have been with us for a very long time. You have always been a loyal, good, and dependable worker. And, come to think of it, you're really asking for a leave of absence on compassionate grounds, if I may call it so. We shan't therefore stand in your way, Mr Grossman."

"T'ank you, Mistah Donken," Jacob said, beaming, "t'ank you very much." He rose. Duncan extended his hand and Jacob grasped it and shook it warmly.

"Speaking of Vienna," Duncan said, his voice becoming more personal, "there was a bit of trouble there last year, wasn't there? Too bad those Nazis murdered Dollfuss. Great little man, eh? Well, I haven't seen anything in the papers lately, so I guess things are back to normal, and everything is settled again." He smiled jovially at Jacob. "And if all they say about Vienna is true, who knows, you'll be waltzing in the streets."

They both laughed.

Jacob took the elevator down. He left the factory, not as he had come in, but through the broad, marble-pillared front entrance, feeling strangely elated, as if he had just concluded a profitable business deal. There were two more things to be done to close the deal. He had to withdraw his money from the bank and then go downtown to book passage. He would do it all this afternoon to make the whole thing irrevocable. He wondered what Rosie would say. He dreaded another row with her, though he didn't really care. Sometimes he felt that he had made a mistake when he moved in with her after his wife died. It meant just another woman dominating him. Oh, well.

Right now he was hungry. He decided to go to Becker's Delicatessen and have a couple of corned beef sandwiches, a little side-dish of cole slaw and sour pickles, and a Pepsi-Cola.

CHAPTER

II

ROSIE followed her father into the parlour. She knew. She could tell by the guilty yet quietly triumphant smile which was spread all over his face and made him look like a naughty child. They stood looking at each other, neither saying anything.

"Well," she said at last.

"Vell," he echoed, and added quickly, "everything is fixed up good."

It merely confirmed what had been plain to her from the moment she saw him. He waited apprehensively for the thunderstorm to break, but nothing happened. Knowing her father, she realized that nothing she could possibly say now would have the slightest effect, and she was too tired to open the argument for its own sake.

As if to consolidate his victory, he said, "Already I have made a reservation on a ship. It leaves from New York on the fourteent' of May."

"Really! All I can say is that once you make up your mind, you certainly work fast."

"Sure," he said. "Vat you vant me to do? Vait for the Messiah?"

"I hope you're going first class," she said. "There's nothing like comfort on a long trip."

He missed the irony. "No, no, no," he said quickly. "I'm goink in the tourist class. The man told me it is joost so good, only much cheaper."

"I'm glad to hear it," she said.

"The name from the ship is the *Illinois*," he informed her.

"It's good of you to support the United States."

"How em I supporting the United States?"

"You're going on a United States liner, the *Illinois*, aren't you?"

"Vat you talkink about? I'm goink on a French ship. Ha-ha! My Frenchman! Fa t'ree years you learned French in high school, an' soon I say a French vord you don' know."

"How d'you spell it?" she asked, a trifle flustered.

"Did I learn French in school?" he said, reaching in his coat pocket and bringing out the folder which he had gotten from the travel agency. "Here," he said, giving it to her, "look alone."

She opened the folder and began to laugh. "Oh!" she cried, "oh! So that's it. You're going on the *Ile aux Noix*, Dad, not on the *Illinois*."

"So that's vat I said right from the beginning. I said right away the name from the ship is *Illinois*, no?"

"You don't say it the way a Frenchman would say it, that's all."

He screwed his mouth up sardonically and waved his hand towards her. "My Frenchman!" he quipped. "My Frenchman direct from France!"

She couldn't help smiling, and she felt her anger evaporating almost in spite of herself, for though she was stubborn she was not vindictive. She did not approve of his going, but she had lost the battle. "Well," she said, as if giving expression to her thoughts, "it's your money. I guess you can spend it any way you like." She rose from the chesterfield. "Morris will be home any minute and supper is ready."

After supper Rosie asked her husband to take her to a movie and Jacob stayed home to watch the baby. He was glad to be left alone, for there were a few things he wanted to do. When the baby was finally asleep, he sat down to write letters to his daughter Ella in Vancouver, to his son in Montreal, and to his mother, and then he made himself comfortable in a soft chair by the radio, half-listening, smoking leisurely, his head full of plans.

Presents! Naturally he could not come empty-handed. What could he bring? He tried to pick out things in his mind, but this proved difficult. He would have to go through the stores. And then suddenly a thought struck him which he at first rejected, but which kept recurring to him again and again with ever greater urgency. It was an old obsession of his. For years he had wanted to buy a white alpaca suit with white, soft-leathered shoes to match, but his wife (God rest her soul) would never hear of it. "A white suit!" she used to exclaim. "Who ever heard of such a thing? You need a white suit like I need a hole in the head." And when Ella and Rosie joined forces with their mother, the opposition was too formidable. He had not the figure for a white suit, they maintained, he was too short, too round, too everything. Their arguments never convinced him, but he was a peace-loving man, and what chance had he against three women? But now he could do it. He would go down to the factory the next morning and order the suit, and if they rushed the job, he could have it in three days. He wouldn't say a word to Rosie, of course. There was no need to complicate matters.

He carried out his plans promptly. He had himself measured for the suit, and then he went downtown to shop for the presents. He went through the big department stores, Eaton's and Simpson's, looking at things, choosing carefully.

He bought a white lawn tablecloth for Manya, his oldest sister; torrential Manya, who used to scold him when he was a boy. Manya scolding. That was the most vivid impression he retained of her. For his second sister, Rivka, whose features were somehow vague and blurred in his mind, he got a pair of golden, flower-shaped ear-rings. And then there was Shaendl. She was the youngest of the family, born to his parents long after anybody had expected them to have any more children. She was a little girl just three years old when he left their little village, the clay-soft, muddy village, with the murmuring brook and the woods stretching on all sides. And even though she was now a woman of thirty-six, the mother of two children, it was difficult for Jacob to picture her as anything but a little pig-tailed girl, in spite of the fact that he had seen recent photos of her. He had always been very fond of her, and he wanted to buy her something distinctive, but since he did not have too much money to spend, this proved difficult. At last he found what he was looking for—a slender, golden bracelet, set with seed-pearls. And in the same store he purchased also a string of white pearls for Rosie.

He did not forget the children. There were really only Shaendl's two little boys. Rivka had two grown daughters, and he did not think it necessary to bring gifts for them, and Manya had no children. He bought a pen and pencil set, and a set of tin soldiers, completely equipped with guns and planes and tanks and even collapsible bridges.

He could find nothing in the big stores that seemed to him appropriate for his mother. But as he walked homewards he stumbled upon a little shop, tucked away in a side street. There he saw a beautiful black lace shawl, a delicate, masterly piece of work, intricately woven into an elaborate pattern, with long, slender, rippling fringes. He fingered it carefully, his thick, uncouth hands almost afraid to touch the dainty fabric. He looked at it for a long time, holding it up to the light and inspecting it, and he tried to make himself see it clinging to the stooped, aged shoulders of his mother. It was a long shawl, and she would be able to pull it over her head if she wanted to. He bought the shawl, and had it wrapped carefully in tissue paper and placed in a cardboard box.

Rosie was out with the baby when he came home laden with parcels. He went into his room and put all the things on his bed. Glancing over them, and calculating rapidly in his head, he found that he had spent more than ninety dollars. It was a lot of money and he could not remember an occasion when he had spent so much for gifts. (There was of course the time he had bought the engagement ring for his wife. But that was a long time ago. So long ago that it had ceased to be real.)

A feeling of achievement and great satisfaction came over him as he looked at the paper-wrapped parcels on the bed. Tenderly he picked them up, took off the paper, and laid all the things he had bought gently on the bed. And then he looked at the gifts spread out before him, almost covering the whole surface of the bed, and he felt that this was one of the moments he would long cherish and remember, for here, tangible and real, was part of a dream materialized. He would come back to visit his mother and his sisters like a merchant arriving after long travels in foreign lands, bearing great gifts.

He was so sunk in contemplation that he did not hear Rosie coming up the stairs. It was not until she was actually in the room, looking at him in astonishment, that he became aware of her.

He was flustered at first, like a man rudely torn away from a beautiful sight, and, vaguely pointing towards the bed, he said haltingly, "I—I bought a few t'ings to take . . . to give . . . to . . ."

Rosie had seldom seen his face radiating such joy and happiness. She took a few steps forward and stood gazing at the things displayed on the bed. She picked them up, one by one, and when she opened the little velvet, satin-lined box with the pearls in it, he suddenly remembered that he had bought them for her.

"The peruls," he stammered. "Fa you, Rosie."

"For me?" she gasped, completely taken aback, "for me? But—but why?"

He stood with his hands fluttering helplessly by his side. "Because . . . because . . ."

"They're beautiful," she said. "Thank you so much, Dad." She clasped them round her neck, and then she turned quickly towards him. "Are you sure you got them for me and not for somebody else, and are only giving them to me because I happened to come in just now?"

"No," he said firmly. "They're fa you only."

Her face softened and she couldn't say anything.

"Rosie," he said, "Rosie." He had to come out with it. "Rosie, I bought for myself a white suit."

"Oh, no, no! You didn't! My God, what next?"

"Once in a lifetime," he mumbled, almost as if talking to himself. "Once in a lifetime," and his eyes had a far-away look, as though they were travelling back and back and back along the highway of his life.

Slowly he began to wrap up the things again, and put them away in a drawer. Rosie watched him. Once in a lifetime, she thought. Perhaps he was right. Perhaps once in a lifetime a poor man, too, may be extravagant and throw money around like a rich man—even if he can't afford it, even if the money might be better spent in other ways. And when he asked her that night if she would lend him her big suitcase—the one she had bought to go on her honeymoon—she said yes.

III

THE *Ile aux Noix* sailed out of New York harbour early in the forenoon of May 14. A small, brightly painted boat, not much more than 15,000 tons, she pushed herself slowly away from the pier, proudly blowing her whistles, puffing thick, magnificent clouds of smoke skywards. It was a dull morning and a thin fog hung over the Hudson. Jacob stood leaning against the white-shimmering railing, and watched the famous skyline of the great metropolis dip into the grey, churling foam. More than thirty years ago, one in a crowd of excitedly babbling immigrants thronging the steerage deck, he had seen that same skyline rising majestically through the morning mist. For it was in New York that Jacob Grossman had first set foot on the New World, and found, to his great disappointment, that the streets were paved with stone and not with gold. After a week's frantic search, he finally got a job as a sewer in a small factory, a grimy sweatshop, and he could only stand it for ten days. Then he was out of work again, and met Sam Silver, a sallow-faced, restless little chap who persuaded him to go with him to Detroit. Somebody had told him there were good jobs to be had there. Desperate, Jacob went with him, but there was no fortune waiting for them in Detroit, either. They tried peddling for a while, without success, until Sam had another idea. Somebody had told him that things were better in Canada. People were always telling things to Sam. They crossed the border and spent some time in Windsor, doing odd jobs and barely getting by. Once more Jacob obeyed one of Sam Silver's inscrutable impulses and followed him to Toronto. There they were luckier than they had been, and almost immediately got steady and fairly well-paid jobs with Perfect Clothes. Sam only stayed six months. No percentage working for somebody else, he used to say. You gotta go in business for yourself. Toronto was no good, Montreal was the place. But Jacob had had enough of wandering about the country. There were no fortunes waiting for him anywhere. One city was like another city, big, sprawling, impersonal. He was quite satisfied with his job, and he felt that it was time for him to look around for a girl and settle down. Sam said he was crazy and moved on alone. Jacob never heard from him again, but he often wondered what had become of him. He thought of him now as he strained his eyes to catch a last glimpse of the tall buildings of Manhattan which were rapidly dissolving in the fog. He could not think of Sam Silver as a man over fifty, with a family, living in one place. He could only imagine him thin, impatient, shifting restlessly from place to place, powerfully attracted by strange cities and always deeply disillusioned in the end.

The fog thickened over the river and the clouds hung low, dark grey clouds made black by the masses of smoke, and the deep moans of foghorns drifted sadly across the river. It was hardly possible to see through the dense fog. Jacob strolled slowly across the deck, smiling a friendly smile at strangers, and went below.

It was almost time for lunch and Jacob was hungry. When he came into the dining room some people were already sitting at their tables, and a three-man orchestra was playing soothing dinner music. The steward showed him to a table set for two and Jacob found himself wondering who his table companion would be. He wanted to wait, but since no one came, he started the meal.

He had almost finished his soup when the steward directed a tall young man to his table. Jacob smiled and half rose in his chair. The other made a short, polite bow before he sat down. Then he introduced himself—his name was Tassigny. Soon they were deeply involved in conversation, chiefly distinguished by the fact that neither understood the other's English. Tassigny tried French, but that didn't work, and he switched back to English. They made some progress, although for the time being they communicated more by sweeping, expressive gestures than by words.

For a while they ate in silence. The orchestra played softly in the background, and the floating strains mingled with the din of conversation, with the peals of laughter, with the regular, rhythmic motions of the steamer. The Blue Danube Waltz filled the air now, the melody carried by the violin and the cello, and the piano playing the obbligato.

Jacob swayed his body to the music and announced, his heaped fork poised in midair and his shiny face bathed in a big smile, "They are playink the Blue Danube now. Ken you hear them, Messiey? Vat a beautiful valtz! I am going to Vienna to visit my family."

"Ah, *la belle vie*!" the Frenchman said playfully. "*A Vienne on est gai comme un pinson*, eh, Monsieur Grossman?"

They nodded at each other and laughed. Rosie should only see him now, Jacob thought. Now she could hear some real French. It did his heart good to be sitting here, talking casually with a Frenchman. A real Frenchman, not one of your phonies. A real Frenchman—direct from France! He was immensely pleased.

After lunch he took a little nap, a luxury which for years he had only been able to afford on Saturdays and Sundays and on the few scattered holidays. For a minute his thoughts travelled back to the dust and sweat of the factory, and he could hear the steady, vibrating noise of the electric power, and could see the tired, listless faces of the workers. Then he fell asleep. He woke refreshed. He washed, and inspected his face in the mirror and decided to go and get a shave. It was wonderful to feel the fresh lather whip his face, his whole body relaxed, stretched almost horizontally in the comfortable leather chair. Next to him a man was being manicured. What would it be like? How would it feel? Should he try it, once? He asked to be manicured. Then, while the barber scraped off his stubble with the sharp steel of the razor, a blonde manicurist scrubbed, polished, and filed his nails until they were clean and pink and softly shining.

Back in his cabin, he dressed slowly for dinner, meticulously tying and untying his tie three times before he was satisfied with the knot. Smiling at himself in the mirror, he flicked a speck of dust from his lapel, darted a quick glance at his shoes to see if they were polished enough, and then walked leisurely to the dining room, bearing himself with great dignity. Everything seemed somehow unreal. The dust, the sweat, the noise of the factory were now almost forgotten, buried somewhere in the distant past, like so many other things in which he had at one time or another been involved in the course of life.

After dinner he strolled into the salon, and a very distinguished-looking gentleman asked him if he would care to join in a game of bridge. Jacob felt flattered to have been asked. The thought of himself punching a time clock every morning was now quite impossible, almost ridiculous, like a foolish dream suddenly remembered. With a politeness that was alien even to himself, and a conscious effort to speak flawlessly, he informed the gentleman, punctuating his remarks with large, apologetic gestures, that he did not know how to play bridge. Ah! If only Rosie could see him now! He sat down in a deep comfortable armchair and crossed his legs. Slowly he let his small, watery eyes wander about the maplewood panels of the salon, and lit a cigarette.

Tassigny came in after a while and joined him. They gesticulated together for a short time, somehow understanding each other, and suddenly the Frenchman said, "*Monsieur*, I shall now play the piano a little bit."

He was a brilliant pianist and his playing attracted listeners. They filled the salon, stood around the piano, listening to the Frenchman's interpretation of Chopin. Jacob felt his heart swell with pride. He felt as if he personally had something to do with Tassigny's playing. It had been like that, only much more intense, when he had sat in Convocation Hall that day David received his degree of Doctor of Medicine. His wife was still living then, and they had both been silent, nervous, tense. He remembered the deep and solemn swellings of the organ, the black gowns and the colourful hoods of the professors, and the academic procession, marching in slow and stately step. Malke had gripped his sleeve, her hand trembling, her whole body quivering, and her eyes filled with big, heavy tears. And he himself had sat on the edge of his seat, his throat tied in a heavy knot, his eyes fixed on David—David robed in the black gown—Doctor David Grossman. Jacob had had a great deal to do with that, and when his son kneeled and the purple hood was placed over his head, a part of it belonged to him and to Malke. Had they not deprived themselves of many things that they might live to see this moment?

Tassigny stopped playing and everyone kept urging him to play some more, and eventually he gave in. Jacob got up and pushed his way through the crowd of people who stood about the piano until he was right behind the Frenchman where he could see the long, agile fingers hurrying across the keys. He looked about him, his eyes shining, prodding the man next to him and whispering, "He plays good, no?" It was a personal matter now. He regarded himself as Tassigny's friend whose duty it was to see that he was properly appreciated.

When Tassigny finished playing and closed the piano, laughingly warding off requests to go on, Jacob patted him on the shoulder and nodded his head admiringly. "You ser-prised me, Messiey," he said. "You ken play marvellous. I didn' know you could play so good." He spoke as if he had known Tassigny for many years and had just discovered something kept hidden from him through all the years of their friendship.

Tassigny smiled and shrugged his thin, slightly drooping

shoulders. People scattered, lounged in chairs, smoked. Some played cards in the adjoining card-room.

Jacob ventured out on deck. The fog had lifted, but he was driven back immediately by the whipping rain with which the wind lashed the waters. Suddenly his stomach began to turn and seemed to mount to his throat. He held onto the railing, limp and drowsy, and sacrificed the good things he had eaten at dinner until he was all empty inside, and little pearls of sweat glistened on his forehead and on the bald spot of his pate like drops of dew. He felt better afterwards and stumbled slowly down to his cabin. He stretched himself on his bunk and lay quiet. He couldn't feel the tossing of the vessel so much there, and his stomach began to settle.

They had reached the open sea now. The night was rough. The *Ile aux Noix* tossed up and down, and the waves were high as houses and came tumbling over her sides. He lay very still, with eyes closed, and listened. Faintly he could hear the muffled sound of the waves as they broke themselves against the body of the ship, and the dull, insistent bickerings of the engines. After a while it seemed to him as if the engines of the steamer were throbbing within him.

Suddenly he remembered that he would wrinkle his suit and got up with a start. He undressed slowly, drowsily climbing into his pajamas, and then slipped between the white, cool sheets and drew the blankets over him.

A clean, cool bed . . . three suitcases . . . Would you care to join in a game of bridge? We need a fourth . . . listening to the brilliant playing of Monsieur Tassigny . . . fingernails manicured . . . I em sorry. I vould very much like to play wit' you bridge. But—but I never learned to play this bridge. Pinochle, yes, poker, yes, but not bridge. T'ank you that you esk me. . . .

He smiled as he reflected upon these things. Nobody had asked him to play bridge when he had crossed that same ocean so many, many years ago. He had come with one dilapidated travelling-box and a single patched suit. He had not had a cabin, and the boat was a little tub of a freighter. There they had been crowded together, men, women, and children, a ragged band of immigrants, some sleeping on the floor, fully dressed, covered with torn overcoats and shreds of blankets. It had been rough the first two nights, and people had been sick all over the deck, groaning and moaning, and children whimpering, too weak to cry. Then the weather had cleared up and for the rest of the voyage the sea had been calm and

30

smooth like a standing lake on a hot summer day. And at night he could hear the sighing and deep panting of men and women as they lay together, and he couldn't go to sleep because he kept listening to them.

But now he was travelling in a cabin, with three suitcases neatly packed, was sleeping in a bed, on white linen sheets, covered with soft woollen blankets. He had at last realized the dream of every immigrant—he was going back, a settled, prosperous-seeming man.

He felt very sick when he woke in the morning. As soon as he sat up in bed his head began to spin, and his stomach seemed to revolve in a wild frenzy. He wanted to vomit, but his stomach was empty and there was nothing to bring up. It was best to remain lying quietly on his back. The steward brought him some hot tea and a few buns. He drank the tea and forced himself to eat the buns because he wanted to have something to bring up when his stomach decided to turn somersaults.

At night Tassigny came into his cabin, gay and exuberant. He wore a raincape over his grey suit and his black hair was ruffled because he had stood at the bow and the wind had played with it. His face was windburnt, glowing with a pale red. Jacob was glad to see him, and the gladness showed in his eyes.

"*Monsieur*, what is the mattaire with you?" asked Tassigny. "This?" He tapped his stomach lightly with his middle finger and a smile crept into his face.

"It is not'ing, Messiey," Jacob assured him. "I feel good now. I vas a little sick this morning."

"Oh, that is too, too bad," said Tassigny. "It is a great pitee you could not stand on the deck and watch the sea. It was magnifizent, *Monsieur*. Most of the ship is sick. It is so quiet in the dining room. Even the music is sick. Only the violin plays. The others are sick."

Jacob said, "T'ank you, Messiey, that you have come see me. I em only sick a day or two. Then I em all right again. I vas sick like this ven I first come from the old contry. Two days, det's all. Afterwards I em like a sailor, Messiey. I stand, I go, I eat, everyt'ing all right. This *Illinois* is a little ship, comparative. So she rocks much. Sit down a little, Messiey."

"Thank you, *Monsieur*." The Frenchman sat down on the edge of the bed. "I shall not be long, *Monsieur*. I go around to all the cabins to comfort the sick. I am the Florence Nightingale of this ship." He laughed. "All day I stood and watched the sea."

Jacob's bad mood was dissolving rapidly in the joviality of the Frenchman. An impish look broke out on his pudgy face, like a sudden rash. "All day?" he said. "All day you vas lookink in the sea?" He cocked his left eye. "So vat did you see there? You joost see water. An' you look long, you see more water. Ef you look all day, you don' see not'ing more."

"Oh, but Monsieur Grossman, you are so wrong. The water changes all the time. It is never the same. Never for one minute. The colour is different every second. A thousand different shades. But the most interesting of all are the waves. Sometimes you see the wave come slow, as if she is afraid, and is not sure what will happen when she hits the ship. She waits there on the top, trembling a little, and then, suddenly she rushes down like mad and breaks herself against the ship. Sometimes the waves come quick, so quick you cannot see, one behind the other as if they cannot wait, as if they have lived enough, and now want only to destroy themselves. And it seems as if each wave wants to be the first to die."

Tassigny paused and laid the fingers of one hand against the fingers of the other. Jacob looked at him. Nobody had ever talked to him like that. The Frenchman spoke with glowing enthusiasm. His eyes seemed to strain beyond the closed environment of the cabin, as if they were trying to recapture what they had seen during the day. He felt the limitations of the foreign language, the limitations of any language, even his own, to express the phenomenon of a turbulent sea.

Jacob was at a loss for words. Tassigny was so serious, so intently sunk in himself that Jacob dared not make a joke. He dared not say anything because he did not want to break the concentration of the man. But he was glad that the Frenchman treated him as an equal, that here at least he was not the worker and underling.

Tassigny said softly, "The sky today was hanging so low over the ship that you could almost touch it with your hand. And the clouds sometimes loosened themselves, so they seemed lower than the sky. They were heavy and pregnant with much rain. Sometimes I was thinking they looked like big, black, ripe grapes when they hang heavy from the stocks just before the harvest."

Jacob sat up, leaning against his right elbow. A spark of admiration flickered in his eyes. "You know vat, Messiey

Tassigny?" he said. "I enjoy better to listen to you than to look on the clouds mit mine own eyes."

Tassigny laughed. His hair tumbled down over his eyes, and he brushed it back with a sweeping stroke of his right hand. "If the wind would not have been so strong, I would have taken my easel and I would have painted on the deck."

Jacob's brows went up in surprise. "You are a painter, too?" he asked.

Tassigny looked him fully in the face. "I am a painter, *Monsieur*," he said. "That is my profession."

Jacob felt a sudden thrill. It gave him a sense of great importance to have a man like Tassigny, a musician and a painter, a real artist, sit in his cabin, talking to him, to have him tell of the sky and of the clouds and of dying waves. Jacob had never been aware of the sky and of floating clouds. A clouded sky meant rain and perhaps the necessity of taking an umbrella and nothing more. The sky in the factory was a dull, grey ceiling, and there was no wind to waft a fresh breeze, but only hot, steaming, suffocating air that swished from the Hoffman presses and made the face grow crimson with heat, and drenched the body with a thick, unhealthy sweat. He was grateful to Tassigny for talking to him like that.

He sank slowly back into his pillows. "You come now from America, Messiey?" he asked.

"Yes. I was sent there on a fellowship. I was in Mexico, too. I did a lot of painting there. Now I go back to France."

Jacob said suddenly, "I have a son a doctor, Messiey."

CHAPTER

IV

AFTER two days Jacob felt completely well again, and now he really began to enjoy the crossing. The weather became bright and on some days the sea was so calm that one could look deep down into the shimmering waters where the sky gazed at its own blue, and the sun was lovely and warm and golden over the dark blue sea.

Jacob lay sprawled out in a deck chair all day, talking to people in his jovial, intimate manner, his body drinking in the sun. Some of the passengers disliked him intensely for his complete lack of discretion, for his uncouth manners and his uncultured speech. But with most of his fellow travellers he got on well. Tassigny especially had taken a great liking to him because he did not pretend to a culture which he did not possess, though he never confessed to Tassigny that he was a poor man. But Jacob himself tended more and more to forget that fact. The illusion was too complete to be wantonly destroyed.

One day, towards the close of the voyage, when he stood watching a particularly beautiful sunset, Tassigny strolled by. Together they looked at the sun setting the horizon on fire, and then the sea quenched the fire and the sun drowned in the sea.

Jacob said, "I vished you should paint somet'ing like that, Messiey Tassigny."

Tassigny smiled. "I have sometimes before painted how the sun goes down in the sea."

"You mean joost like that. Like we've seen now."

Tassigny considered a moment. "No, it is not the same. I looked at another time, and I do not feel the same each time. So I cannot paint the same."

"But it looked like it looked now?" Jacob insisted.

"Yes."

Jacob curled down his lower lip and shook his head doubtfully. "But ef the sun fell down like now," he argued, "an' ef you painted it, I don't care two years ago, it mus' look the same, no?"

"Ah! But if you feel different it doesn't look the same."

"Feelinks, feelinks! There are different kinds feelinks the vay you love somebody. A modder, a svitheart, a vife, a child —it's different altogether. A different kind love, a different kind feelink. But the sun is the sun. Sometimes she shines bright, sometimes not so bright. In the morning she rises, an' in the evening she goes down. But always the same. It makes no difference to the feelinks."

Tassigny threw his head back and laughed. "Oh, it makes all the difference. It is not always the same. But I cannot explain to you in words."

"You mus' excuse me, Messiey," said Jacob, smiling a somewhat embarrassed smile, "but I am a ord'nary man and I know not'ing about such t'ings."

Tassigny nodded his head slowly and thought for a moment. Then he said, "After dinner you will come to my cabin and I will show you some pictures." He knew that Jacob would not understand them, but he liked the simplicity of the man and he wanted to see his reaction.

When Jacob saw the three paintings which Tassigny showed him, he was at first completely stunned. He could see nothing but patches of colour thrown, so it seemed to him, quite haphazardly onto the canvas. He did not know what to say. He just stood and glared.

"These are the pictures which I have," said Tassigny. "The rest have gone to France already. I will have an exhibition in Paris next week. This, here, is a sunset." He propped the picture against the wall and drew Jacob back a little.

Jacob laughed. "I don' see not'ing," he said. "I ken see the colours, but where is the picture?"

Tassigny tried to explain. He became impatient, and a little angry, too, because Jacob did not seem to comprehend anything he said.

The other two paintings were done in the cubistic manner and made no sense at all to Jacob. They seemed to him just a jungle of lines, running criss-cross, and he said so. Tassigny grew irritated, and talked more rapidly. He talked with his hands, gesticulating wildly. He talked about design and form. He talked about his conception of painting. This, he explained to Jacob, pointing to one of the paintings, was the way he had felt a skyscraper in New York. He talked about feeling things, not seeing them; about ridding himself of sensations by painting a picture. He interpreted the lines, the colours, the design of the painting. All this meant little to Jacob, but he was nevertheless much impressed by Tassigny, and though he still did not understand what he saw, there were flashes when he seemed to see a skyscraper where before he had only seen lines. When Tassigny's long, expressive hands described graphically what the lines were meant to convey, something dawned in Jacob and the forms seemed to take on life, but in the next moment what had been the semblance of a skyscraper became again a jumbled mass of curves and triangles and straight lines.

Jacob picked up the third painting, and brought it close to his eyes, studying it incredulously.

It was a narrow, crudely framed canvas, about thirty inches long and ten wide, with garish greens and yellows predominating, remotely suggesting a human figure, though this was not at first easily apparent because a geometric construction built up of spheres and rectangular planes obscured it. The figure had a long, fleshless neck, but no face. Where the head should have been, there was a thick, cylindrical, megaphone-like contraption, painted jet-black, and pointing sideways. The legs were somewhat more readily recognizable. They were completely out of proportion to the rest of the body, filling almost three-quarters of the canvas, and clad in wide, sailor-like trousers. Lurking behind the right leg, there was visible, sketched with a few bare strokes, a thin and distorted female face.

"Vat is this?" Jacob asked after a few minutes, during which he tried in vain to make something of the picture. "Vat is it suppose' to show, Messiey?"

"Step back a little, *Monsieur*," Tassigny said. "You will see better. I call the painting *L'Entrepreneur*."

"Le vat?"

"*L'Entrepreneur*," Tassigny repeated. And seeing that Jacob did not understand, he tried to explain. "It means a man, who . . . who . . . who . . . how shall I say, *Monsieur*, who . . . who has something to show off and he shouts and screams so people will hear and come and pay to see. They come, they pay, sometimes only money, sometimes more, the whole body and the soul. And what do they see, *Monsieur*? . . . They see nothing. A few cheap eghzibisions." He paused dramatically and pointed a finger at the misshapen grimace whose body lay concealed behind the right leg of the figure. "But the man cares nothing, for he is full of falseness. And more and more people come, *Monsieur*, because his voice is so . . . so powerful and loud. When he shouts, the people can hear nothing else. They are caught by the voice. One goes and all follow, like a herd of sheep. Do you know what I mean, Monsieur Grossman?"

Jacob nodded. "I understan' vat you say, Messiey, but I can't reco'nize it in the picture. This here looks like his legs all right, but the rest doesn' look like a man at all. He is all legs in the first place, an' he hasn't got no face."

"Men like him have no faces," said Tassigny, earnestly, "so I couldn't paint him with a face. The people seldom see the face, most of the time they only hear his voice—from the radio, from loudspeakers, or they read in the newspapers what he says. The face is not important, so I gave him no face."

"So how you expec' I should reco'nize him, Messiey?" Jacob asked. "Ef you don' stand here to explain me these t'ings, how would I know?"

"I cannot help that," Tassigny said, somewhat testily. "I mus' show what I feel, and then I mus' express the truth the way I see it. It is up to people who look on the picture to understand."

"But how can a ord'nary man like me understan', Messiey?" Jacob asked. "I like a picture should tell a story, or it should show a person that looks like a person, so I know right avay vat it means."

"I am sorry, *Monsieur*," Tassigny said, shrugging his shoulders. "You cannot come to me for that. There are a lot of painters who paint the way you want. But to me painting is something altogether different. I have already told you. It is an expression of the most inner feelings. I think that a painter, an artist, must be a fighter and a prophet. I do not paint pictures so people will hang them up to decorate apartments. If people do not understand, I cannot help it. Perhaps they will understand sometimes. Perhaps never. I hope they will, but if they don't, it is nothing to me. So long as I have always told the truth, the way I see the truth."

Tassigny's voice rose, filled with a burning enthusiasm and a driving intensity. He talked on for several minutes, excitedly mixing French words with his English, his dark eyes, as on that night in Jacob's cabin, again focusing on a point in space. Jacob sat motionless, dumbly comprehending.

Abruptly Tassigny stopped. He gathered up the paintings and stacked them against the side of the cabin. With his back turned to Jacob, he said, "I hope I didn't bore you, Monsieur Grossman."

"No, no, Messiey," Jacob said quickly. "It was nice that you talk to me like that." He was deeply grateful. His hands groped

for words. And suddenly he burst out, "Messiey, I should like
—ef you could—I should like you should give me a picture to
take home perhaps."

Tassigny was taken by surprise. He stared at Jacob as though
this were the last request he should have expected him to
make.

"But why, *Monsieur*?" he asked. "Why do you want a picture of mine? Do you like these pictures?"

"No," Jacob said honestly. "I don't like these pictures. But—
but I like you Messiey. I vant to have a picture to remember."

Tassigny smiled. Was this a whim? Would he hang the picture in his drawing room, and would he show it to his friends, as a kind of joke? Or would he boast of it before people to whom it meant no more than to him?

"*Oui, Monsieur*," Tassigny said after a short pause of consideration, "these paintings, they are not sold yet, so you can buy one."

Jacob gasped. "You—you are selling these pictures?"

"Of course, *Monsieur*," Tassigny said sharply. "A painter mus' live, just like a businessman." Then, very business-like, he placed the paintings side by side on the table again.

Jacob was cowed by the Frenchman's sharp snap, and he could not bring himself to withdraw his offer, once this offer had been made.

"How . . . how much you askink for these pictures?"

"Sixty-five dollars for this, for this fifty dollars, and this one," he pointed to the picture titled *L'Entrepreneur*, "is thirty dollars."

The cheapest thirty dollars? It seemed to Jacob an outrageous price. Almost a whole week's wages. He was too stunned to reply.

"I do not force you to buy any of the paintings," Tassigny said. "You asked for one. But if you think they are too expensive for you, please, *Monsieur*, don't buy."

"I buy this one," Jacob said grimly. He would buy the painting that cost the least money, but he would not withdraw. He did not even attempt to bargain with Tassigny. Reluctantly, and with a strange glimmer in his eyes, he paid the money and took his picture, feeling that Tassigny had taken advantage of him. What nerve, he thought, to ask thirty dollars for a painting which, in spite of Tassigny's elaborate explanation, seemed to him a mere mass of jumbled lines and indiscriminate splashes of colour that any child might have put together.

When he came back to his cabin, he placed the picture on

the table, facing his bunk. Then he undressed and lay watching it for some time, but it became more and more confusing the longer he looked at it. He wanted to rush to Tassigny's cabin and give the painting back to him, but his pride would not let him. Finally he fell asleep and had a fearful dream.

It was late at night and he was all alone in the factory, working. Beside his machine a huge pile of white suits was stacked up on a table. They had to be pressed before morning. He worked feverishly. A cloud of steam enveloped him, and the machine was hot, but he gave it no rest. Suddenly a faceless giant with enormous legs came stalking through an open window, roaring, "There's no percentage working for somebody else, you gotta go in business for yourself." The voice grew louder and more insistent and more threatening. The monster came closer and closer, walking very slowly, very deliberately. Jacob tried to flee, but his legs refused to carry him. He could not take his eyes off the giant. Looming behind his right leg there was a thin, mask-like face, and when Jacob looked closer he saw to his amazement that it was Sam Silver. Now the ghoul was within arm's length, and he could feel its breath, and he wondered where the breath was coming from since there was no face. Two powerful, hairy arms reached out and grabbed him, and the last thing he saw was Tassigny sitting on the window-sill, eating a corned beef sandwich and laughing. Then he woke up.

Next day he was very cool at breakfast and the Frenchman noticed it immediately. He sensed the reason, too, and when they were drinking their coffee, he leaned forward and said, "I am sorry about the painting, *Monsieur*. If you will return it, I will gladly give you back your money."

"No," Jacob said firmly. "I bought it. I keep it. I ken afford a few dollars, Messiey."

"It is not the money, *Monsieur*. But I thought over the whole mattaire last night. You do not like the picture. You do not really want it. What will you do with it?"

"I keep it," Jacob repeated stubbornly. "Besides, you are a young man. You're tryink to make a livink." His eyes began to twinkle, and his voice took on a patronizing tone. "I like to help out a young man. I vas young, too, once. I know vat it is to earn a few dollars. I vas strugglink, too, once."

Tassigny smiled awkwardly. He drank down his coffee quickly. He resented the remark, but he did not counter it. Jacob, however, was extraordinarily pleased with this new interpretation which he had given his purchase.

And more and more, from that day on, did he come to think of himself as Tassigny's patron, an attitude which he could not help expressing, and which antagonized the Frenchman intensely. He avoided Jacob whenever he could, and at meals he spoke very little. The painting, though they did not again mention it, always remained vividly before them. Tassigny came to hate it so much that he wished he had never painted it, and Jacob almost began to like it, not because he came to appreciate Tassigny's art, but because he fancied that with the purchase of the painting he had become, not only Tassigny's equal, but even his superior. He felt his ego grow, and become inflated like a balloon. For was he not now a patron of the arts?

CHAPTER

V

THE first sea-gulls, wide-winged and stately, came sailing in from the crags and cliffs of the yet indiscernible coast. Mewing, they circled the boat, swooping down like arrows into the sea, snatching up the morsels of food which the passengers threw them. The atmosphere became strangely tense, and people thronged the deck, waiting impatiently for the first sight of land. And at last, dim and shadowy, a thin, black line breaking through the water, and a lively commotion, and a rapt pointing of fingers as if no one on board ship had ever expected to see land again.

The *Ile aux Noix* docked early in the afternoon, but it was not until some time later, after all the formalities had been duly completed, that Jacob, resplendent in his white alpaca suit and white shoes, stepped out onto the quay. He had only two hours before his train was due to leave for Vienna. He sent a telegram to his mother, saying that he would arrive at the Westbahn station on the following evening at seven-thirty, had his luggage sent off by express, and then strolled about a little, not straying far from the station.

He stopped at a little café and sat down at one of the small marble-topped tables outside on the pavement. He ordered a cup of hot coffee with whipped cream, and some pastry. The waiter's trained eye quickly perceived that here was a newly arrived tourist. He became very friendly and rushed away, bringing the coffee, disregarding other guests, because he knew that foreigners were usually more liberal with tips. Jacob sipped his coffee slowly, enjoying it. The sun came down softly upon the pavement, and he leaned back in his chair and let it warm his throat. It made him feel wonderful. He had changed a few dollars into French money, and when the waiter brought him his check, he was surprised that he had to pay so little. The bill came to only about fifteen cents, and when he tipped the waiter as much, the man seemed exceedingly pleased. Jacob acknowledged his bows and profuse outbursts of thanks with a slight wave of his right hand and a thin, somewhat embarrassed smile, and mumbled, "Oh, don't mention it, Messiey. It's not'ing, ebsolutely not'ing."

He rose, his stomach wagging softly. He flashed a bright smile at the waiter and threw a combination of three words at him. "*Oui, Messiey, oui, oui. Au revoir, Messiey!*"

Then, having completely exhausted the resources of his French vocabulary, he crossed the road to the station, his face beaming.

Jacob could not afterwards say that he had particularly enjoyed the train journey. He only vaguely remembered that the train passed through Belgium, and when he later tried to recall what the Belgian countryside looked like, he found that his memory was blurred and hazy. The air in the compartment grew warm and sticky, and he dozed off repeatedly during the evening.

Then the conductor came through, reminding the passengers in a dry monotone to get ready for the passport and customs examination at the German border. At Aachen the Germans boarded the train. Two men entered the compartment, a customs official in ordinary dark blue uniform without any special insignia, and a tall, heavy-booted officer in the black uniform and the visored cap of the storm-guards, on his left arm, just above the elbow, the deep red band with the black swastika in a white disk. Jacob sat rigid and upright in his seat. Fumblingly, he lit a cigarette and puffed at it nervously. There were only four passengers in the compartment, all sitting in front of him. The examinations followed a stereotyped, formal routine. It was Jacob's turn now. He saw the two men coming along the passageway, and it seemed to him that they moved heavily and with exaggerated slowness. Having watched the procedure four times already, he held out his passport with a slightly trembling hand without waiting to be asked for it. The storm-guard officer took it and checked it carefully.

"*Kanader*," he said to the other official. "*Bloss auf der Durchreise nach Oesterreich.*"

Since Jacob was only passing through Germany, and would not get off the train, the inspection of his personal luggage was cursory and superficial.

The officer handed back his passport. "*Haben Sie irgend-welche Zeitungen oder Magazine?*" he asked.

Jacob understood him easily. He shook his head. He carried no reading material of any sort.

Now the officer performed the last function of this border ritual. He bent down and searched under the seat with a flashlight, very seriously and solemnly. It was then that Jacob saw the strange and ominous insignia on his cap—two crossed bones and a leering death's-head. He had once read newspaper accounts of this, but now that he saw it with his own eyes, the effect was terribly menacing and monstrous. He never forgot that moment.

He was glad and relieved when they crossed the Austrian border the next day shortly after noon. He grew nervous, and although he knew perfectly well that the train would not get into Vienna before seven-thirty in the evening, he kept pestering the conductor every time he came face to face with him. He paid no heed to the beautiful scenery. The snow-capped mountains, rising magnificently; the quiet, sleepy villages, the picturesque little mountain houses appearing suddenly behind a bend, tucked cosily into a bed of forest; the rapid mountain streams that rushed by wildly, straining to marry their floods to a river—Jacob saw nothing. He kept thinking of his mother and his sisters, and he wondered how it would be, seeing them again after so many years of separation.

At five o'clock in the afternoon he went into the washroom to shave. His hand was shaky and he cut himself. Now the train was racing through the fertile plains of Lower Austria, and was nearing the capital. At St. Poelten there was some delay and they lost thirty minutes. At seven-thirty they had barely reached the outskirts of the city. Jacob could no longer bear to sit down. Why couldn't the train move faster? At last the spire of St. Stephen's cathedral became visible, rising clear against the night sky, and ten minutes later the train thundered into the smoky Westbahn station, hollow and loud.

As soon as Jacob stepped onto the platform, he could see them. They were standing together in a little group, their eyes searching the train. He recognized them before they had seen him, and breathlessly he pushed his way through the milling crowd. When he came near them, he waved his hat above the moving mass of people and shouted, "Mama! Mama!"

And then they saw him. The little old woman freed herself from the arm of her daughter and took a few steps toward him, and he caught her in his arms.

"Yankel," she sobbed, "Yankel." Her furrowed, leathery face was distorted with emotion, and he could feel her body shake and quiver as she pressed him against her.

She called his name again and again. "Yankel! Yankel!"

It touched him strangely to be called Yankel again. It brought back to him a wealth of recollections and an overpowering sense of a long forgotten past. It brought back a picture of himself as a small boy, running about barefoot in a little village, and the memory of harsh scoldings and gentle caresses. He was very moved. He had not thought that he would ever see his mother again, and now, when he felt her cling to him, it touched him deeply. His mother let him go at last, and he turned to the others and greeted them. They were all dressed in their Sunday best, and no one knew quite what to do.

First he embraced Manya, her tight-lipped and stern face made gentle by a wry smile. She was a tall woman of sixty, and she wore her hair in a big, heavy knot at the back of her head. Her quick tongue was silenced by the waves of emotion which flooded her, and when she finally found her speech she could only mumble, "Yankel, you are getting a bald head."

His sister Rivka pushed herself forward now and demanded his attention. Jacob did not know what was going on. Everybody tried to touch him, to embrace him. He felt like a pampered child, long lost, and now found again.

The crowd milled all about them, and they were pushed towards the exit almost against their will. They were all talking mumbled sentences and nobody made an effort to

44

understand what was being said. The old mother kept repeating over and over again, "Oh, God, God, that I should have lived to see this day. Your father should only have lived to see you again."

When they were outside the station, they could breathe a little more freely. Jacob shook hands with the men. There was Reuben, Manya's husband. He was the only one of the men whom Jacob knew. His sister had married him eight years before he had left the little village, and he had not changed much. He was a good deal bigger, to be sure, and his head was now completely bald. He had the same, childish, innocent smile, and he did not say much. But then, he never had spoken very much when Manya was present. She was the talker in the family and he had soon reconciled himself to that fact.

"It's about time you remembered your family, and you come to see us," he said, and he smiled his round smile, and wagged his finger playfully.

Rivka's husband, Manfred, was a short, sharp-nosed man. He shook hands stiffly, without saying anything.

"This is Shaendl's husband, Albert," said Manya, "and her two little boys."

And now, for the first time really, Jacob became aware that Shaendl herself was not there, and he looked about in consternation. Then he asked, "And where is Shaendl?"

There was a drop of silence. Everybody tried to talk, but no one did.

At last Manya whispered confidentially, "Shh! Don't ask, Yankel. She is all right. She is waiting at Mama's place, preparing a few things."

"But why didn't she come to the station?" Jacob asked.

"You ask too many questions," said Manya. "Just like always. You always asked a lot of questions. You are the same. No, but she is all right. She is in a condition where it is not good for her to come to places where people push and press. It could do her harm."

Jacob smiled a broad, happy smile. "Ohhhhhhhh!" he exclaimed, "ohhhhhh! That's a different matter altogether." He turned to Shaendl's husband. "Noo," he said, "if it is like that, I must wish you Mazel Tov."

Albert grasped Jacob's outstretched hand. He was a tall, pale-looking man of about thirty-seven. His hands were long and slippery to the touch, and he had a thin, rather sad face, and striking eyes, set deep in their sockets and blinking nervously behind a shield of thick, horn-rimmed glasses. He wore no hat, and his matted-brown hair was straight.

He said softly, "It is not time yet to wish us happiness. In a few weeks, I hope."

"So what's a few weeks?" laughed Jacob. "In any case, where is the harm? You can wish happiness to people any time."

Then he bent down and kissed Shaendl's two little boys. Herman was eight, and Bernhardt was eleven. They were a bit awed by the presence of their uncle who had just come from Canada, all the way across the sea. Canada was to them a region that did not somehow belong to this world. It was too far away. They felt strange, and their usual boisterousness had dried up like a little brook exposed to the scathing rays of the sun. Manya had not wanted to let them come to the station, but they had put up a great fight, and she had finally given in because otherwise they would have pestered their mother to death.

And now all the welcoming was done, and they stood there in silence. They had so much to tell each other that nobody said anything. The little old woman clung tightly to her son's arm, and she did not take her eyes off him. Nothing else existed for her at the moment. She was completely oblivious to the surroundings. She had even forgotten that others of her children and grandchildren were there, too.

There was a great deal of noise—porters shouting, and taxis hooting, and people talking and laughing. And yet they did not notice it. They were for the moment isolated within themselves, alone among the multitude.

Little Herman looked up at his father, and said softly, but they could all hear it, "Papa, is this our rich uncle who's just come from Canada?"

Manya threw an irritated look at the child and stamped her foot impatiently on the concrete. Jacob smiled. He was not sure whether he liked being called the rich uncle or not.

Nobody answered the boy, and he tugged at his father's coat, and insisted, "Well, is he, Papa? But he looks just ordinary, Papa. And he *has* just come all the way across the ocean, hasn't he? But his belly is almost as big as Uncle Reuben's, and he is much smaller than Uncle Reuben."

They all forced a strained laugh, and Herman's face grew red.

"That's enough," his father said. "Now be quiet."

They walked slowly out into the street, and then Jacob

46

hailed a taxi. There was not room for everybody. The women climbed in, and Jacob after them. The two little boys stood there, longing to ride home in a taxi. It was an adventure for them to ride in a motor car. They seldom did. Only the rich owned cars in Vienna.

They pleaded with their eyes, and Herman asked softly, "Can we go in the auto, Auntie Manya?" She was the boss, and the children knew it, and disliked her for it. She was always managing affairs and making decisions.

Jacob said immediately, "Sure, sure. You come in the taxi, children. There is plenty of room for you."

They loved him for this. Laughing happily, they piled into the taxi. The men went home by streetcar.

It was Jacob's first glimpse of Vienna. They drove along the broad, tree-lined boulevards. And lilac was everywhere. The sweet fragrance was wafted into the car by the gentle May breeze. The streets were alive with people; old men and women promenading slowly up and down, sitting on benches in the mellow evening air, young couples walking arm in arm. The cafés were full of patrons, some sitting outside in the improvised gardens and vine-hung terraces, chattering and drinking coffee.

"Did you have a good crossing, Yankel?" asked Manya.

"Yes," he said, leaning back comfortably in his seat, "very good, very fine." He revelled in the fact that he could speak his own language again. "The first two days, well, it was not so good. The rocking was not so good. I was sick a little."

The mother sat up straight, and stretched out a trembling hand, and her eyes bored themselves into his face, searching it in the semi-darkness of the car. "Sick? How sick? And what was it? Did you have a doctor there? Tell me, what was it? What sickness? Manya, you must bring the hot water bottle tonight yet. It is in your place. You took it for Reuben a week ago when he had his stomach bad. I'll make a hot water bottle tonight for Yankel."

Jacob laughed. "Mama, Mama, I'm all right, Mama." He patted her hand, and then he stroked her face and leaned her gently back into the cushions.

But she sat up again, and the anxiety had not yet gone from her voice when she said, "Yes, yes. You are all right. I pray to God you should only be all right. So what was it? What was the sickness?"

"I was only a little seasick, Mama. Everybody gets it when

you travel in a big ship on the ocean. But it's nothing, Mama. The stomach is a little bad, that's all."

Her voice rose higher, like dying embers suddenly stirred, and a note of triumph slipped into it. "So I knew from the beginning. A mother knows always. Manya, you will go to your place right away and bring down the hot water bottle. You will take the hot water bottle tonight, *mein Kind*, and in a few days you'll be well. Oh, Manya, I don't know if he should eat the meat on a bad stomach. No, no, I think better not. But the soup will be good for him. Hot chicken soup can't do any harm."

"Mama!" Jacob was exasperated, and his voice had a pleading note. "Mama, it is all right. I was sick about six days ago. And it hasn't to do with the stomach really. It is the rocking of the ship, Mama."

"Yankele, *mein Kind*." The words came floating from her mouth, spoken with infinite tenderness, and they lodged themselves deep within him. They made any further protests completely useless, almost sacrilegious. She spoke to him as though he were a little boy of ten. For her the passing of time meant nothing. He was her boy. She had lost two sons. He was the only son who survived, and now he had come to her. It mattered little that he had a son of twenty-five himself, and married daughters, and grandchildren of his own.

Herman's voice piped up and broke the silence. "Uncle, how does the ship rock? Does it rock this way or that way, Uncle?"

Jacob said, "It rocks both ways. It depends how the waves go, Herman."

"Are the waves big, Uncle Jacob?"

Jacob remembered Tassigny, and the way he had talked about the waves. "They are very big sometimes," he said, "and sometimes they are very small. When there is a storm they are very big."

"Then how is it that they don't turn over the ship so that all the people drown?"

"Now don't ask so many questions, Herman," Manya said irritably.

The boy slunk back into the corner of the car. Rivka, who sat in front beside the driver, turned round.

"Herman is just like you, Yankel," she said. "He asks questions all day long like a machine. We always wonder how he knows so many questions to ask. Poor Shaendl and

48

poor Albert. My children never asked so many questions in a week as Herman can ask in two hours."

"So he asks questions," said Jacob. "He is a bright child. Let him ask questions. I should only like to know the answers to all his questions."

Herman's eyes filled slowly with raging, impotent tears. Not even the pleasant jolting of the car could compensate him for the pain which his aunts had inflicted upon him.

Rivka sighed. "Poor Albert. As soon as he comes home in the evening, tired, and with all the worries on top, Herman asks questions."

Now Bernhardt came to the defence of Herman. Although he was two years older, he was far less aggressive than his brother, and he was very much devoted to him. He was a slight lad, and he had inherited his father's striking eyes. He had a thick crop of brown hair that was disorderly even when it was combed.

"Papa does not mind us asking questions, Uncle Jacob," he said firmly, and with the charming importance of a child. "He is never too tired, and he always answers them, and when he doesn't know, he says he doesn't know. And he said to ask as many questions as we like."

"Sure, sure, children," Jacob said reassuringly. "Ask questions. It's a cheap pleasure, asking questions."

"It's a cheap pleasure—yes!" Manya's voice was hard. "It's a cheap pleasure, and it can drive a person crazy, too."

Herman sat up straight and peered out into the street. "Look, Bernie," he cried, his voice filling with enthusiasm, "look, there's the Tegetthoff monument! Can you see it, Bernie? And it didn't take us long at all to get here."

They had almost reached the end of the long Praterstrasse where it gets shabbier and is suddenly redeemed by the huge, obelisk-like monument of Admiral Tegetthoff. The monument fills a big square into which flow five long avenues. Steps lead up to it, and its wide base is covered with straining figures of warriors and foaming horses, writhing wildly against the harnessing bridles. A thick, marble, pillar-like column, adorned with beaked prows of warships, shoots out against the sky, and on top stands the admiral, gazing far out into space, his hand gripping a telescope.

Herman turned to his uncle and looked straight at him. "Oh, Uncle . . ." For a long moment he was silent, afraid to ask another question. He could feel Manya's look on him, and it frightened him. But then his natural inquisitiveness got the

49

better of him, and the words came spurting from his mouth as if he wanted to prevent anyone from interrupting him. "Is it true, Uncle, what Bernie told me, and he asked his teacher two days ago, and his teacher told him, is it true that when you're right in the middle of the ocean you can only see water as far as you can see, and the sky over your head, and nothing else?"

Manya groaned audibly, and Rivka shook her head, but Jacob said very slowly, and very seriously, and his voice was friendly, "Yes, Herman, that is so. You can see nothing else except the sky and the water. No land at all."

The two boys looked at each other, and Bernhardt nodded his head. The taxi circled the square and went past it.

Herman said slowly, "Some day when we are bigger, Bernie and I are going away from here, and then we shall see the ocean. It is not good living here. Papa said so to Mama. I heard it. He said that it is bad for Jews here. He said people hate us. Why do people hate us, Uncle Jacob?"

A thick cloud of silence fell into the car and settled. Herman waited for an answer, and when none came he grew red and drew back. He was afraid to insist on an answer as he would ordinarily have done, because he thought they were angry with him.

At last Manya said, "Please, Herman. Your uncle is tired. He has come a long way. Enough for tonight." She turned to Jacob. "You see what I mean. He asks and asks and asks. No end to it. Who can answer all he asks?"

Jacob stared out of the taxi. The scene was no longer sparkling and colourful. They were now come into the east end of the city, and the streets were narrow and small, and no trees lined them. Big blocks of shabby tenement houses flanked the streets on both sides, looming darkly. This was not the Vienna, gay and careless, which innumerable motion pictures had prepared him to expect. Urchins ran about the streets, barefoot and dirty, and couples made love in dark corners. Through the open windows women stared down into the street apathetically or made conversation with neighbours. Jacob could not imagine these people dancing in the street. Of course, he had never really believed that people broke into song and dance at a minute's notice, leaving their work and filling the streets with mirth and laughter, but it was comforting sometimes to think that it might be true, especially after a hard day's work when he sat in the delicious darkness of a cinema (he always went to the Bellevue on College Street), watching handsome men and beautiful women act out enchanting illusions on the screen.

The taxi turned round a corner and came to a stop at Hillergasse No. 4.

A few people were waiting there, eager to catch a glimpse of Frau Grossman's rich son. In their eyes anybody living on the North American continent must needs have money. This axiom needed no proof, for it was self-evident. A few casual passers-by stopped and watched silently, wondering who the well-dressed man might be, because the sight of a well-dressed man arriving by taxi on an ordinary week-day was something extraordinary in these parts of the city. A few unkempt children came running from the other side of the street, and crept up quite close to the taxi, peering inside with hungry, devouring eyes.

Little Herman went over to them and said importantly, speaking in the broad Viennese dialect, "This is our taxi. My brother an' I've just been riding in it. Boy, it rides smooth."

One of the boys kept throwing a tennis ball up into the air and catching it. "So what?" he said casually. "I been riding a taxi two months ago when my big sister got married. An' it was much biggern this one, an' it rode a hellova lot smoothern this one, I'm telling you."

"How do you know? You never went in this one."

"Oh, I c'n tell." He stopped throwing his tennis ball about and focused his eyes on one of his friends. "I know plenty 'bout taxis, don't I, Pepi?" He looked contemptuously at the car. "This taxi's old an' creaky. I wouldn' ride in it for nothin'."

"Geh, schleich di," said Herman. "Go, climb up a tree. Listen, my uncle's just come from Canada. Say, do you know where that is?"

They stared blankly at him.

"It's way, way, way over the ocean," Herman explained. "He lives in a city called Toronto. D'you know where that is?"

They shook their heads.

His superiority firmly established, Herman said proudly, "It's right close to Chicago, an' my uncle's rich, an' he knows all the gangsters, an' he wouldn't ride in a taxi that's old."

This argument was absolutely irrefutable. They stood open-mouthed, looking with awe at Jacob Grossman, at his neatly pressed white suit and his white shoes. He paid the driver, slowly and with deliberate, almost studied poise, conscious of the silent eyes that were on him, conscious of the great sensation which he was causing. He liked it. He liked it very much. The mother still clung tightly to his arm. For her this was a great moment, and she looked about, critically scanning the houses on both sides of the street to note how many of the people she knew were watching from the windows to see her in this hour of triumph, and then her eyes came back to Jacob, following his slightest motions with great pride and tenderness. And Manya and Rivka, too, were filled with the importance which was emanating from Jacob, and which for a moment lifted them from the drab surroundings of their daily lives and raised them, if only for a fraction of time, to a position far superior to that of the people who were watching them.

THE mother and Manya lived in the same house, but they did not share a flat. The mother had consistently refused to move in with one of her daughters, preferring to keep her independence and her privacy.

The house was old and shabby. There were wide cracks in the grimy walls, and in places the plaster crumbled down in large, paper-thin patches. The lamps in the hallways were weak and threw a very small radius of light. The steps, though of stone, were worn down by the tiredness of the feet that had climbed them through the long years.

Shaendl heard them come and opened the door for them. Jacob rushed forward when he saw her and embraced her.

"My little Shaendl," he cried, veiling his emotions in a flood of words, "my little Shaendl! Let me have a good look at you. You were only a baby when I left, and I liked you best because you were a baby and you never nagged me. Your sisters (God should only bless them and they should live long) but they can nag a horse to death!" He took her face between his hands and held it away a little and looked deep into it. It was a thin, rather pretty face, with a straight, aquiline nose that broadened somewhat at the base, and her lips were full and sensuous. She had high, arched eyebrows, and her eyes were black and restless. She wore a dark-green, loosely-fitting dress and low-heeled shoes.

Suddenly she took his hands from her face and pushed him gently away, and she blushed deeply because she felt his eyes go over her body and the child was big within her.

Jacob was radiant with the reality of his happiness, and he hardly noticed the small, shabby hall, and the dark, old-fashioned kitchen that led off from the hall. They showed him into the living room, which was also the bedroom, and now for the first time his mother let go of his arm. From the time he had stepped off the train she had been in a state of hazy comprehension in which it was difficult to accept the fact that he was really with her. And so she had clung tightly to him to feel him move, and slowly her hands had convinced her eyes that he was actually there.

Jacob looked about the room. It was a fairly large, but poorly furnished room, and its two windows led out on to a big stony yard, with a few desolate patches of grass miraculously interspersed between the mass of stones, and two high, slender, but almost leafless trees eking out a meagre existence and starving a slow death.

A big wooden bed stood in one corner, neatly made, with a beige, velvety-looking cover spread over it. In the opposite corner was an old-fashioned sofa whose lining was worn threadbare in places and showed bulging springs, welling up softly like little hills in an otherwise flat stretch of land.

On the dark brown mantlepiece Jacob noticed two elaborate silver candlesticks. They had survived all the tribulations of the past six decades, and had always been his mother's most treasured possession. Jacob walked over slowly and fingered them.

"Mama," he said softly, "you still have the candlesticks."

They had always reminded him of the figure of a beautiful young girl. They had a slender throat, and then they swelled out a bit and the silver was hammered into a rounded form, like two young breasts, and then they became slender again, and then again they broadened, and the ornaments which were worked out of the silver and into it were very elaborate.

"Mama would never give away the candlesticks," said Shaendl. "You know that, don't you, Jacob?" Her voice was much more cultured than that of the others.

"I keep them always," the old mother said, as though she were defending herself. "Some things I must keep. We had never much, and we have lost twice what we have had, but a few things I keep always. And the candlesticks are so beautiful. The only really nice things which I have. When we were coming here in 1915, and on the roads a few soldiers stopped us and they wanted something, Papa said to give them the candlesticks, but I said no, not the candlesticks, because what will I light on Friday nights and on the holidays? And we have left everything, I said, only not the candlesticks. And then Papa gave them a little money and two—three bottles schnapps, and so they let us go."

Over the mantlepiece was a large photograph of Jacob's father. He looked rather forbidding and intensely serious with his long, grizzly beard and his earlocks. On his head he wore a *yarmolka*, a little black velvet skull-cap. He had been a very orthodox Jew, but in some respects he had given in to emancipated ways of living, and photographs especially had so fascinated him that he had finally consented to have his picture taken, even though some people frowned upon this practice. And indeed the stern gaze with which he faced the camera, and the deep scowl engraved around the edges of his lips made it seem likely that he himself had not been able to square the act with his conscience.

A big chest of drawers filled almost one side of the room, and tucked away against a corner was a wooden casket with iron hinges and two iron locks. A massive, oaken clothes-cupboard stood facing it.

The floor was of soft, wide-rilled wood. It had been scrubbed very thoroughly that morning. No carpet covered it.

"Noo, come on, sit down by the table, Yankel," said Manya. "Drink a little schnapps, eat a piece of cake. Come on, Yankel."

"I'll wait," he said. "I'll wait till the men come. I like to drink with everybody." He let his eyes wander over the table.

"This table is set out wonderful," he said.

The table was beautiful. It was burdened with fruit and cake and bottles of wine and schnapps. The drabness of the room was brightened by its fresh colours. Herman and Bernhardt were standing very close to the table, looking it over with watering mouths. Now and again Herman stretched forth a cautious hand and tickled a peach or stroked the smooth surface of a pear. But he did not dare disturb the symmetry of the table by removing anything, although he would have done so if Bernhardt had not been standing close by. If he took something, Bernhardt would take something too, and then his mother would probably notice because Bernhardt was clumsy.

"Here come the men," said Manya. "I can hear Reuben's steps."

Bernhardt made a tactical mistake and ran out to greet his father at the door, and Herman's hand climbed slowly up on the table, made straight for a big fruit bowl, like a thief who has thoroughly reconnoitred the territory and is sure of his way, and embraced a luscious yellow pear. He lifted it from the bowl, carefully and without disturbing anything, withdrew it slowly and slipped it into his pocket. Then he turned casually and strolled nonchalantly away to find a quiet corner where he might eat it in peace. Jacob had watched him all the time, and now he broke into a delighted laughter.

Shaendl looked at Jacob, and then her eyes wandered quickly to Herman and a smile crept into them. She knew what he had done by the way he strolled away and kept his eyes fixed on one spot as if he could see something magnificent there. She knew, too, by the way he grinned, self-satisfied and in eager anticipation of the treat to come.

"Oh, Herman," she said. "Come here, child."

The sweet tone of her voice made him cringe. "I haven' taken nothin', Mama, honest I haven'."

"Talk properly, Herman. You know I don't like it when you talk like that in the dialect. And you really shouldn't act like that. You see how Uncle Jacob laughs. He must think you get nothing to eat at home."

"Oh, we don't get much pears and peaches, Mama, because you always say they are so expensive. And Mama, it would've fallen off that bowl if I hadn' taken it."

"That's enough, Herman." She was angry because he had spoken the truth about their not being able to afford expensive things. "Go and put back whatever you took."

Jacob said, "Noo, noo, Shaendl dear. Let him eat the pear."

"No," she said. "First let him put it back. He'll get one later. And please don't spoil the children, Jacob. Now put back whatever you took, Herman."

Herman slurched back to the table and put the pear reluctantly into the bowl again. "It would've fallen off anyway if I hadn' taken it," he mumbled. "And if Uncle Jacob hadn' started to laugh, I would be eating it now."

Manya filled the little schnapps glasses, put them on a tray, and handed them round to everybody.

"To our mother!" Jacob toasted. "May she live long and be healthy!"

They all clinked glasses and drank to the mother.

Jacob smacked his lips. "Ahhh!" he exclaimed, his whole body suffused with warmth. "Good schnapps! Another drop, Manya, please, another drop!"

She filled his glass again. He raised it high in his hand and looked about the room and his eyes came to rest on Shaendl. "And now to Shaendl! To our little Shaendl!" His voice was trembling with joy. "And to the next grandchild, Mama," he concluded, quickly glancing from Shaendl to the mother. "God grant it may be born in a happy hour!"

"Amen," the mother said solemnly, and Shaendl blushed deeply as all raised their glasses to her and drank her health.

"It is time to eat," the mother said. "Yankel must be hungry after such a long journey on the train." She remembered his seasickness and her brow became furrowed. She turned to

Manya. "You think he can eat the white meat of the chicken?" she asked, and answered herself, "I think he can eat the white meat. White meat can't hurt even a sick child."

Rivka took the fruit off the table, and Reuben and Albert brought another table from the kitchen because the one in the room was not nearly big enough to seat all comfortably. Then Manya came in with a huge loaf of braided bread, fresh and crisp, and Shaendl behind her, carrying dishes of horseradish, and sour pickles, and thick red slabs of tomatoes, and a big plate of lima beans, mixed with eggs and onions, considered a great delicacy. The energy of all the women had for days been focused upon this great occasion, and each had contributed the dish she knew best how to prepare. With glistening eyes and watering mouth Jacob watched them load the table with good things until it seemed to cave in almost, and the white table-cloth was quite invisible.

They took their seats, the guest of honour fittingly at the head of the table, resplendent in his white suit. Reuben filled the glasses with red wine, and then he took the big loaf of bread and gave it to Jacob. Jacob stood up, broke off a big piece of bread, and spoke the ancient benediction, "Blessed be God, Who maketh the bread to grow from the earth." Then he broke the big piece into smaller pieces and passed them to everybody, and they broke the bread together, and drank the wine.

There was first the traditional *Vorspeis*, the entrée, *gefillte Fisch*, white fish, carefully cleaned and chopped up fine and flavoured with many spices. It had always been one of Jacob's favourite dishes, and the mother had not forgotten it. She herself served the plate to him.

Ah! It did her soul good to watch him lift his fork to his mouth. He closed his eyes in transport, as if to shut out everything in order to savour to the full the delectable dish. It did not escape her eager eyes.

He turned to her. "It is delicious. Nobody in the world can make *gefillte Fisch* like you, Mama."

She sat on his right, beaming as he paid tribute to her skill. *Gefillte Fisch* was not, she thought, the most salutary food for a man who had so recently suffered from seasickness and whose stomach must therefore still be tender, but it would be too cruel to remind him of it now. And anyway, a hot water bottle would remedy everything. She had infinite faith in hot water bottles.

At the other end of the table Herman piped up suddenly. "I don't like fish. Mama, can I have an apple instead of fish?"

"No," said Shaendl. "You eat your fish. And be sure you eat everything, or you get no dessert."

A dire threat! He turned to his brother. "Bernie, d'you like fish?"

Bernie thought fish was all right. Herman pulled a sour face. Deserted, then! Left all alone in his fight against fish! Grudgingly he kept on nibbling bits, only the thought of the ultimate goal sustaining him.

He was still jabbing at the fish with his fork when the soup was brought in, steaming and fragrant in the bowls. Herman won his battle against the fish. Shaendl took his plate away and gave him the soup. He grinned, even though he wasn't too fond of soup either. Why was Uncle Jacob ahh-ing and ohh-ing now about Auntie Manya's *Knoedeln*, the little dumplings that were swimming about in the soup and didn't taste like anything much to him? He would give the whole meal, the fish, the soup, and the chicken, for one piece of that wonderful chocolate cake with the almonds and walnuts sticking out all over, which he had seen in the kitchen in the afternoon. He hoped nobody would notice that he had picked a walnut from the cake. He made himself believe that the little yellow dumpling which he had just fished out of the soup was chocolate cake. It was easier to eat that way. Now everybody was joining Uncle Jacob in singing praises about the *Knoedeln*, and Auntie Manya was sitting there in full glory. And, horrors upon horrors, even Bernie was saying now that the soup was good! You could expect that from grown-ups whose ideas about food were all mixed up, but your own brother! He decided, however, that he had better finish the soup without any public protests, because he deemed it too dangerous to risk a showdown with his mother. But meanwhile, to help him endure the burden, he thought he could ask his uncle a few questions about the fascinating world across the ocean which, in his imagination, was peopled entirely by gangsters and Red Indians, the whole scene dominated by Tom Mix, whose struggle for righteousness and law and order he and Bernie followed faithfully every Sunday afternoon in a little neighbourhood cinema in the Wohlmutstrasse.

Manya was even now bringing in the big roast chicken, brown and juicy and altogether magnificent. She carried the platter with all the pompousness of a high priestess performing a mystic rite, and placed it carefully before Jacob for him to carve. There was a lull in the conversation. Jacob stood up in his place and grasped the big carving knife firmly in his right hand.

58

Herman leaned forward and asked in a loud, clear voice, "Did you ever meet Al Capone, Uncle Jacob?"

There was a moment of silence and then a wave of laughter swept the room. Herman was confused. What was so funny about the question?

"Well," Herman insisted, defending himself with relentless logic, "Al Capone lives in Chicago, and Chicago is right next to Canada."

"Canada is a big country," Jacob said, proudly flourishing the knife over his head, and he was addressing not so much Herman as all those gathered in the room. "You know, it takes you four whole days and nights to travel over the whole country, on the one side the Atlantic Ocean and on the other side the Pacific Ocean."

"Four whole days!" said Manfred, awestruck. "And all one country! To think you can go for all this time and you never have to show a passport." This aspect appealed to him most, for he was a travelling salesman, and frequently had occasion to travel in the countries surrounding Austria, in Hungary and Czechoslovakia, and one could not go anywhere for more than twenty hours without having to pass a border-control.

"What is even more amazing," said Albert in his cool, controlled voice, "is that in all this vast and mighty land there are not much more than ten million people."

Reuben shook his head and his eyes twinkled. "T-t-t-t-t. Everybody must have a city all to himself."

"Yankel," Manya implored, "please cut up the chicken. It will get cold."

He addressed himself to the task with gusto. "Right now," he said, as he cut deep into the meat, "right now unfortunately things are not so good. All over people are out of work. In Toronto alone thousands of people go around looking for work. It is hard to find a job these days."

"Everywhere the same story," said Reuben sadly. "All over the world the same story. Toronto is a big city, yes?"

"Oh, very big. Not so big as Montreal or Chicago or New York, but plenty big. It is right on a great lake. Lake Ontario. A lake, I tell you, big enough to drop in a few little countries, and you wouldn't notice it even. A lake big like the sea. Sometimes the waves are even bigger than the waves in the ocean, such a big lake it is. I like to go to the harbour in summer when it is nice and watch the ships come in and go out." He had finished carving the fowl, and sat down again.

"I like to watch ships, too," Reuben said, his eyes lighting up.

"On a warm afternoon I go down to the Danube and sit there a little and watch the ships. I have always loved to go on ships, although in my whole life I have only been twice on a ship." He chuckled. "Manya is afraid to go on the water. She is afraid something will happen and she can't swim."

"Why, Reuben!" Shaendl cried. "I never knew about your secret passion before. Why didn't you ever make Manya take swimming lessons?"

"Don't laugh, don't laugh," Manya protested. "It is dangerous to go on the water. Now I can tell you because Yankel is here with us and nothing happened. But all last week I was praying that nothing should happen to him, and that he should come here safe. Always I remember the *Titanic*. Such a big ship! And did all the bigness help her? Go fight with icebergs."

"Nine-tenths of an iceberg is under the water," said Bernhardt.

"On Lake Ontario there are no icebergs," Jacob said amid general merriment. "You go on the ship in Toronto, and in three —four hours you are in Niagara Falls."

Niagara Falls! A magic, famous name!

"Niagara Falls!" Rivka cried in astonishment. "You mean it is right close to Toronto?"

"Sure."

"You—you have been there?"

"Once? Ten times maybe in all the years."

It was astonishing.

"Is it big?" Rivka asked. "Like they say in the newspapers and like you see in the moving pictures?"

"It is so big," he said with all the pride of ownership, "I can't tell you in words. The noise from the falling water is so powerful, you can't hear even your own voice."

"All the rich people from everywhere in the world go to Niagara Falls," said Rivka, still awed, "and our own brother has been there, not once, but maybe ten times. To think that all this time we didn't know that the famous Niagara Falls is only a cat's jump from where Jacob lives."

Albert put his napkin to his mouth to stop from bursting into unrestrained laughter.

The atmosphere in the room was fairly charged with immensity. The mighty land, stretching from Atlantic to Pacific, the great lake, the ocean, Niagara Falls—and something of all this grandeur clearly reflected upon Jacob who had with his own eyes seen all these gigantic things.

And with the accent still on bigness, Manya asked, "The factory where you work, Yankel, is it a big place?"

"Oh, yes," he said, dipping a piece of bread into his gravy, "it is a very, very big place. There are now over two thousand people working there, and until a few years ago there were even more, only now on account the depression there are less."

"And it was not difficult for you to go away?" the mother asked. "They will be able to manage without you?"

Jacob began to feel a bit uncomfortable. He brushed the question aside quickly. "Now is not a busy time."

"You know," said Manya (was there suspicion in her voice, or did it only seem to him?), "I have always wondered. In your letters you used to write so little about what you do."

"Ach," he said with a short wave of his hands, "I am not a big letter writer, anyway." He knew the answer was not adequate. He felt Manya's eyes looking steadily at him. He had finished his chicken, and he pushed the plate away, and then wiped his mouth with his napkin. He thought frantically. And then he said, as casually as he could, "You mean to say I never wrote you that I am a designer?"

The effect of his words was gratifying.

"Sure," cried Rivka, "sure he wrote," and the sudden look of enlightenment on Manya's face testified that she seemed to remember, too.

Jacob stretched back in his chair expansively. "Ah!" he said. "You think it was easy? When I first came to America I didn't know where I would take the money for the next meal. But God was good to me. Now things are easier. I come to my office at ten, ten-thirty, I work a little, not too much any more." It was such a delicious lie. And who could say that it was not the truth? Did he not himself believe it at this moment?

An air of well-being and gladness spread through the room, for there is nothing more pleasurable and satisfying than to relate stories of hard toil and failure in times of prosperity and success. They were happy for his sake that things had worked out so well for him.

Manya leaned forward and asked confidentially, "You make a lot of money?"

He hesitated a moment. "Enough," he answered, curtly and with finality.

She did not press him further, for she had caught Reuben's disapproving glance. After all, a man's pocketbook is his own affair.

Herman suddenly clapped his hands. "The cake, Bernie!" he

rejoiced. "Look, Mama's bringing the chocolate cake!" Victory at last! The end of the long struggle with fish and *Knoedeln* and meat!

"What a cake!" cried Jacob. "But I couldn't eat any more if you killed me. I couldn't, positively."

"All right," said the mother. "You'll eat later."

Herman and Bernhardt exchanged significant glances. This time they were on the same side of the fence. How was it possible that a man should exult over fish and soup and meat, and so glibly pass up the crown and purpose of a festive meal, for which all else was but a prelude? Ah! Strange and mysterious are the ways of grown-up men.

Manya went out into the kitchen and came back with a pot of tea and a kettle of hot water. She poured the tea into big glasses and put a piece of sliced lemon into each. Jacob brought out a package of cigarettes and offered them round. Only Manfred and Shaendl smoked. Reuben took one, too, but only puffed at it a few times and then stubbed it out. Jacob struck a match and lit Shaendl's cigarette. The other women thought it outrageous and disgraceful for a woman to smoke, and the disapproval showed clearly in their faces. For years they had been fighting a losing battle against Shaendl's modernism, but out of deference to their guest they refrained now from making any comments.

Jacob reached out for a piece of lump-sugar, put it on the tip of his tongue and sipped the tea slowly, sweetening it as it passed through his mouth. "You know," he said, "last year I was reading practically every day something about Austria. And always the news was bad. Shooting. Civil war. I was trembling for you every time I looked in the paper. Then for a few months the papers didn't say much, and then suddenly in the summer I was reading that the Nazis were trying to make a *Putsch*, and they had murdered Dollfuss, and everywhere in Austria was martial law, and for two days, I'm telling you, I couldn't sleep hardly, thinking about you."

"It was a terrible year," the mother said softly. "In February, I remember at night when I went to bed, I could hear the noise from the guns. They were bombarding the Goethe Hof just across the Danube. And I lay in bed and I prayed because the children of other mothers were dying."

"Soldiers with tommy-guns were patrolling in the streets all the time," said Herman, "and we didn't have to go to school for a whole week. We had a holiday all week."

"God forbid another such holiday," said Reuben.

Manya sighed deeply and passed her hands over her face. "It was a terrible year," she said.

"What happened exactly?" Jacob asked. "To me everything was confused. It seemed to me everybody was fighting with everybody, and everything happened so suddenly."

"It didn't really happen so very suddenly," said Albert. "Things are going on inside a volcano before it erupts. The shooting was only the last act of this tragedy. The most spectacular and the most sensational, and the most easily understood. But everything must be prepared before the shooting can start. Everything was ready here." Albert sat bent forward in his chair, his elbows leaning against the table. "One day in March of 1933 the news came, with all the force of a thunderbolt, that the Chancellor had carried a bloodless *Putsch*, and that from now on we would be ruled by decree. The legal basis for this dictatorial act was an ancient statute, dating back to the days of the Monarchy, which Dollfuss and his lawyers had dug up for the occasion. About six months later Dollfuss said at a great parade that the old Parliament was gone forever. 'I announce the death of Parliament,' he said. And so a government that didn't have an absolute majority in Parliament killed democracy. Where did this leave the other parties? Above all, where did it leave the Social Democrats who had almost as many seats as the government, and who had for fifteen years or more formed the municipal government of Vienna? Everybody knew that things couldn't go on this way. Either Parliament had to be restored, or else the opposition had to be smashed completely. Starhemberg and Fey and the Heimwehr were crying for blood, and Mussolini was supporting them. And when Dollfuss threw his full support to them, too, it was clear what would happen. Democracy was dead here in 1933, and when the smoke cleared away after that dreadful week in February a year later, it was buried too. The workers didn't have a chance. It is a wonder that they held out for seven days. You can't fight howitzers with rifles. And so another country was swallowed up in the Fascist tide. And to us here who had to look on helplessly it seemed that nobody in the whole world cared. This is such a little country. Only six million people. We don't matter."

Jacob listened nervously. For the first time he became aware that Albert was different from the rest of the family. For the first time, too, Jacob noticed the quality of his language. He could not easily fit him into the picture. He had not expected to find such a man in his own family. Albert made a very undistinguished impression, and until a few minutes ago Jacob had almost completely ignored him. He was very tall and carried himself awkwardly. He never knew quite what to do with his hands. He twitched them nervously or let them dangle aimlessly and they underlined his awkwardness. He wore a grey suit that had been badly pressed. His tie was twisted and looked sloppy.

"You know," Albert went on, "years ago when the Social Democrats first started to build the *Gemeinde Häuser*, the great blocks of model apartments, the other parties cried, 'The Socialist municipality is throwing away the taxpayers' money. The building materials are so inferior that the new houses will fall to pieces in the next big storm.' Editorial after editorial proclaimed the same truth. But they didn't fall to pieces, neither in the next storm nor in the storm after that. People from all over the world came to admire them. They became showpieces of the city. But last year the cry was different. 'Now we know why these houses were built!' Starhemberg shouted. 'They are fortresses built by the workers!' Fortresses, indeed! The noble Prince didn't say why they built gardens and playgrounds for the children, and libraries and halls for concerts and plays."

Reuben suddenly got up and closed the windows.

"Why do you close the windows?" Jacob asked. "It is hot in the room."

"Somebody could hear," Reuben said.

Jacob's eyes grew large. He felt a shiver running down his back. Reuben's words sounded ominous and frightening to him. All at once he found himself thinking of the insignia on the cap of the storm-guard in the train. It brought the sweat to his brow. Haltingly he told them about the incident. They listened calmly, but it didn't seem to make a startling impression. After all, nothing had happened to him.

Albert shrugged his shoulders. "Ah, but you have a Canadian passport. That's a wonderful thing. Remember all the hundreds of thousands who must travel unprotected, hunted from place to place, like wild animals."

"Politics," Manya said, pronouncing the word as if it were obscene. "Dirty politics. Better not to mix."

"For years I used to say that, too," Albert retorted. "I took little interest in contemporary politics. What did politics have to do with me? My interest was elsewhere. Politicians were crooks and intriguers. But I found that even if I didn't take an interest in politics, politics took an interest in me. I heard Hitler's voice, loud and strong, and it kept on getting more

64

powerful. Suddenly I heard that I was of an inferior race, and that my blood was poison, and that I was the cause of all evil, and he thundered that when he came to power he would destroy me and my children. All that he says may be nonsense, but now he is in power in Germany, and he is already casting eyes on us. How then can I afford not to take an interest in politics when it is a matter of life and death? Even though I am powerless, I must take an interest. Already we are living under a dictatorship. Not yet the worst. But when a few people get together and want to talk, they must close the windows and they must lower their voices and whisper like conspirators. This is twilight terror. God knows how soon the full night will break over us."

Jacob's eyes were glued on Albert. There was something about him that reminded Jacob of Tassigny. His voice, when he was agitated, had the same driving intensity as the Frenchman's.

Manya said, "I am going to the kitchen to wash the dishes." The mother rose, but Manya motioned her to sit down again. "You stay here. Rivka and Shaendl will help me."

The three women left the room.

"Albert is a pessimist," said Manfred. "He paints a black picture. Too black. Sure since last year there is a dictatorship here, but like Dollfuss said himself, it is a moderate dictatorship."

Albert's hands twitched nervously. "Moderate dictatorship!" he scoffed. "What a lovely, harmless-sounding phrase. How can you say that, Manfred? Only because you personally haven't been attacked yet? Is that your test? What about February, 1934? Didn't you see the shattered and gutted buildings? Didn't you read the accounts of the trials that were conducted after the shooting was over? Were those accounts of justice which you saw there? The juries picked or cajoled into bringing in a verdict that had been determined long before the accused had even entered the court. And then Dollfuss could stand up and proclaim a Corporate State patterned on the model of Mussolini's Italy, and call it a moderate, paternal dictatorship! Who wants such moderation, such paternalism? And at any rate, a dictator is only moderate and paternal in his own eyes and in the eyes of his followers. But what if a man doesn't want such a fatherly patron? Where can he show his opposition since there are no more elections? How can he protest if there is only one party and everything that is published must be censored first? Dictatorship of any sort, however benevolent it pretends to be, can never be acceptable to me. I have never been able to believe that there can be such a thing as a moderate dictatorship. Some dictators are less bloody than others, but all are bloody. No dictatorship can function without a secret police and the denial of some of the most basic human rights. A murderer who kills only one man is moderate compared to one who kills ten, but both are murderers." He reached for a bottle and with slightly trembling hand poured himself a glass of red wine and gulped it down.

"What do you want?" Manfred asked petulantly. "Is Hitler better?"

"You ask me to choose between two evils when there is a third way. You give me Dollfuss's argument. 'I must be strong to ward off Germany's threat to the independence of Austria,' he used to say. So he crushed the trade unions, he hung their leaders or drove them into exile, and destroyed the only democratic force that could help him in the fight against Nazism, and then he turned round and cried that it is better to stifle the Social Democrats in their own blood than that Hitler should rule in Vienna. What logic is that? Hitler must have been the happiest man that February, because he was the real victor. The Austrian government was doing his dirty work for him, they were destroying his most powerful enemies. Anyway, Dollfuss got his answer five months later. Who shot him and let him bleed to death in July? And it is not Dolfuss's doing that Hitler is not now ruling in Vienna. We have to thank Mussolini for that. He doesn't want to see Hitler in Austria because he would lose control here as soon as his lackeys are removed, and Hitler would certainly remove them and put his own boys in."

Jacob listened with increasing apprehension. It had grown hot in the room with the windows closed. He wiped the perspiration from his forehead and crumpled the handkerchief in his hand. He leaned forward a bit, closer to Albert.

"But now," he said, and his voice was full of urgency, as if he hoped thereby to allay his fears, "now everything is quiet, eh, Albert? Things have settled down, eh?"

Albert shook his head. "Only on the surface," he said. "Beneath the surface there is a boiling cauldron. Hitler wants Austria and I can't see anything that could stop him. I think sooner or later he will make a deal with Mussolini, and the country will fall to him like a ripe plum."

"Never!" Manfred cried. "Never!" His face grew red and he banged his fist hard against the table. "England and France will never allow it. Never!"

"That's our only hope, but I'm not sure about it. The world is getting too used to the spectacle of one country after another slipping to destruction. A few newspapers will raise their voices. Perhaps one or two governments will even send so-called sharp notes of protest, but that's all."

Jacob raised his eyebrows and his forehead became furrowed. His hands hung helplessly by his sides. "Noo," he asked sharply, "you think then Hitler will come here?"

Albert did not answer immediately, and Jacob waited anxiously, as if the course of history depended entirely upon what Albert was about to say.

"Yes," Albert said at last.

"No!" Manfred shouted. "Never!"

An awful silence fell upon the room. Herman slipped quietly down from the sofa, went up to Jacob and whispered something into his ear. Jacob took two peaches from the big fruit bowl and gave them to him. Herman gave one to Bernhardt. The two boys sat silently, munching them.

Jacob rubbed his chin. "If—if you think the way you do," he said to Albert, "then why do you stay here? Why don't you go away?"

"I have a family," said Albert, smiling sadly. "But if I had the money, and (that's even more important), if I could then find a country that would let us in, I would leave tomorrow. With no money that is out of the question. And we would need a lot of money. For people who have no money the doors of foreign countries are barred with steel. The time has gone when a man could step on a boat and leave the way you did, Jacob."

Albert's words, spoken almost dispassionately, left a note of grim finality which made Jacob squirm inwardly. He turned to Reuben. "You haven't said a word all this time. What do you think?"

"I haven't said anything because I don't know," Reuben answered slowly. "What will happen, will happen. I don't trust in kings and presidents. My trust is in God. Everything is in His hands."

"God will watch over us," the mother said suddenly, as if to confirm Reuben's words. Jacob had almost forgotten that she was in the room, too.

"God's children live in Germany, too," Albert said. "If He could forsake them there, why not here?"

Reuben reached out absent-mindedly for an apple and began to peel it. "Satan is powerful," he said. "Sometimes it seems that he is even more powerful than God." The apple-skin curled up like a snake. "But never for long."

"Long enough for thousands of innocent people to get killed," said Albert. "Perhaps long enough for all of us to be destroyed."

"Perhaps," Reuben said. "Does God have to come to me to explain to me why things are the way they are? Who am I that I should argue with God?"

"I have no argument with God," Albert said. "My argument is with men."

Jacob rose abruptly and threw open a window. There was a breeze of fresh air and he leaned out of the window and stared down into the dark and empty yard. Reuben and Albert were arguing back and forth. Jacob thought suddenly how wonderful it would be if he could say to them, "Here, here is money for you. I am a rich man. Here, how much do you need? Here, take all you can. Things are bad and you're afraid the worse will happen? Then pack up your things and leave immediately. I will give all the money you need. With money a man can go anywhere and do anything."

The three women came back from the kitchen, and he heard Manya's voice, "Noo, you settled all the world's problems already? I always said that Albert should be a prime minister."

The presents! it flashed through his mind. He did bring something, after all! He felt as if he had stumbled upon a hidden treasure unawares, and he turned quickly away from the window.

"The suitcases?" he asked. "Have the suitcases come already?"

"Yes," answered Manya, "they are here. They are outside in the hall."

"I almost forgot," he said. "I brought something for the children and for you."

The words worked like a spell. Herman and Bernhardt jumped up immediately and ran out into the hall. Silently they inspected the suitcases. Then Herman tried the locks to see if they opened, and announced to his brother that they did not. Jacob came out of the room now.

"Uncle," Herman asked, taking the peach-stone out of his mouth and holding it in his hand, "have you got keys to open the suitcases?"

"Yes."

"Can I put the keys in and open the suitcase after, when you take it inside?"

"Yes."

Herman put the stone back into his mouth. It was a big stone and it was not easy for him to manipulate it. Jacob lugged the big suitcase into the room and the children trailed slowly behind him. He put it up on the sofa and took out his keys. Herman opened it.

Right on top was the cardboard box with the black shawl which Jacob had brought for his mother. He took the string off with nervous, slightly trembling fingers. The tissue paper rustled like dry leaves when he drew it back.

"This is for you Mama." He spread the shawl out and held it up for them to see. Nobody said anything, but he could tell by the way they looked at it how much they liked it.

The two boys stared into the suitcase, exploring it with their eyes. A lace shawl held relatively little fascination for them. It was only important as an indication of what was to come, and silently they set to speculating what he had brought for them.

The old mother was crying. Almost too much happiness had come to her in one evening and it was difficult for her to bear it all. Jacob went over to her and placed the shawl round her shoulders, and then he stepped back to look at her.

"Yankele," she said tenderly. With short, almost jaunty steps she hurried to the mirror to look at herself. The long, slender, rippling fringes of the shawl danced up and down as she went.

"Mama, you'll be the most beautiful old woman when you'll go out into the street now," said Shaendl. "Everybody will look at you."

"Oh," she said, gazing at her image in the mirror, "a mother suffers much with her children till she sees them big. Especially with Yankel I had worries. It is nice now I am old that he remembers me and comes to see me over the ocean. All the neighbours will look on me and they will say, 'Such a son Frau Grossman has.' That's what I lived for all the years. Why else do you bring up children? You hope and pray all the time that they will grow up well and that they will bring you pride and happiness." Tears were rolling down her cheeks and she wiped them away and went over to Jacob and kissed him.

He went back to the suitcase and fumbled about in it. Herman and Bernhardt watched him as though he were a magician in a side-show. And there was indeed a great deal of the showman in Jacob Grossman. He had the most appreciative audience any performer could wish for and he knew it. He could feel their eyes on him, and he moved with deliberate slowness, increasing the moment of suspense and tasting the sweetness of the hour. He took out the little case with the bracelet for Shaendl. Her black eyes smiled at him when he put it round her wrist. She stretched out her hand, turning it slowly so that they could all see the bracelet, and Albert went over to her and stroked her hair softly.

She looked up at him. "Do you like it?"

"Mhm. It's very nice. It suits you well. But then beautiful things always look more beautiful on you."

"Oh, Albert," she laughed, "you're being silly. After all, it's fourteen years now."

"I know," he said, "but you like it just the same. That's why you ask me, don't you, because you want me to say these things?"

"Oh, now then," she said, pursing her lips like a little girl. "Now you go and spoil it all." She pushed him away playfully. "Telling me you only say these things because I want you to say them. That isn't nice, is it? It's not nice at all."

He smiled at her. "Well, you asked for it. You should have taken the compliment without belittling it."

In the meantime Jacob had given the golden, flower-shaped ear-rings to Rivka, and they aroused quite some commotion because they could be screwed on to the ears and did not have to be pushed through the tiny lobe-holes.

"How can they stay on?" Manya asked doubtfully. "A little movement with the head and they must fall off."

"Don't you worry," said Jacob, his voice full of authority, "they don't fall off. They were made in America, and in America they don't make things so they fall off. You don't put holes through ears any more. A little girl doesn't have to suffer no more. This is a modern age. The women are the same as the men. A girl wants to wear ear-rings, the mother doesn't have to go with her and make holes in the ears. There's no time for such foolishness in the New World. Come on, Rivka, put on the ear-rings."

The children were getting impatient. Herman was still sucking the peach-stone. He took it out of his mouth now because he wanted to say something.

"Eh, Bernie," he whispered, "le's ask him what he brought for us. We won't have to show it around like they do. We c'n just take the things and go out in the kitchen and play with them."

"No, let's not ask. He might get mad and not give the things to us at all. Besides, how do you know he didn't bring us something like shirts or pants?"

That of course was a dangerous possibility. Herman's face fell. "All right," he said, "le's not ask, then. Le's just wait. But I don't think he did. He's a swell guy, Bernie, an' he wouldn' bring us shirts and pants." He put the peach-stone back into his mouth and kept on sucking it.

The ear-rings did not fall off. It was a great triumph for Jacob. But when he gave the tablecloth to Manya his triumph was somewhat impaired. She did not receive it with the same enthusiasm with which his mother and Shaendl and Rivka had accepted their gifts. She smiled and thanked him and laughed, but the laughter was feigned.

"I am an old woman already, what, Yankel?" She tried to make her voice sound jocular without succeeding. "I am an old woman already, eh? I am too old to wear bracelets or ear-rings!" She wriggled her body a little and laughed a hurt laugh.

Rivka took the tablecloth and looked at it. "It's a beautiful tablecloth, Manya," she said. "It's almost more beautiful than my ear-rings. Use it well, Manya."

"Manya and Rivka are acting like little children," Albert whispered to Shaendl. "Jacob should have brought the same thing for everybody. Manya doesn't like that tablecloth, and she'll bear a grudge against him as long as he lives."

"Shhh. Be quiet, Albert, or they'll hear you. And don't exaggerate just because you don't like Manya. She'll get over the tablecloth as soon as a few people say that it's beautiful."

"Uncle Jacob!" Herman could wait no longer. Impatience was eating him up. "Uncle, you said you got something for us. Have you got something for us?"

Albert looked severely at his son. "Herman, behave yourself. Wait till Uncle Jacob gives you what he brought for you."

"Yes, Papa."

Jacob said, "Today is a different kind of day, Albert. Sure I brought something for the children. I should have given to them first, but I forgot. Well, it doesn't matter."

"You'll spoil the children," said Shaendl. "By the time you leave here we won't know what to do with them."

"Oh, they will be all right," said Jacob. "I wish only somebody should have come to spoil me once in a while when I was a boy. Mama was so busy with the house and with everything, she had no time for such things, and so the only one left to spoil me was Manya, and better don't ask how she spoiled me." He chuckled. Then, like a magician who has just pulled a rabbit out of a hat, he flourished a small package in his hand. "Here is a pen and pencil set for Bernhardt."

Bernhardt opened the case and gazed transportedly at the green-shimmering twin pair. "Wow!" he exclaimed. "Oh, oh, thank you, Uncle Jacob A fountain pen and a pencil that lasts forever! Look, Herman! Where's a piece of paper? I'm going to write with them." His voice almost snapped with excitement and pleasure. He searched his pockets for a scrap of paper.

Herman watched him with eager eyes. He whispered, "See, I told you he wouldn' bring us shirts and pants."

"Yeah, I know. You—you got a piece of paper, Herman?"

"No."

Albert took a notebook from his pocket and tore out a page. He gave it to Bernhardt. The boy knelt down on a chair, his body bent over the table. He printed his name slowly, first with the pencil and then with the pen. His tongue stuck out a little from the side of his mouth as he wrote. He wrote carefully. Every muscle of his body was strained, tensely occupied in the writing.

Herman looked over his shoulder. "You won't have to dip your pen in ink now every time," he observed. "The ink keeps coming all the time in this pen."

"And for you, Herman, I brought a whole army."

Herman turned round quickly. In his excitement over the fountain pen he had almost forgotten that Jacob had not given him anything yet. Bernhardt stopped writing and climbed down from the chair.

Herman took the big box and opened it slowly. He stared into it for a long time and his face lit up. He placed a few soldiers in line-formation and trained a miniature machine-gun on them. "Ratta-ta-ta-ta-ta-ta," he went. Then he puffed out his cheeks and blew the soldiers down with a powerful blast of air. "How you like that, Bernie, eh?" he cried exultingly. "The boys'll like that, won't they, Bernie. Holzinger made himself soldiers out of paper. Wait'll he sees this! Look at this bridge here, Bernie. You can take it apart and put it together again, see? Oh, Uncle Jacob, thank you for this."

"You could paint half your soldiers over in a different colour," said Bernhardt, "and you'd have two armies. We could invent a really nice game."

Herman liked the idea. "Le's go in the kitchen," he said. "We c'n play better there."

Rivka kept on putting her hands up to her ears, trying to see if the ear-rings were still in place. She shook her head in wonderment. "You ever heard of such a thing?" she said to Manya, who was sitting beside her. "Ear-rings to screw on the ears! For a whole half hour I have worn them now and they didn't fall off. Imagine! Such marvellous things they can do these days!"

Manya nodded her head stiffly, hardly looking at her. To

72

bring everybody something personal, and leave her out! She felt neglected and the thought rankled and gnawed within her. A tablecloth! How could she show off a tablecloth to the neighbours in the street? She saw Shaendl taking a cigarette and lighting it casually, and she was suddenly roused to fury. Her lips tightened into a straight line.

"You *must* smoke, Shaendl," she hissed, "You *must* show Yankel you smoke! Shame on you!"

Shaendl drew back. "Manya, please. What's got into you, for God's sake? Don't make a scene now, please. There's no harm in smoking."

"No harm in smoking!" Rivka joined the ranks against the youngest sister. "No harm, eh? And the child, you think nothing of the child, what? Before the child is born even you teach it to smoke." Her voice rose higher. "The child will choke with the tobacco. No harm, she says!"

"Stop talking all this nonsense, Rivka," Albert said in a voice that carried finality. "Don't aggravate Shaendl. If she wants to smoke, she can smoke. Nothing will happen to the child."

"Hah! Nothing will happen to the child! Look who's talking. How do you know, Albert? You had so many children already? You talk and talk and talk. Go have children, and then talk."

"Look at her," Manya railed. "Like a . . . like a . . . like a prostitute!"

"Children! Children!" the mother implored, her parchmentlike skin pale, and her hands shaking with excitement.

Albert turned furiously and faced Manya. "Hold your tongue!" he roared. "You're just a bunch of ignorant fishwives!"

"Albert! Albert!" Shaendl rushed over to him and drew him away.

The other three men had been talking and had paid no attention to the women, but Albert's infuriated voice roused them, though they didn't know what had caused the turmoil.

"What's the matter?" Manfred asked. "Why all the shouting and the excitement?"

"Why? he asks. Are you deaf or something? A fine husband I have. Manya and I are fishwives, you hear? Ignorant fishwives! That is what he said."

"Ssh—shh. Don't excite yourself." Rueben tried to calm her. "So he said a little word. He didn't mean it like that. Don't make a big thing out of nothing."

"It isn't nothing." Manya was bracing herself for the attack. "Rivka was only saying a sensible word. So you tell a person what is good for her, and right away you're a fishwife. That is the thanks you get."

"That's the trouble with you," Albert lashed back at her. "You're mixing too much in other people's affairs."

"Look who's talking," Manya sneered. "My Chancellor! My President! The whole world's problems he can solve, and for himself he can hardly make a living. The only thing he can make is debts."

Albert's face grew pale. His whole body began to shake, and it seemed as if he was about to break into violent invective, but Shaendl quickly put her hands on his shoulders and restrained him.

"Albert, please," she said quietly. "You know what the doctor told you. You're not to get yourself all worked up. Please, it isn't worth all that excitement, really it isn't."

"Enough," the mother pleaded, "enough."

"That's how it is," said Reuben, breaking the momentary silence. "They take a little thing, and in a minute, no, in a second. . . ."

"You keep quiet," snapped Manya. "Before, when you should have talked, you didn't. Now be quiet. In all the years that we have been married, I cannot remember once that you have argued on my side. Not once." She gulped down a few rising sobs of indignation. "Always it is me who talks, and you sit quiet. Now say nothing. Albert always take Shaendl's side. Always. You see, that's a husband. Now be quiet."

And Reuben, smiling helplessly, sank back in his chair and was quiet.

Jacob was still in a haze. "Children, children," he asked, "what happened? Tell me, what happened? Who started all this?"

"Nothing happened," answered Rivka curtly. "It's all over now. I don't want to talk about it any more. It's a shame, that's all. The first night you are here, and . . . and . . . Nothing. Better not to say anything. You didn't hear, well, so much the better." She fumbled for her handkerchief. She blew her nose and wiped an angry tear from her face. Then she blurted out quickly, giving an impression of casualness, "Shaendl smokes, that's all. She smokes. It's not right for a woman, and it is not good for her, that's all."

Jacob looked at her, hardly believing what she said. Then he broke into a laughter that shook his sides. He laughed long and deep and hollow. The others sat there and watched him laugh.

"And that's all?" he said when he had finished laughing. "And that's all, eh? For this you cut your throats? So she smokes. So what? This is a modern world. This here is not a little village in Galicia. Women are not what they used to be. A woman can now be a doctor, a lawyer, an engineer." His voice was full of conscious superiority. "A woman is now just like a man. She wants to smoke, she can smoke."

"You hear this?" Manya's wrath was up again. "He is taking Shaendl's part."

The mother could not endure this brawl any longer. She drew the black lace shawl closer about her shoulders. "Yankel has come all the way so that you should fight? Just for this he has come? Today is a holiday for me, and you fight." Her thin, bloodless lips quivered, and heavy tears rolled slowly down the furrows of her cheeks.

"Don't get upset, Mama," Shaendl said tenderly. "It's nothing. Nobody meant any harm. It was just a little argument." She lifted her head and looked at the others. "But really," she said, "we ought to be ashamed of ourselves. Look how upset Mother is."

Jacob went up to the mother and put his arm round her shoulder. "Mama," he said affectionately. "Why do you excite yourself over nothing?" He smiled at her and laid his broad hand over her thin, emaciated one. She was no longer crying. The tears had dried quickly in the rills of her face, leaving small traces behind. When she felt the touch of Jacob's hand a surge of happiness swept over her. Her face was radiant and the tears came again, like a light shower of rain diffused by a beaming sun. She was jealous now of every minute in which she had to share his attention with the others.

"It is late," she said. "I think you should go home. Yankel has come a long way on the train and he is tired. He should go to bed, I think." Suddenly she sat up straight with a jerking motion. "Manya," she said, "how many times have I asked you. In the end we will all forget. You haven't brought down the hot water bottle yet. Go right away, Manya."

Manya groaned. "I'm too tired." Her fury had entirely spent itself. "Reuben, go upstairs for the hot water bottle," she said wearily. "It hangs behind the gas-stove in the kitchen."

Reuben rose heavily. He did not say anything. Manya gave him her keys. He grinned and walked out.

Jacob was dissatisfied. He did not want the evening to fizzle out on a note of discontent. "Stay a little while longer," he said jovially. "It is not so late yet." From his side-pocket he brought out a heavy, old-fashioned gold watch which was appended to a golden chain, and snapped open the lid. "Ohhhh!" he exclaimed, "what are you talking about? Late! It is only a quarter after eleven."

"My God," said Shaendl. "The children won't be able to get up tomorrow morning."

But even as she was about to call them, they came into the room, their faces red with excitement. Herman was just about to conclude a most complicated agreement, on which he had been working hard most of the time they had been out. Bernhardt looked dubious. He was not yet convinced that the bargain was a good one. Herman pressed him hard. He wore a pair of long trousers that had once belonged to his brother and hardly reached to his ankles when he walked. His shirt collar had been nicely laid out, but was crumpled now, and hidden underneath his coat. He hated ties and would never wear one. He said they choked him.

"D'you get it, Bernie," Herman was saying, "if I let you play with my soldiers for two hours, you've got to let me write with your pen for one hour. And I don't want to write with your pencil at all, see? But you can play with all my soldiers, and you can play with my bridges, too."

"Yes, I know," said Bernhardt, "but every time I play with your soldiers, you've got to play with 'em too, because there's no fun playing alone. But you're going to write all alone with my pen."

That was the problem which for the past half hour they had been unable to solve. Their negotiations always broke down when they came to it.

"All right, then," said Herman, making a final concession, "you can bring your friends up, and you c'n play with 'em, and I wouldn't even come near you. Are you going to let me write with your pen then?"

It seemed as if that might break the deadlock. "I might, then. But I'll tell you tomorrow."

"Why can't you tonight?"

"Because."

Bernhardt turned to Jacob, holding out a piece of paper. On it he had sketched, with a great deal of freshness, two graceful, long-necked horses. He had early shown some promise as a painter, and Albert and Shaendl were secretly setting much hope on him. He was only eleven and one couldn't predict anything, of course. But he had a sharp, discerning eye, and a natural and easy touch.

76

Jacob looked at the little sketch. He let his tongue tripple admiringly. "T-t-t-t-t. A real painter! Two horses! And they look just like real horses. I could go up and touch them almost."

Bernhardt stood there, smiling proudly.

"I c'n draw a horse, too," chirped Herman. "Can't I, Bernie?"

"No, you can't. All you can draw is lines, and not even straight ones."

"I can so. Didn't I draw a horse yesterday?"

"You said it was a horse, but nobody else knew."

Reuben came back with the hot water bottle and put it down on the table. There it lay, amid the fruit bowls, and the empty bottles and glasses.

Bernhardt said, "I'm going to be a painter when I grow up, Uncle Jacob."

"Ah!" Jacob cried. "I have a good friend who is a painter. A Frenchman. He came over with me on the same boat. A fine man. And I'm telling you he can play the piano better than . . . than, better than Paderewski. On the ship he had a few paintings, and when he showed them to me, I bought one. It's a fine picture. Wait a second. I bring it."

He ambled out into the hall to get Tassigny's painting which he had stowed away in one of the other suitcases. The family was getting impatient. They were tired and wanted to go home. Jacob came back with the painting. He stopped a few paces away from the table, holding it up for them to see. Albert was immediately interested. He looked intensely at the work. The others were puzzled at first. Then they laughed and shook their heads.

Jacob asked aggressively, "You don't like the painting? You don't understand, that's all. You should know Messiey Tassigny. Such a gentleman."

"What is it?" Manfred asked.

"A man."

"A man? Where?"

"Here. Look and you will see." He put the picture on top of the chest of drawers and propped it against the wall. "But this here man is not an ordinary type of man," he explained. "He hasn't got a head."

"Oh," said Manfred, "in other words he is a dead man."

"No. He walks around. He shouts. Only he has a megaphone instead of a head."

Manfred seemed puzzled. "What kind of a man is this? How

77

can a man walk around without a head? And you say he shouts, too? How is that possible?"

"Because he is that type of a man," Jacob reiterated. Tassigny's words came back to him, a bit jumbled and confused. He struck a rhetorical pose. "Men like him have no heads. And why? Because everything is only hullabaloo that's the reason why. From this type of man only empty words come out. Only hocus-pocus. He shouts so loud, you think it is the truth, and you believe him. All right. So you come in. Noo? What do you see? A cheap woman, that's all." He pointed dramatically at the female grimace glowering behind the right leg of the figure. His glance was fixed sternly upon Manfred, but the verdict came from Reuben.

"I don't like it," he said calmly. "Bernhardt can draw a nicer picture."

Jacob turned about sharply. "Bernhardt can draw a nicer picture!" he echoed Reuben in a mocking tone. "What are you saying? You know how much I paid for this picture?" He waited a moment to get every ounce of their attention. Then he said slowly, heavily underlining each word, "I paid thirty dollars."

The revelation was received in silence. Jacob glowered at them. His watery little eyes were fraught with meaning. Now then, they seemed to be saying, what do you say now? Now that you know the price of this painting, are you still not going to like it?

Manya's mind set to work instantly, painstakingly changing thirty dollars into Austrian currency. Thirty dollars, she calculated, were one hundred and fifty schillings. She gasped. That was a great deal of money when she considered that the weekly income of an average family in Vienna hardly exceeded fifty schillings. She herself had had to manage on less than that when times were bad. A hundred and fifty schillings for this picture! For a few splashes of colour! And not even a gilded, fancy frame! It was incredible to think there were people who would dare to ask such a price for this monstrous hoax, but even more incredible that there were people who would willingly pay that money. And her own brother! It was unbelievable. A man must have a lot of money if he could so easily throw away so much. But—but perhaps she had not heard right.

"How much you say you paid for it?" she asked.

"Thirty dollars," he said proudly.

She drew back, bewildered. Words failed her.

Albert had taken the painting into his hand and he and Shaendl were looking at it together. He let his fingers glide lightly over the surface, and then held the picture out at arm's length and leaned back.

"Quite fascinating, eh?" he mumbled.

"I don't know," Shaendl said. "It gives me the creeps."

"That's what he wanted." He drew his eyebrows together. "Tassigny. Tassigny. The name sounds familiar, but I can't recall where I've seen it. I may have come across it in some journals."

"Well, Albert," Reuben said. "What do you think? You know about such things."

Albert wouldn't commit himself. "It depends. Some people like that kind of art, others don't."

"Only crazy people," Rivka scoffed.

"I wouldn't take it even if you paid me thirty dollars to take it," said Manya, and her voice left no doubt that she meant what she said.

A sly glint slipped into Albert's eyes. He turned to Jacob. "You know, some day when Tassigny is famous, this painting may be worth a thousand dollars."

Jacob fairly jumped with pleasure. "You heard this?" he cried. "You heard what Albert said just now? Sure, why not? People get famous, you pay more. It's always like that. When, Albert, when?"

"Oh, perhaps in twenty years, perhaps in twenty-five."

Jacob's enthusiasm was somewhat dampened. It was a long time to wait. Still, if it really paid off, it was a good investment for thirty dollars.

Albert peered sideways at Manya, because it was for her that his remark had been chiefly intended. In matters of art she respected his opinion. She sat, stiff and tight-lipped, with her arms crossed over her bosom, but her face was blank. This was too much for her. What had happened to the world? Was the world crazy or was she crazy? She could remember a time when things had values which were fixed and incontrovertible. But now every thing was afloat. What had been true yesterday was, without warning, pronounced false today. When she was a girl, it had been God and the Kaiser. Who could ever have thought that the Kaiser would one day be driven from his throne and out of the country, like a pariah? Who could have thought that a housepainter, a corporal, would become the most powerful man in Europe? And if such an upheaval could come to pass, why, then perhaps Jacob's picture would one day be worth the stupendous sum of one thousand dollars. Nowadays she hardly ever dared to contemplate the awful state of affairs. For her world was everywhere crumbling and falling to pieces. Better not to think about all this. Better to trust in Providence, for the human mind was too weak to fathom the why and the wherefore of things. Better to perform faithfully all the duties of a good wife—keep the house clean, cook, and look after her husband, and leave the rest to God. The others were talking. Jacob was still showing off his picture, but she would say no more about it.

"We really must go," said Albert, turning to Shaendl.

"Yes," she said, "it really is high time. Herman, Bernie, come on, children."

They all rose. Manfred stretched himself. Manya got up and gave a little shriek of pain, because her legs hurt her. "I think it will rain in the night," she said. "I can feel it in my bones." The mother bustled about the room. At last she would be alone with her son.

Jacob wondered where he would sleep, because it struck him suddenly that this was the only room. "Oh, Mama," he said, "you have no room for me."

"No room for you?" Her voice was hurt. "There is a lot of room here for you. You will sleep on the sofa, my child." And, as if she sensed what was on his mind, she said quickly, "You are not ashamed to sleep in the same room as your own mother, Yankele?"

He bit his lip. "Mama, why should you say such a thing?"

And then he turned away from her and said good night to the others.

CHAPTER

VIII

WHEN they had gone, Jacob was really beginning to feel how tired he was. He went over to the sofa and stretched himself on it, bending his arms behind his head.

The mother came over to him and sat down. "Yankele," she said, "you look very tired. You will soon go to bed. I will just go out to put on hot water for the bottle." She stroked his face gently with her hand. "You want another glass of tea perhaps?"

He nodded.

"Yes, yes." She spoke as one speaks to a little child. It sounded strange and incongruous to him, but yet strangely natural, as though she could not possibly have spoken otherwise. "A hot glass of tea with lemon," she said.

He smiled. He felt like a child, and not like a man of fifty-three whom people sometimes called an old man. They were silent. He looked deep into her face, scanning it. It was old and tired and wizened. He could see traces still of what she had once looked like. She had had a well-formed face. Time had not changed the bones. Their outlines were as he had always remembered them, sharp and firm. Only the skin had sunk and had become leathery so that her face, once voluptuous and full, was now lean and sallow.

She stood up. Taking the shawl from her shoulders, she folded it carefully and put it away. Then she removed the *sheitel*, her wig, and covered her head with a big, three-cornered kerchief and tied it under the chin. Not since the day of her marriage, when she was nineteen years old, had she worn her own hair. According to eastern orthodox tradition it was cut off that no man but her husband might ever be attracted to her. Manya was the only one of her daughters whose hair had been shorn off at her wedding, but as soon as they had left their village, she had let it grow again. The mother, however, respected tradition too much to go against it.

She put the *sheitel* back into the chest of drawers. Tassigny's painting was still on top, propped against the wall. She took it into her hands and looked doubtfully at it.

"Do you like the picture, Mama?"

She shrugged her shoulders. "It's a picture," she replied enigmatically, and went out into the kitchen. He looked after her, watching her thin little figure go through the door. It was amazing how active she still was at eighty.

Jacob's eyes strayed across the room, up to the ceiling, and along the walls. On the wall over the sofa he noticed a nail sticking out. It bothered him there. He wanted to pull it out, but it would not give way. Suddenly a thought struck him. He went over to the chest of drawers and took Tassigny's picture. Then he hung it up, balancing it. He could not get it straight. Finally he left it, tipped slightly to one side. He stepped back to look at it. It pleased him there. He could not see how singularly out of place it was in this old-fashioned, poorly furnished room, a room whose only other decorations were two silver candlesticks and a faded portrait of Solomon Grossman.

Through the open door he could hear the hissing of the kettle as the water started to boil. He would very much have liked a hot bath, but there was no bathroom.

The mother came back. She poured the tea and put lemon into it. Then she went to the big wooden chest and took out fresh linen sheets to make his bed. She wrapped a towel around the hot water bottle and put it between the sheets.

"Tomorrow morning," she said as they sat drinking their tea, "you will go to Diana bath. You can take Reuben with you. I have put a big kettle of water on, so you can wash yourself now." She noticed the painting on the wall. "You think the picture is nice there?"

He nodded his head.

"I don't think it is so nice there."

"I think it is very nice," he said defiantly. Would it not one day be worth a thousand dollars? "Let it hang there, Mama."

She would do anything to please him. "All right. But your father, he would not have liked it." She took a long sip of tea. "It is now almost fifteen years exactly since he died. We had a flat then just around the corner. When Shaendl married, I moved out to this flat here. He died such a nice death. I wish I should die like that."

"Mama," he said, "why must you talk like that now?"

"Why not?" she said. "I am thankful to God that your father died so nice. He wasn't sick, he didn't suffer, nothing. One night he came home, and he said, 'Sarah, I don't feel so good.' So I made strong tea for him, and I gave him two aspirins. In the night he groaned a little bit, twice, three times. He woke me up because I sleep so light, and I asked, 'Shloime, what is

82

wrong with you?' And he said, 'Nothing, nothing. But perhaps you can make me a glass of hot tea with much lemon.' I got up and I walked out soft, because Shaendl was sleeping, and I made tea. I brought him the tea, and I put on the light in the room. I could see he was weak because he had to have both hands to sit up, and so I put a big pillow under him. Then he said, 'Sarah,' he said, 'I wish we would have already a husband for Shaendl.' 'Why do you worry about Shaendl all of a sudden?' I asked. 'It is nothing,' he said, 'but I am old, and I can die today, tomorrow, who knows when? And I would like to know that Shaendl is a bride already. I spoke with Abramo-witch today, and he said he knows a young man just right for Shaendl. I told him, good, let this young man come to see her. So he will come to see her next Sunday. It's time already that Shaendl should be a bride.' Then I went back to my bed, an' I heard him groan again, not so heavy any more. Then he was very quiet, an' I didn't hear a single noise. In the morning I looked at him, and he slept so quiet and he looked very nice. I didn't want to wake him up, so nice was he. But then I thought I will make some tea for him. An' when I brought in the tea and came close to him, I saw his eyes, how they were open, so strange I had never seen. An' I knew then that he was dead."

Jacob listened silently without even once interrupting. His fingers tapped the table softly, and he swayed his body lightly to and fro.

"With the money you sent," the mother said, "we bought a nice marble gravestone. You will see it when you go to visit his grave. Now go out into the kitchen. The water is hot already. I have put a basin on the chair for you, and I have put a towel there, too."

He finished his tea, and fished the piece of lemon from the bottom of the glass and sucked it dry. Then he rose abruptly and walked out into the kitchen. The kitchen had been cleaned and scrubbed, too, that day, but in one corner of the greyish-white ceiling a flimsy bit of neglected cobweb was still dang-ling. Leaning over the chair, he washed his face and his hands, and then splashed water over his chest.

The mother was already in bed when he came back into the room. She was lying with her head toward the open window, away from the door. All he could see was her face and her white nightcap. He thought she was sleeping, and he walked on his toes in order not to disturb her. But when she heard him move about, she turned towards him.

"Was the water hot?" she asked.

"Yes," he said.

"Tomorrow you will go to the steam-bath," she repeated, "and you can take Reuben with you."

"Why don't you sleep, Mama?" he said. "It was a heavy day for you."

"*Ach!*" she said deprecatingly. "I'll sleep. I'm not so tired."

He undressed slowly. He folded his trousers carefully and hung them over the back of a chair, smoothing the crease with his hands.

"Turn out the light, my child," she said.

The springs of the sofa squeaked as he climbed in. He stretched himself. His back hit the hot water bottle, and he sat up with a start because he had forgotten that his mother had put it there. He reached for it and let it glide gently down to the floor. He grinned and sank back into the pillows.

"Yankel."

"Yes, Mama?"

"You're in bed already?"

"Yes, Mama."

"Is it soft enough for you?"

"Yes, Mama."

"You have the hot water bottle there?"

"Everything is fine."

"It must be cold already. It is such a long time since I filled it up. Perhaps I should get up and put more water in it."

"No, no, no, Mama. It is so hot, I almost burned my back."

"Good so. Put it on your stomach and press it on hard, so the heat will get in."

"All right, Mama, don't you worry."

"I don't worry. Perhaps you should have taken a few aspirins too, to sweat a little bit. But—it doesn't matter."

"No," he said, "everything is all right. I don't need no aspirins."

The moon was out and the night was cool. He could see the tops of the two leafless trees swaying slowly in the breeze, like praying men. Across the yard there was another block of tenement houses. The lights in the corridors flashed on and off at irregular intervals. A few flies buzzed in and out of the windows.

Jacob asked suddenly. "Did the young man come to see Shaendl?"

"He came," said the mother. "He came a few weeks later. He was such a fine boy."

"Who was he? Albert?"

"No," she said, "not Albert. A fine, fine young man. He would have made her so happy! And money, he had money, too."

"So why didn't she take him?"

"Why? Why? I don't know why. A foolish girl."

"Did she know Albert then already?"

"No. But she met him a year later, and immediately she didn't want to look even on the other man. And he liked her so much. He used to bring her candy, and flowers, and even a ring he bought for her, only she wouldn't take it. And everybody like him, only not Shaendl. And he was such a fine man. Golden mountains she could have had. So she went and took Albert." The mother sank back into her cushions and sighed.

"And Albert?" asked Jacob. "Isn't she happy with Albert?"

"I don't know." Her voice seemed to come from afar. "I don't know. Sometimes she is very happy and sometimes she is very unhappy, but I don't know why. Shaendl doesn't tell me. It is all Albert's fault."

"Why are you angry at Shaendl, Mama? Can she help it if she was in love with Albert and didn't like the other man? Such things happen all the time."

"Love . . . Love," she said musingly. "In a marriage you have to think of other things besides love. When there is no money in the house, can you live on the love alone? In my time you didn't think of love when a daughter married. Was I in love with your father when I married him? I didn't even know him until a week or two before the wedding. The two families came together and they made the match. And didn't it turn out good? Didn't we live happy for almost fifty years?"

"Hhm," he said slowly. "So it used to be. But it's different now, Mama. It's a new world. The children want to be in love first and then marry. That's how it is." He paused. Then he asked, "Noo, and what is wrong with Albert, Mama?"

She did not answer immediately, and he began to doze off. But her voice roused him again.

"He is poor," she said, "very poor. He is poor as a mouse. And the other one, such a fine boy."

Jacob sensed that this was not the real reason. "But Mama," he said, "my father was a poor man. And Reuben is also a poor man. But if she is happy with him, what's the difference? And if she is unhappy sometimes, does it matter so much? Were you never unhappy in all the years? Was I not unhappy plenty of times?"

"It is a different sort of unhappiness with Shaendl and Albert. If I only knew why she is unhappy, I could help her perhaps. But she doesn't tell me."

"How many times is she unhappy?" he said. "As many times as all other married people. It's nothing. Why should she tell you all the little things?"

"But she tells nothing." Her voice became bitter. "Albert has made her a stranger to the family. She thinks of things such as a woman shouldn't think about."

His eyes were heavy with sleep. Her voice seemed to him more and more like a whisper coming from afar. He could hardly understand her last words. He turned over on his side, and his head came to rest on his hand.

The mother waited for him to say something, but she could only hear his deep, regular breathing, broken occasionally by a short, stab-like snore.

She called him softly. "Yankel!" And again. "Yankel!"

There was no answer. He slept.

She lay awake for a long time, thinking. She opened the storerooms of her memory and lived over again in the course of minutes the events of years. And so Jacob was born again in the mind of his mother as surely as he had been born of her body, and he grew up again, and the whole thing did not take longer than five minutes. She thought of 1902. That was the year he had left. Many had left that year and in the years that had gone before. People from their own village and from the neighbouring villages, people from the towns and from the cities, lured by the rich, free countries across the sea. They were mostly young men, searching for opportunity and hoping to escape from the great hatred. And so she had known long before he ever spoke of it that he would go, too.

For the years at the close of the old century had been bad years, years of restlessness and dark rumblings, aggravated by floods and lean harvests, and followed, almost inevitably, by bloody pogroms. Theirs was only a little village and nothing much had happened there, but reports had come to them, telling of ghastly and horrible things. She and her husband and the people about them had always accepted pogroms as natural disasters, visitations from above, like droughts, or storms, or disease. They blew over eventually, and then one might hope for a few years of peace again. Innocent victims were left dead or maimed, and innocent children were made orphans, but such were the workings of destiny, inscrutable and

86

perplexing. As well ask why lightning strikes one house and leaves unscathed the next. Life was a struggle in which much had to be endured and little could be enjoyed. It was to another world that the righteous must look. There God would mete out reward and punishment, to each according to his desert.

She remembered and lived over again the day in which Jacob, fidgeting about, first broke his decision to them. Though she had known that it would come, the shock was great. He was such a young boy, not yet twenty, the only surviving son, and it is not easy for a mother to let a son go out into a strange and far-off land, perhaps never to return. Had she not heard stories of wicked women in the big cities, luring ignorant and trusting boys with their painted faces and their false and winning smiles? Had she not heard of gangsters and sharpers, and how easy it was for unsuspecting youths to fall in with them, and go down to perdition, ending their lives in ruin and shame? And knowing all this, she tried to make him put off his plans for a few years, until he would be older and wiser in the ways of the world. But he could not be budged, and when his father realized at last that all protestations were in vain, he borrowed money and gave it to him. He left in March. They all came to the station with him. It was not a station, really, but just a wooden shack, and the trains only stopped if somebody wanted to get on or off. When the train finally chuffed and jolted its way to a halt, Jacob climbed in, holding the tattered old travelling-box tight under his arm to prevent it from falling open, because its locks were rusty and no key could be found that would fit them. He leaned out of the window and waved to them, his hair fluttering in the breeze.

And that was the last she had seen of him. But now she was glad that he had gone, for he had fared so much better than the other children, and he had at last returned to her, a prosperous man. She strained her ears to hear him breathe. He was an unruly sleeper. The sofa creaked and groaned under his weight whenever he shifted or turned his body.

The moon rose higher in the sky and the room became brighter. She could see him now, and she could also see Tassigny's painting hanging on the wall. It seemed weird to her, and mysterious. She did not like it at all.

After a while she fell into a light slumber. She always slept very badly. The least little noise woke her. She would wake if the wind rustled through the trees; falling leaves would rouse her, and twittering birds. She slept best toward the early hours of the morning when all living things are at their lowest ebb.

The misty dawn rose in the east, and her sleep tightened. Her breath came as regular as Jacob's, though not so deep, and she did not shift about at all, but lay sleeping quietly upon her back.

CHAPTER

IX

On the following morning at about ten o'clock Jacob went to call for Reuben. He walked up one flight of stairs and knocked on the door. Manya opened it. She was pleasantly surprised when she saw him.

"Yankel," she greeted him, "how are you? Did you sleep well? You must excuse me in this dress, but I am cooking in the kitchen. Today is Friday, so I must make all the things ready for tomorrow." She beckoned him in. "Reuben!" she called, "Reuben! Yankel is here."

"Who?" came his voice from the bedroom.

"Yankel," she shouted back, "Yankel!"

Reuben opened the door and stuck his head out. "Oh," he said, "a guest! A guest! Come in, come in."

Manya's flat was kept spotlessly clean. She was a very meticulous woman, and a hard worker. From the kitchen came the sweet, hot smell of baking, and a pot hissed on the stove. Manya's large hands were red and covered with the scales of a carp which she had just been cleaning.

"Go in to Reuben," she said. "I must go back or else my cake will burn."

"I don't want to stay long," Jacob said. "I only want to take Reuben and go to the *Dampfbad* with him."

"Oh!" she said, broadening her lips to a pleased smile, "Oh, that is nice of you. I am very glad that you take him. So he will not bother me for a few hours. I'm very glad. This way he does nothing. Go in to him. I will come in in a few minutes. Go in to Reuben."

Reuben was listening to the radio. It was an ancient model, and the reception was very poor. He had to sit close to it so that he could fiddle with the knob every time the static threatened to drown out the broadcast. He had on a pair of old, shoddy trousers, worn thin at the knee. He wore no coat, but sat in his shirt, with the sleeves rolled up.

"Well," said Jacob as he shook hands with him, "if you have a little bit of time I wish you to come with me to the bath."

"Yes," said Reuben, picking his ear, "yes. I have a little bit of time. I have really a lot of time. You know, since I got the pension two years ago I don't know often what to do with myself. Before, I liked to think always of the time when I would stop work and could rest up a little."

Jacob nodded his head. "In a few years I will stop work too, mit God's help. But I don't think I will be so sorry."

Reuben went on as if he had not heard him. "Funny how it is in this world. A poor man has nothing. He works away his life, and when he stops working, he is even sorry yet that he has stopped working. You are lucky. At least you can go around the world a little bit. But we, we have just enough to live. Not even that sometimes. You want a little drink perhaps?"

"I think we should go now. It will be late."

"So we'll be late a little. All my life I was early. So!—What have I got? I am sixty-seven years now. It's time I am late a little for a change. Manya," he called into the kitchen, "bring in the bottle schnapps."

"What?" she called back.

"The schnapps! The schnapps!"

Manya brought the bottle and two glasses. When they had drunk, Reuben got up to get his coat. Manya looked at him and then her eyes wandered to Jacob.

"No," she said, "no. Reuben. Look a little bit after yourself. How can you go out in a suit like that? Yankel is wearing such a nice suit and you want to go like this. You will look like a tramp when you walk with him. He will think you have nothing else to wear."

"Shhh! Shhh!" he said. "A little more quiet. A little more quiet." He passed his hand over his bald head. He fumbled about in his embarrassment and stood rooted to the spot, turning this way and that, uncertain of where he wanted to go. Then with a sudden jerk he strode over to the clothes-cupboard and took his suit out.

Manya said to Jacob, "He is like a big child, Reuben is. Never will he know himself what he should do."

Reuben stood with his suit thrown over his arm. "Enough, enough," he said. He tried to make his kind and gentle mono-tone sound indignant, but it seemed only louder, and he could not ban the gentleness from it. "A little bit at the time, Manya, a little bit at the time. Go out into the kitchen, so I will put on this suit."

"Oh!" she said, mocking him, "t-t-t-t-t. My husband is ashamed of me! You ever heard of such a thing? Forty years almost we have been married, and all of a sudden my husband is ashamed of me. You hear this, Yankel, my husband is ashamed of me."

She went out of the room, banging the door behind her. Jacob chuckled. In a way she reminded him of his own wife (may she rest in peace). But Manya seemed more bitter. And Jacob thought it might be because she had no children. She had borne two, but they had both been dead at birth and the doctors had told her that she must not have any more. Neither Reuben nor she had ever gotten over this great disappointment. Their life was empty because of it, and they felt that they had nothing to live for. It had made Manya envious and quarrelsome. She was forever longing for something which she could never have. It was much harder for her than for Reuben, and in some inarticulate way he understood that it was so. When she became querulous she usually let her anger loose on him. But instead of becoming enraged under the whip of her anger, he grew more gentle still, and he endured the lashes of her tongue with patience and in silence. There was no love between them. There never had been. Theirs was a marriage contracted by the parents. They had married because it had been deemed good by their parents that they should marry. It was generally believed that their marriage was a happy one, and indeed they themselves would have been the last to say that it was not. They never thought that their union was not what it should have been, except for the fact that they had no children. That, however, was a thing that could not have been foreseen, nor was there anything that could be done about it. But there had grown up between them a strong bond, forged by the long years of living together, and made stronger and more durable by the many hours of sorrow and hardship, and by the few hours of pleasure and happiness which they had shared together.

When Reuben had finished buttoning his trousers he went before the mirror and began to struggle with his tie. His fingers were very clumsy and one hand was always in the way of the other.

Jacob walked over to the window and looked out into the street. Women were bustling up and down, carrying big baskets filled with groceries. A fruit vendor stumbled by, pushing a handcart, shouting and praising his wares. He stopped in the middle of the road and from all sides women began to cluster round him like a swarm of bees attracted by the fresh colours of a beautiful flower. They handled the fruits, weighing them in their hands, examining them carefully. A big, brown-coloured truck swung round the corner and could not go forward because the road was blocked. The driver leaned out, cursing and blowing his horn, and the fruit vendor, shouting at the driver and at his customers alike, picked up the handles of his cart and pushed it over to the curb, followed by the throng of bargaining women.

"Jacob," said Reuben, his hands working away furiously, almost choking his throat, "Jacob, perhaps you can tie a tie?"

Jacob turned round, his body leaning against the window-sill. "Hm?" he asked.

Reuben's hands tied themselves into a knot around his throat. "A tie," he stammered, "a tie. Can you tie a tie?"

"Sure," answered Jacob, "sure. It's easy to tie a tie. Why do you ask?"

"Come here, please. Tie me my tie." He let his hands drop down. "I can never learn how to do it," he said helplessly.

Jacob quickly did the job. "There," he said. "All right like that?"

"Yes, yes," said Reuben. "Usually Manya does it, but I didn't want to call her in again. She is busy in the kitchen. And you know how women are. When you call them away in the middle of their work, they are angry."

Reuben put on his coat and then the two men walked out, bidding a brief good bye to Manya, who answered them from the kitchen without opening the door.

"It is not very far," said Reuben when they were out in the street. "Only about twenty minutes to walk. So I think if you want to, we could walk there."

It was a beautiful warm spring day. A light blue sky hung overhead, sprinkled with little white clouds, and the sun was mellow and soothing. It was one of those days in which even the most poverty-stricken districts appear more hopeful and less dirty.

Reuben led the way. After they had passed through some side streets they came to a long, broad avenue, lined with chestnut trees on both sides. It seemed incongruous that such an avenue should be so close to the narrow, crooked, cobble-stoned streets from which they had just emerged. But then, this was a city full of incongruities and sharp, striking contrasts.

Jacob and Reuben walked along very leisurely. Jacob's alert and eager eyes flitted about quickly, absorbing the scene, fascinated by the strangeness of the foreign city. He was astonished at the number of cafés. There seemed to be hundreds of them. By just looking at their exteriors one could judge the financial status of the patrons who frequented them, even if one could not see the patrons themselves. The cafés took on the character of the streets in which they happened to be situated, and they seemed to be an organic part of them. Jacob noticed that even at this early hour of the morning the cafés were far from being empty. Men were sitting at the marble-topped tables, sipping coffee, reading newspapers, ogling the people who passed by with bored expressions. Jacob wondered why they were not at their work. How did they make their living?

He turned to Reuben. "Tell me," he said, extending his hands and turning the palms upwards, "tell me, what do these people do?"

Reuben fixed his eyes on the pavement, and for a while he did not answer. Then he shrugged his shoulders and shook his head. "You ask me what they do?" he said phlegmatically. "They sit. They just sit."

"And what do they do?"

"I told you," said Reuben, "most of the day they just sit. They read the newspapers and then they talk. A few do a little bit of business, too. But mostly they just sit."

Jacob stared. Then he chuckled. "A fine occupation," he said, wagging his head, "a fine occupation. But how do they live? I see a lot of young men sitting there, too. When old men do nothing, I can understand. But the young men!"

"Most of the young men you see there," said Reuben, "are out of work probably. It is nicer to sit in the café than to walk around in the streets if you have no place to go to. This way they buy a cup of coffee and they can sit all day."

"One cup of coffee, and they can sit all day?" asked Jacob. "And nobody throws them out?"

"No. They don't throw them out. Why should anybody throw them out? What difference does it make if they sit there? They don't eat away the tables. The only thing they wear out is the seat of their pants. I like to go and sit in the café too, but Manya doesn't like it."

"But still," said Jacob, "they have to live. Even if they only drink one cup of coffee, they have to pay for it. And a man can't live on one cup of coffee a day. Or perhaps you are going to tell me that they get wages for sitting in the coffee-houses?" He smiled at his own wit.

But Reuben's face remained quite serious, and not a muscle twitched in it. "You know," he said, "often I have wondered how we poor people live, how we still can make a joke and laugh over it, too. Only yesterday I read in the paper that there are now in the city three hundred thousand unemployed men. And in the whole city there are not even two million people altogether."

"When you look at these men," said Jacob doubtfully, "you think they have not a worry in the world. They sit there so peacefully. Why don't they run around and try to get a job for themselves?"

"Where should they go and find a job?" said Reuben. "There is no place for them to go. As long as they have a few groschen left they would rather do this. This way at least they save their shoes."

Jacob's attention was suddenly caught by a strange and captivating sight. "Look!" he cried, pointing his finger, "Musicians! Musicians in the street!" So it was true after all. There was music in the streets. The movies didn't lie, then. Here, before his very eyes, was a four-man band, rending the air with lusty tunes.

But Reuben soon disillusioned him. "They don't play for pleasure," he said. "You will see street singers everywhere, and after a while you will not even notice them any longer. It is only another way of begging. Sometimes the players are real musicians, but they are out of work, sometimes only poor people who have maybe long ago learned how to play on a violin or on a trumpet, and now they are trying to make a few pennies this way. It is less like begging. But it is strictly forbidden to play in the streets. So people usually warn them when a policeman is coming, and then they stop playing and go away."

"Oh," said Jacob, "so that is how it is."

They stopped and listened to the music for a short while, and when one of the men came up to them, cap in hand, they dropped a few coins into it, and walked on again.

After a few minutes they could see the winding band of the Danube canal, and the palatial buildings which flanked it on both sides.

"Over there," said Reuben, "that great building. That's the bath."

Jacob had never seen a more luxurious public bath. He was amazed when they passed through the arched portico into the spacious rotunda whose centre was taken up by a large round marble pond. From the mouths of sculptured figures water was spouted into the pond, and goldfish swam about

94

in it, twisting and turning amid floating leaves of water lilies and thick clusters of green reeds. The walls were covered with frescoes, depicting the part that water had played in the progress of the human race through the centuries. Not all the frescoes were of equal artistic merit, but a few were executed with a magnificent, sweeping power, and the painter's brush had caught a moment of man's gigantic struggle to wrest energy from the roaring masses of water and had given it form and substance on the wall.

Jacob let his eyes feast upon the magnificence of the scene. He inhaled deeply. The air had the fresh, clean smell of a body just emerging from water.

"This is really marvellous," he said to Reuben. "Do you come here often?"

"Not very often. I usually go to another bath. It is smaller and not so nice, but it doesn't cost so much."

Jacob bought the tickets. He paid two schillings for both, about fifty cents.

When they had undressed they went first into the hot air chambers. There were four of these. Jacob could only stand two. The third was too hot for him and he was forced to leave it after a minute or two. He did not even venture to cross the threshold of the fourth. The waft of hot air which hit him when Reuben opened the door was enough to send him staggering back. Reuben, however, experienced in the art of enjoying artificial heat, strode boldly in. Sitting in a hunched position, with his legs stretched out before him, he remained there for a good five minutes while Jacob watched him through the glass door. His body was fiery red when he came out, but he was in an exceedingly good mood. He chattered gayly so that it seemed as though the heat had released some of the tension which was stored up deep inside that gentle man.

With great zest he led Jacob through the steam chambers. There the men lay stretched out on broad benches, with buckets of cold water ready. Now and again they reached out and threw the water over their bodies, and a white pillar of steam rose swishingly.

When Reuben and Jacob had had enough of steam and enough of heat, and had soaped and washed themselves thoroughly, they went for a quick dip in one of the four small tanks. From there a door led straight into a big room where attendants stood ready with soft warm towels and rubbed them dry. Then, clad in greyish-white bathrobes and yellow straw slippers they entered an elevator which took them up

95

one floor to the rest room. On both sides of this room were long ottomans, low couches without back or arms. The slats of the Venetian blinds were so adjusted that only a faint glimmer of light came through. And though the room was very large, so that one could almost speak of it as a hall, the semi-darkness in which it was shrouded and the beckoning couches gave to the atmosphere an extraordinary degree of restfulness and peace. They went up to the far end of the room and lay down, covering themselves with soft camel-hair blankets.

"Mmmmm." Jacob clenched his fists and stretched his body. "You know, Reuben," he said, "taking a bath here is hard work."

"Yeeees," Reuben said, "but it is wonderful. I feel like a new man."

Jacob brought out a packet of cigarettes. Reuben took one. For a while they smoked in silence. Jacob lay flat on his back, his eyes staring up at the ceiling. He watched the smoke curl and dissolve in the air. It was now about one o'clock, and a small river launch, passing by in the Danube canal down below, blew a shrill whistle. Jacob started. Involuntarily his thoughts travelled back to that other Jacob who used to wait impatiently for the factory siren to blow at twelve-thirty that he might go down to the cafeteria to eat his lunch, two sandwiches which Rosie prepared for him every morning.

"Here you can at least smoke a cigarette and there are no silly women to argue with you," said Reuben, smiling.

Jacob glanced over at him and laughed. "Yeah," he said. He raised his body slightly, propping himself against his elbow. "Tell me, what sort of a man is Shaendl's husband?"

Reuben bent forward, put out his half-smoked cigarette and deposited it in an ashtray. "This tobacco is too strong for me," he explained. Then he leaned back and did not immediately continue.

"I can never understand Albert," he said at last. "He is—I don't know. He thinks I don't like him because Manya doesn't like him, and he thinks I think he is crazy because sometimes I say he has crazy ideas. Although I will tell you honestly, Yankel, that sometimes I have seen after a long time that his ideas were not so crazy after all. But really, I like him. I like him in a different sort of way . . . a sort of . . . a sort of . . . How shall I say it? . . . where you can't tell the person how you like him—if you know what I mean. Sometimes I don't like him—not at all, and sometimes I like him very much. With Albert I never know. He is a strange kind of a man."

"Then how did he come to marry Shaendl?" asked Jacob.

"With them," said Reuben, emphasizing his words with strong, expressive motions of his large hands, "it was a love. A great love like you read sometimes in the books or you see in a theatre. It was about a year after your father died, and another man was calling on her, and we all hoped that she would marry him. He was a nice man, a—a serious man, and he would have given her a nice home, a nicer home I am sure than Albert. But she met Albert. And as soon as she knew him she wouldn't have anything to do with the other man. It was Albert, Albert, Albert, all the time Albert. But when she brought him home, nobody liked him. Manya kept saying all the time, 'Reuben, Reuben, we must do somthing.' And I said to her, 'Manya, you talk like a child.' I remember the words exactly as if I had only said them yesterday. 'Can you go with your head through a stone wall?' I said. 'So it is no use if you try to hinder Shaendl. You will only drive yourself crazy, but she will marry Albert, because your young sister is a very independent girl.' And so she married Albert."

Reuben let his body sink back into a lying position, and straightened his legs.

"But why didn't they like him?" Jacob asked. "You just say they didn't like him. But why? You must have a reason if you don't like a man."

Reuben put his hands behind his head and shifted his body into a more comfortable position. "You have been away for a long time, Yankel. So you have forgotten many things. Manya doesn't need a lot of reasons. If she doesn't like a person, she doesn't like him, and that's all. She doesn't give reasons. It wouldn't be like Manya to give reasons. And in this respect she is a little bit like your mother. Don't think, please, I am saying something bad. After all, Manya has been a good wife to me, but that's how it is."

Jacob smiled. He blew a smoke ring accidentally and watched it. It was a trembling, transient, wavery little ring, with its outside edges tapering, slowly expanding, finally breaking, yet faltering a split second, at last dissolving into the air.

"Now it happens, with Albert they had reasons," Reuben continued. "In the first place, they liked the other man. They were wishing only the best for Shaendl. And besides, Albert can get very excited. And especially he can get excited about his ideas. It is not so bad now any more, but ten, twelve years ago when he was a young man of twenty-five maybe, he did a lot of foolish things. Even if you have certain ideas, do you have to go around telling everybody? But he did. So he came, and immediately he began to argue with me and with Manya and with your mother, and generally with everybody. Now to me it doesn't make any difference what somebody tells me. Let everybody believe what he wants, so long as he lets me believe what I want, too. Most things are foolishness, anyway. But when it comes to your mother, it's a different story." Reuben sat up on the couch and put his feet on the floor. "He used to sit in the flat, saying how all the religions are hocus-pocus. Now I don't get excited about this. God is God. I don't know what I would do if I couldn't go to the synagogue, but if another person doesn't want to go, if he thinks it is hocus-pocus, it is his business. But do you think your mother liked it? How could she have liked it? All her life now she has been doing things just as they are written down. Your father was a very orthodox man, and he lived and died according to the laws in the Bible. And Albert used to talk about the war, and about how there shouldn't never be another war, but he didn't speak so we could all understand what he said, but he was talking with big words and nobody knew what he was saying. How can you like a man when you understand some of the things he says, only they are like poison to you, and other things that you would like to hear he says in a way you cannot understand? And so nobody liked him. Only Shaendl. And when she spoke about him when he was not there, she talked about him like you talk about a god." Reuben put his legs back on the ottoman and lay down again. "And he changed Shaendl. As soon as she married him, she became a different woman. She went with him to the night schools. Both together they were learning about I think politics and philosophy, or God knows what. And it seems to me that he got all these ideas from the night schools, because soon Shaendl was like him, and she talked like he did. Only she had a little bit more sense and she didn't come home to argue with your mother. But she wasn't the same any more, and your mother knew that she wasn't the same, and she was very sad because to her it was almost as if she had lost a child. To me this was not so sudden, because I had noticed, long before she met Albert, that she was going her own way."

"Well," said Jacob, "and what does Albert do for a living?"

"That is the whole trouble with him. He is a great, great talker, and he is full of ideas. But he is not a practical man. He knows about philosophy and about literature, and about this and that, but all put together are not worth ten groschen. Who will give him money for it? And when you have two little children at home, you need to give them milk and bread, and you need to buy clothes for them. Can you feed them with your ideas? In a week they would be dead. And now, now Shaendl is going to have another child. Why, I ask you? Why is she having another child? In a time like this when it is so difficult to earn enough money to make a living, and when you don't know what will happen tomorrow in the world, she goes and has another child. Foolishness! Foolishness!"

"What can you do?" said Jacob. 'In former days a woman had six, seven children, often more."

"That's all she needs," mumbled Reuben, "six, seven children. Three is not enough?"

"What does he do to make a living?" repeated Jacob. "Is he a teacher or something like that?"

"No. It would be good if he were a teacher. No, he has a little bookstore in a little street. It is not easy to find the street, but to see his little store is altogether impossible if you don't know exactly where it is. And most people who live around there have no money to buy books, anyway. There are a few students who buy second-hand books. So mostly he sells second-hand books now. On top of everything Albert has a good heart. So the students come into the store, mostly poor boys, walking about practically without shoes so they can study, and they tell him how they have nothing to eat and no money, and this and that, until he is practically crying for them, and then sometimes he gives them the books for even less money than he paid for them himself, and sometimes they take them away on credit, and God knows when they have enough money so they can pay him back. At night he gives a few private lessons to earn a little extra money, and Shaendl takes in a bit of sewing now and again. Otherwise they couldn't even make a living at all. . . . Be so good, Yankel, and give me a cigarette."

"Sure, sure. Here." Jacob threw the packet to him. "It's a pity, a great pity," he said. "What good is it if you know many things and you can do nothing with them? My David was a clever boy, and he wanted all his life to be a doctor. Two years ago he finished. Now he is working in a hospital. In a few years he will earn a nice living, I hope."

"Yeah," said Reuben, puffing out the smoke without inhaling it, "but you had money to send him to school. Albert is a very clever man, too. He is an educated man. He finished the *gymnasium* and after they were married he even went for one year to the university. But he is not a practical man, and that's his whole trouble. Talk, talk, talk. But what good is this if you starve on it? As soon as it comes to something that the world pays you money for . . ." He finished the sentence with his hands. "Mind you, he used to earn more money a few years ago. He was an agent for a big firm here. But he lost his job. He got another one, not so good, and then, about six years ago, I think, a terrible thing happened. He fell sick. A strange sickness. A nervous breakdown they call it. I don't know how he got it, but he was in the hospital for two months, and then for months afterwards he couldn't work. And when he was all right again, he couldn't get his job back any more. Here, if you fall sick, it is too bad for you. Then he borrowed money and opened his little shop. But in the three years that he has had it, I don't think he has been able to pay back even a schilling. I wouldn't be surprised if he was forced to make more debts. And now on top of all they must have this child. Foolishness! Foolishness! Noo, what's the difference?"

He paused for a moment and turned his head toward the window. The light came through the half-drawn blinds in thin, yellow bars.

"If Manya could only have had one child," he said sadly. "But—that's how it is. One too many, and the other nothing . . . I'm hungry, Yankel. Manya is probably waiting with the dinner, and angry already because I am not yet home." He got up quickly and stretched himself.

Jacob remained lying with his eyes half closed. A wild charge of thoughts stormed through his head, a jumbled, blurred mass of impressions without seeming significance.

"Come, Yankel."

Jacob roused himself and sat up heavily. "What time is it now?"

"It is almost two o'clock," said Reuben.

"Then I will still have time to go to the bank. I want to cash a cheque."

They went down to their lockers and dressed quickly. Outside the sun was warm and lovely, and almost blinded them when they stepped into the street. Jacob cashed his cheque, and then they crossed the bridge which spanned the Danube canal and boarded a streetcar.

The mother was waiting impatiently for him. She was a bit angry. "At last you come," she said, wagging her finger at him.

"I have warmed the dinner three times already, and I should really give it to you cold, except that I have put it on the stove again a few minutes ago, so it wouldn't be nice to take it off the stove now."

She went out into the kitchen and he came after her. "Here," he said, "here, Mama, I have brought you some money." He held out a bundle of notes.

"You are a good son to me," she said, looking at him tenderly. "I have nowhere to put it now. Keep it meanwhile." She raised the lid of a pot and stirred the soup with a big ladle. "This is the first time that I have cooked dinner in a long time. I eat with Manya and Reuben. But now that you have come, I wanted to cook. I like to cook and to bake. Here," and she turned and removed a white piece of linen which covered a long baking pan that stood on the table. "I made some cake today. Cottage-cheese cake. You always used to like it so much."

He smiled.

"When I am alone," she said, "I don't do these things. There is no pleasure if I cook for myself, and so I eat at Manya's place. I am so happy that you have come. I would have given ten years of my life."

He wished Rosie could hear this. She would never have objected to his going if she knew what happiness he brought to his mother. No, he thought, this was no pleasure trip.

"Everything is ready," the mother said. "Come in the room." She had bought the very best food, rich and wholesome things such as she would hardly have afforded for herself.

"I almost forgot," she said. "Shaendl's boys came here, and they left an envelope for you." She got up and fetched it. "Here."

He finished eating, wiped his lips and his hands, and then opened the envelope, curiously. It contained a piece of paper folded several times, and on it Bernhardt and Herman had scribbled messages.

Jacob read aloud,

Dear Uncle Jacob!
    I am writing this with the fountain pen you gave me yesterday. It is a very nice pen, and all the boys like it a lot. The day after tomorrow is Sunday and I want you to come with me to the Prater where I will show you

all the things I know. Herman also wants to come, but he wants to write it alone, so I'm going to let him.

Many kisses your nephew Bernie Reich.

Bernhardt's writing was neat and straight, but it was not so easy to decipher Herman's scribbling. It was crooked and heavily interspersed with ink spots.

Dear Uncle Jacob!

Bernie has given me his pen but I can't write so good yet cause [here he had evidently given the reason, but it was impossible for Jacob to make it out]. But the pen is very nice. I wish I had one too. I want to come with you to the Prater too, on Sunday.

Many kisses from your nephew Herman Reich.

Jacob leaned back in his chair and laughed. "A fine pair of boys Shaendl has," he said.

"Yes," said the mother, "they are wonderful children, but Albert is making heathens out of them."

"Don't worry, Mama," he said. "What is this Prater?"

"It is not far from here. There are merry-go-rounds there, and acrobats, and things like that. You will take them, Yankel, won't you? For weeks already they have been talking about that."

"Of course," he said. "Of course I'll take them."

The afternoon passed quickly. The mother bustled about the room, making things ready for the coming of the Sabbath. She took a white, embroidered tablecloth from the wooden chest and spread it over the table. From the kitchen she brought two *chalehs*, specially braided loaves of bread, and laid them at the head of the table, covering them with a plain white cloth of linen. She went over to the mantelpiece and took the two silver candlesticks. These she placed just behind the braided loaves and put big white candles into them.

Jacob strolled out for a while. When he came back, she sat close by the window where the light was strongest. On her lap she held an ancient, page-worn Bible, bound in brown leather. She kept on reading and he did not disturb her.

The day waned softly and the shadows lengthened on the wall. The afternoon slipped slowly into evening. The room grew hazy and dim in the dusk.

The mother rose and went over to the table. She struck a match and lighted one candle. Then she took it and put the flame to the second candle, speaking the blessing as she did so.

The room grew suddenly bright and then dim again, and the objects that were farthest away from the table remained shadowy and visible only in outline.

A few minutes afterwards Reuben came in and called for Jacob. Together they went to the *shul*, the first time in many, many years that Jacob had gone on a Friday night.

The synagogue, a small, bare place, was in the basement of a big house. The Holy Ark, adorned with a light blue, star-embroidered curtain, was its chief ornament. To the side, facing the east wall, stood the Reader's desk, and on it two thick candles burned in brass candlesticks. A few wooden benches and prayer desks made up the rest of the interior. About twenty men, most of them old and bearded, were gathered together now. The service had not yet begun and they stood about in small groups, talking. Some of them had been there for several hours, for the *shul* is not only a place of worship, it is also the social and intellectual centre of an orthodox community, where men come to study and to talk.

When Jacob and Reuben came in, the soft hum of conversation ceased, and all eyes were upon them. A few men came forward to greet them.

"This is Shloime Grossman's son," said Reuben.

There was a ripple of excitement, and several voices speaking together.

"Oh, Oh!"

"Solomon Grossman's son!"

"Who?"

"Shloime Grossman's rich son!"

"Oh!"

"Welcome! Welcome!"

They crowded round him, pressed his hands, escorted him to one of the front benches, right behind the Reader, a seat of honour. He was proud of all the attention lavished upon him, and he wished that his father could be here to witness it.

The Reader, a wizened old man with a beard as white as newly fallen snow, wrapped himself in his long prayer shawl, bowed his head before the ark and kissed the fringes of the light blue curtain. Then he took his place to begin the prayers. He intoned the opening psalm in a thin and trembling voice.

Oh come, let us sing unto the Lord!

They joined in with him, a chorus of gruff and untrained voices, chanting,

Let us come before His presence with thanksgiving,
For great is the Lord,
A King greater than all the mighty.
In His hands are the depths of the earth;
His also are the heights of the mountains.
The sea is His for He made it;
And His hands formed the dry land.
Come, let us worship and bow down;
Let us bend the knee before the Lord.

Jacob looked about himself and saw the old men swaying slowly to and fro in prayer. For a moment it seemed to him as if his father were standing by his side. He could see him clearly —the long, black caftan, the grizzly beard, the little bluish-black skull-cap. And there he was himself, a small boy in short trousers, a bit restless, his thoughts wandering away from the prayers. And then the firm grip of his father's hand on his shoulder, and stern eyes silently calling him back. And he remembered vividly how his father had examined him every Friday after supper to see how well he knew and understood the portion of the Bible prescribed for that week. He loved the story of Joseph and his brothers above all others, and especially that part in which Joseph at last reveals himself. "How does he make himself known?" That was the way he always put the question, year after year. "He sends everybody away," Jacob answered, "but the Egyptians could hear him weeping." His father's eyes glistened, and his voice trembled when he asked the next question. "What does he say to them?" "He says, 'I am Joseph. Is my father still living?'" So the examination went, and when his father was pleased he used to hand him cakes from the table and keep on examining him while he munched them.

Reuben's voice broke into his recollections. He sang with fervour, trying to make his gentle monotone as flexible as possible.

Come, my friend, to meet the bride.
Let us welcome the presence of the Sabbath.

They all rose and faced the door where the Sabbath was now symbolically entering. Reuben's face was radiant, and his voice rose higher.

Come in peace, thou crown of thy husband,
With rejoicing and with cheerfulness.

Here, in this unadorned and unpretentious place, was the source of his strength and of his patience.

"Of all the days in the week," Reuben said as they walked home, "Friday evening is to me the dearest, even dearer than the Sabbath itself. For a few hours I can forget all the troubles and worries, and I am not afraid what the future will bring, because my heart is so full of peace that I cannot think how it is possible that there is such a great hatred in the world. And when I say the prayers I think often, how is it that men have written such noble words and yet they can go out and murder, worse than the wild beasts of the jungle?"

Manya and Reuben came for supper. Jacob was in a festive and jovial mood, filled with great contentment, and his mind was perfectly at ease. They ate slowly, as people do when they have a lot of time. After supper they sat around the table, talking softly and drinking tea. They did not put on the electric light. It was much more intimate and cosy to sit by the flickering glimmer of the candles. Their voices were low and one might have thought that children were sleeping in the next room and they were trying to be careful not to wake them up. They spoke only about pleasant and joyful things, as befitted the time and the occasion.

After an hour or two the candles were burnt low, two tongues of flame, flickering up and down. The room had grown quite dark. For a while they sat in silence, watching the flames perform their dance, enjoying the peace and the restfulness which was spread over the room, filling it.

Manya and Reuben went home. The mother and Jacob undressed in the dark. The night was sufficiently bright for them to see what they were doing. They did not talk very much. The mother asked him a few things and he answered her, but that was all. They were both very happy, filled with a happiness they could not express but could only feel, because its source lay not in some accomplishment or in some fortunate event having come to pass, but sprang from a state of mind. It was a happiness that could best find expression in quiet, peaceful sleep.

CHAPTER

X

THE Sabbath passed quietly. All through the day the mood of festivity and perfect contentment never vanished, but was even increased. It waned a little towards the end of the day, when a note of sadness and regret that it would now soon be over mingled with it.

Manya wanted Jacob and the mother to have dinner at her place on Sunday, but the mother would not hear of it. During the first week of his stay, she insisted, she had a monopoly on him. The two women finally compromised, and it was agreed that Manya and Reuben would come down and have dinner with the mother and Jacob, an arrangement that did not please Manya at all, because she had wanted to exhibit the mastery of her cooking and the art of her baking. In order not to deprive herself wholly of that pleasure, she came down laden with sample dishes in sufficient quantities to supply a full course meal for two grown men.

They had hardly finished dinner when Bernhardt and Herman came bursting in, breathing heavily because they had run all the way. They threw themselves at Jacob without paying much attention to the others. Bernhardt wore a pair of knickerbockers and Herman had on short leather pants and a dark-green *Bauernjanker*.

"Did you get our letter, Uncle Jacob?" they asked, both speaking at the same time.

"And are you going to take us to the Prater?"

"We know a lot of places there."

"And I bet you've never seen what we're going to show you there, 'cause nobody knows about those places except us."

"Yes, and one of the side shows has got a new program, all new. They got a knife thrower, and *die Dame ohne Unterleib*. She's a woman that hasn't got any lower body at all. Gee, I'd like to see that."

"Yes. We're going to see all that, but first we're going to show you our cave in the Krieau."

"Mhm. We're going to let you crawl in, but you've got to promise us that you won't tell anybody where it is or how you get in there, 'cause it's secret, see? Are you going to promise, Uncle Jacob?"

The mother said, "Quiet, children. Quiet, please."

"We discovered that cave, and only three people in the whole world know about it. You'll be the fourth, Uncle. We're going to show it to you because you'll be going away from here soon and you won't have a chance to tell anybody. But you mustn't let a word slip out of your mouth while you're here. And you know, when you're in the cave you can see everything that's going on outside, but anybody that's walking around outside can't see you at all when you're hidden inside."

"That's true, Uncle. That's the kind of a cave it is."

"Children! Children!" cried Manya, holding her hands to her ears. "Quiet! Quiet! Uncle is eating. Don't bother him now. Let him eat."

They ceased talking abruptly, and it was as though a heavy rain of machine-gun fire had stopped, making the stillness yet more pronounced.

"All right, all right," said Jacob laughingly, "we'll go in about an hour, and you will show me everything."

"One hour!" they exclaimed, and their voices had the long-drawn ring of disappointment. "One hour! But that'll be too late."

"What do you want?" said Manya. "It's only just after one o'clock. Everything is closed yet in the Prater."

"Not on Sundays," said Herman. "They open early on Sundays. And we want to go to a lot of places. Besides, our cave is a far way off, and we want to sit in it when we get there. So we've got to leave here early."

"All right, all right. You'll have plenty of time." Manya's voice was becoming irritated. "Now sit down, and be quiet."

Reuben reached for a knife and cut two big slices of cake for the boys. "Here," he said, calling them. "Eat this and sit down quietly for a while."

"Are you going to come with us soon?" said Herman filling his mouth with a big piece of cake.

"Very soon," said Jacob.

"They come, and the whole house is upset in a minute," said Manya, looking at the mother. "Sometimes I'm glad I have no children. At least it's quiet in the house."

"Is your mother at home?" Reuben asked. "And have you eaten dinner?"

"Yes," answered Bernhardt, "we've eaten long ago. Mama and Papa are both at home. Mama is sitting like this." He walked over to a chair and assumed the pose of a person reading, "and Papa is making a sketch of her. My Papa can draw well, Uncle Jacob, and I'm going to be a painter when I grow up. I'm going to be a famous painter with pictures hanging in the big galleries. And I'm going to send you a picture all the way to Canada. You're going to like that, won't you, Uncle Jacob?" He spoke with such conviction and in such earnestness that one was almost ready to believe that he would be a great painter some day.

"I'm going to be a carpenter," said Herman, his mouth full of cake. "You know what, Uncle? I'm going to make you a big chest of drawers out of mahogany wood and polish it real nice for you."

"Oh, you don't know what you want to be," came Bernhardt's disparaging remark. "You change your mind every day. Last week when the man came to fix our broken window, you watched him, and then you said you wanted to be a glazier because you liked the way he cut the glass and kneaded the putty with his knife."

"Yeah, I know," admitted Herman. "But I didn't want to be that, long. I'm going to be a carpenter, I know for sure, 'cause I like it."

"You only like it because you watched a man planing a piece of white wood, and another was polishing a chest and he made it all shiny. You change your mind every week, but I don't."

"Well, you're eleven. I bet when I'm eleven I'll still want to be a carpenter."

"All right," said Bernhardt. He got off the chair and walked over to the sofa on which Herman was lounging. "All right, then. What do you want to bet for?"

Herman considered a moment. "I bet my honour against yours," he said then firmly. "If I've changed my mind and want to be something else when I'm eleven, you can have my honour."

"All right," said Bernhardt.

They shook hands.

"Uncle Jacob," said Bernhardt, "did you hear what the bet was?"

Jacob's sides shook with laughter. "Yes," he said.

"All right. Now you've got to part our hands."

They came up to Jacob, their hands firmly clasped.

Jacob looked at them with a puzzled expression on his face. "How shall I do it?" he asked.

"Just part our hands," said Herman impatiently.

Jacob took hold of their wrists and pulled their hands apart. The bet was concluded.

"Are you going to come with us now?" asked Herman.

"Let your uncle finish his dinner in peace." said Manya. "He'll go with you when he is ready."

"Oh, but he's finished his dinner long ago," said Herman. "I c'n eat much faster'n that, can't I, Bernie?"

"Sure you can. I can, too."

With suspicious eyes they watched Jacob smoking a cigarette. At last he rose. "Reuben," he asked, "you will come with us?"

"Oh, no," broke in Herman, exchanging a swift glance with his brother. "Uncle Reuben can't come with us today. We can't show him our cave. We can only show it to you 'cause you won't stay here long enough to tell."

Reuben smiled. "Go with them, Jacob," he said. "Go with them. They want you for themselves. What do they want me for? They've known me all their lives."

"Come on, Uncle," they said.

The boys walked on either side of him, talking rapidly, and both at the same time, so that Jacob had a great deal of difficulty understanding what they said, and no chance at all of saying anything himself. His difficulty was further increased by the fact that they began talking in the broad Viennese dialect as soon as they were in the street, and Jacob could only get every tenth word or so. It was obvious, however, that they were talking about their cave, describing it carefully, sketching its position and the way of approach, emphasizing again and again that he was the fourth person to be let into the big secret, and making it quite plain that he was to regard this as a great honour and distinction, indeed the greatest privilege which they had in their power to bestow upon anyone.

Suddenly Herman stopped. "Look Bernie. There's Holzinger," he said, pointing his finger at a small boy who was hopping along curiously on the other side of the street. He took three big steps, and then he stopped. And then he made three very small ones, just setting one foot in front of the other, and stopped again. He completed the process of moving himself forward by hopping three paces. Then he started the cycle all over again.

Herman formed his hands into the shape of a long O and placed them in front of his mouth. "Oh, Holzinger!" he shouted. "Holzinger!"

The little boy lifted his head slowly and peered across the street.

"Holzinger," shouted Herman, "Come across here! This is my uncle! The one I told you 'bout! The one that's just come from Canada!"

Jacob laughed. Putting his fingers to his lips, he cautioned, "Sssh! Not so loud!"

A few people stopped and glanced at Jacob and passed on. Holzinger came running across the street. He was exceedingly short-sighted, and on his little snub-nose he had a pair of thick, round, metal-rimmed glasses.

"Hello, Herman," he said. His voice was hoarse. "I'm hoarse," he said. "Where are you going?"

"This is my uncle. The one I told you 'bout. The one that came all the way from Canada. The rich one. The one that gave the soldiers to me, and the fountain pen to Bernie." He took Jacob's hand and held it, moved by a subconscious desire to show that Jacob belonged to him.

Jacob chuckled, his face beaming with pleasure. He was not embarrassed at all. The boys stood there, radiating charm and happiness. Holzinger opened his eyes wide, and let his lower lip curl down. He moved his head very slowly, letting his eyes wander carefully over Jacob, observing every detail.

"Is that him?" he asked. He was evidently very much impressed by what he saw. He scratched his head. He had red hair. Then he rubbed his nose. "He's got white shoes," he observed, addressing himself to Herman.

"I know," said Herman.

Holzinger finished his critical examination. "Where you going?" he asked.

"We're going to show him our cave, and then he's going to take us to the Prater and to all the shows, and he's going to let us ride on the merry-go-rounds."

"Say, c'n I go with you?" Holzinger asked timidly. "I mean just to see the cave?"

Herman shook his head sadly. "No, you can't. We can't show you the cave. Bernie an' I discovered it. Only my father's seen it except us, and now we're going to show it to our uncle. But nobody else can see it."

"I got a cave too," said Holzinger. "If you show me yours, I'll show you mine."

"Oh, but ours is much better. And besides, my uncle wants to be with us."

"Wait'll my uncle comes," said Holzinger, pouting. He looked up at Jacob once more, and then he left them, walking slowly, with head bent, rubbing his nose with his finger.

They went on, and soon they came to the same broad, tree-lined avenue along which Jacob had walked with Reuben. But instead of walking along it, they crossed it and went on beyond.

Here, only five minutes from the poor district in which Jacob's family lived, there were no houses, but only open ground and meadows, so that it seemed as if one had left the city and were out in the country.

Not many people were about at this early hour of the afternoon. Jacob and the boys walked along the gravelled pathways, flanked on both sides by cultivated lawns. They passed the Rotunde and the exhibition buildings, and then the race-track which lay desolate and hot in the midday sun because no races were run that day. Jacob shuffled alongside the boys. They had grown silent suddenly, and led him quietly. They had now walked about fifteen minutes, and Jacob was beginning to wonder where they were leading him. He looked about, searching in vain for merry-go-rounds.

"Boys," he asked at last, "where are we going? Where are the shows? There is nothing here."

"I know," said Herman. "We're going to show you our cave first. Then we can sit in it for a while, then we'll show you all the other things."

They turned sharply to the right, swerving from the cultivated lawns.

"This here is the Krieau," said Herman proudly. "Now you've got to walk real slow and careful, Uncle, and you've got to look around you to see that nobody follows us, see, 'cause we don't want anybody to find out where our cave is."

Jacob laughed. The children looked at him quickly, their eyes berating his improper conduct. They walked slowly, their bodies bent forward, and now and again they stopped, pretending to have heard a noise. Occasionally they did hear something, and then they fell flat on the ground, though the noise of crackling twigs and shuffling footsteps was usually produced by no one more startling than a woman pushing a baby carriage on the beaten pathway. Jacob of course did not go down on the ground, but remained standing, and since the bushes were not very high there he could see the people who walked by and they could see him. One woman stopped, startled by the figure in the bushes, and looked at him with an astonished expression as though she wondered what he was doing in there.

The children, stretched flat on the ground, tugged at his trousers and whispered furiously, "Uncle, get down, Uncle! Look, Uncle, the way we do! It's easy, Uncle!"

But he only laughed, and after two or three attempts they gave up urging him on.

Herman was rather disappointed. "When we took Papa in here," he said, "he went down just like we did." And turning to his brother, he added, "Somebody's gonna see us and come after us and find out where our cave is."

The brush grew thicker now, and soon it reached over their heads. Interspersed among the bushes were birch trees, and the ground was a maze of roots and leaves and twigs. Here and there wild lilac sprigs blossomed, and Jacob plucked a little sprig and put it through his buttonhole. He tripped a few times when his foot got caught in the noose of a root, but then Bernhardt, who walked behind him, got hold of his arm and prevented him from falling. Jacob tried to keep his eyes screwed to the ground, but now the sharp edges of shoots and branches began to whip his face so that he did not know whether to keep his head down or up. His suit became covered with leaves and twigs and clinging things of all kinds.

"Children!" he begged. "Children! Enough for today! I've seen enough for today."

"Oh," said Herman, "but you haven't seen our cave yet. You haven't seen anything yet. Oh, Uncle, you aren't getting weak, are you? You're not soft, are you? Oh, please, Uncle, you're making a lot of noise. Walk soft and careful, Uncle! Try not to tread on a twig when you see one. Somebody's sure to hear us and come after us."

In spite of his discomfort Jacob had to laugh. He stumbled along, his arms stretched out wide before him, parting the brush furiously, and the sweat trickled down in big drops from his forehead.

At last they came on to a clearing, and Jacob could stand up straight. He inhaled deeply. The boys dashed across the clearing and disappeared in the bushes on the other side. Jacob walked slowly, enjoying the sensation of walking along in a normal posture.

Suddenly Herman's head appeared, framed in a mass of leaves, and he shouted, "Come on, Uncle, run across, Uncle! Somebody's gonna see you."

And Jacob, startled by the voice, obeyed the command quickly and without questioning, like a soldier stealing through the enemy's positions. He cut a funny figure as he shuffled across the clearing, flat-footed, taking short, rapid steps, panting and perspiring, his belly wagging quickly up and down. But strangely enough, he did not mind it now. He was indeed beginning to enjoy this little adventure. For a moment he was a young boy again and thought back to the time when he had discovered hide-outs and had played with his friends.

He was across the clearing now, and the bushland swallowed him up again. He ruffled the hair of the two boys as soon as he came to them, an action which brought him a reprimanding look from both.

They pushed along, and he pressed on with them, no longer half-hearted and grumbling, but now in the game with all he had, ducking when they ducked, dodging imaginary foes when they did, and pretending with them that dozens of silent eyes, peering from behind every tree and every bush, were following them to find out the secret of the cave.

Suddenly the boys stopped, motioning him to be silent. Herman went on alone, carefully parting leaves and brush, sharply scanning the terrain about him. After a few minutes of perfect silence, broken only by twittering birds and scampering squirrels, he raised his hand and beckoned them to come.

"We're getting close to the cave," whispered Bernhardt.

Herman went on, and they followed him. At last he said, pointing his finger, "This here is the cave."

It was not really a cave, but simply a deep hollow in the otherwise flat stretch of ground, surrounded by a dense mass of bramble bushes and brush. From a nearby depository the boys had lugged three big, flat-topped stones, which they used as seats. They had also slightly parted the twigs on one side, thus making an opening through which they could look out, but could not themselves be seen.

"This is our cave," said Herman when they were finally in it. "Do you like it, Uncle?" He was happy and proud. Columbus could not have been prouder after he had discovered America. "We discovered it. Do you like it, Uncle?"

Jacob looked around. "Yeah," he said. "It's all right."

"Sit down, Uncle," said Herman.

Jacob took a handkerchief from his pocket and dusted the stone before he sat down. The march had quite exhausted him. He wiped the perspiration from his forehead. Then he took off his shoes and emptied the sand and the stones which had accumulated there.

At a given signal Herman and Bernhardt crawled up to him. "Now you've got to promise that you won't tell anybody how you got in the cave," said Herman. "We should really have put something over your eyes, but you're our uncle."

Jacob looked from one to the other.

"You've got to give us both your hands," said Herman.

Jacob held out his hands.

"Now you've got to say it," said Herman.

"I promise," said Jacob.

"You've got to say it all," said Bernhardt.

Jacob looked puzzled. "I promise," he repeated.

"No," said Bernhardt. "You've got to say, I promise I won't tell anybody where the cave is, and I'll be a true confederate."

"I promise I won't tell anybody where the cave is, and I'll be a true confederate," said Jacob.

"Now you're one of us," said Bernhardt.

"Yes," echoed Herman. "Now you're one of us."

"I'm glad," said Jacob. "I'm really glad."

The boys crawled back to their stones and sat down.

"Now there are four big confederates," said Herman. "There's us and our papa and you, Uncle. And then—there's Holzinger and Steiner and Freud and Gruber. But they're only small confederates. They're our friends, but they can never really get inside the cave."

"Yes, but our papa is still the greatest confederate," said Bernhardt, "and nobody can ever become as great as he."

"Our mama would be one, too," said Herman, "but naturally we can't have girls, so she can't be in, although Mama isn't really a girl, she's a woman, and that's not the same, is it Uncle?" His voice had the tone of someone answering his own question even while asking it.

Jacob said, "Well, children, tell me what you do. Do you go to school?"

"Sure," said Bernhardt. "School will be over soon for this year. I'm going to finish the first year of the *gymnasium*. I'm learning Latin already. Do you want to hear me say something in Latin, Uncle? *Patria nostra olim provincia Romana erat.* Do you know what that means, Uncle? It means: Our country was once a Roman province." He paused to let his words sink in. "Herman is still in public school," he went on, "and he's got two more years to go before he can enter the *gymnasium*. I've only got seven more years to go before I finish, and then Papa said he's going to send me to the College of Art if I still want to go. Papa said he's going to see that we can do all the things he wanted to do, but could never do. I love him."

"I do, too," said Herman, sitting with head bowed, and staring down on the ground. "So far I like geography best of all. And whenever I want to, Papa sits down at the table, and we have a big atlas at home where all the countries are painted in with different colours, and then he tells me all about the foreign countries, Papa does. Mama likes it, too, and sometimes she comes and sits down, and listens, too. When I'm big, Uncle, I'm going on a ship. I'd like to be a sailor."

Bernhardt looked quickly at his brother. "You just said at grandma's place that you wanted to be a carpenter. You lost your bet now."

"No, I didn't," Herman shot back. "I c'n be a carpenter on a ship, can't I?"

"No, you can't. You lost your bet."

"I can so," Herman cried aggressively. "I didn't lose my bet."

"Yes, you lost your bet. I've got your honour."

"You have not!" Herman jumped up, ready to throw himself at Bernhardt.

"You lost your honour," Bernhardt jeered.

Herman sprang forward and hit him. Bernhardt struck back. In a second they were rolling on the ground, tightly interlocked, wrestling furiously.

"Children! Children!" cried Jacob. He tried to part them. He went down on the ground too, dirtying his suit. After a great effort he pulled the boys apart. They stood there, scowling at each other. Jacob was hardly able to restrain them from rushing again at one another. They were straining like wild horses to shake off his hands.

"A fine pair of partners you are," said Jacob. "What kind of a federation have you got? You make a federation and then you fight."

They became calmer, and he let go of their arms. Reluctantly, and still glaring at each other with hostile eyes, they went back to their stones and sat down.

"You still lost your honour!" hissed Bernhardt.

"I did not," Herman snapped back.

"Children, children," Jacob begged them, "I'm not going to be a confederate if you're going to be like that. And if you keep on fighting, I'm going to tell where the cave is, that's what I'll do."

"Oh, no, you're not!" they both cried, and immediately they banded together again. Herman stretched out his hand, a sign of submission, and Bernhardt took it.

Jacob smiled. "That's right. That's what I like to see."

"You're not going to break your word?" they asked.

"No."

"It doesn't mean anything if we fight," said Bernhardt,

"honest it doesn't, Uncle Jacob. We fight all the time, but we still love each other, don't we, Herman?"

"Sure," said Herman. "Sure we do."

"You can fight and still love each other," said Bernhardt, his elbow propped against his knee and his hand cupping his chin. "Mama and Papa said so, too. Mama and Papa often argue, and often they shout at each other and are angry. But it is always all right after a while. And once, when Papa left angry and slammed the door behind him, Mama stood there and she cried, and I went up to her and put my arms around her like this—" he bent over and embraced Herman, "and I kissed her and asked her if she and Papa didn't love each other any more, and she said yes, and she said that I must never think like that, and that she loved Papa more than anybody else in the whole world, except us, and that Papa loved her too, just as much. And I know, because I asked him, and he said so. And Mama said that people can love each other very much and still fight and hurt each other, even more sometimes than people who don't love each other at all. She said I'm still a little boy and that I couldn't understand all these things, but that I would some day. But I told her that Herman and I always fight, and yet I love him, and she said that's almost the same thing."

"Sure I do," said Herman. "Sure I love Bernie." And he leaned over and embraced his brother and kissed him on the cheek.

A great tenderness came over Jacob when he saw this. He bent forward and patted the hair of the two children. "You're all right, my boys," he said. "You're all right."

Suddenly the boys sat up straight. Then they leaned their bodies slightly forward and listened intently. They could hear voices not very far off, and the noise of crackling twigs, breaking under approaching footsteps.

"What's the matter?" Jacob asked.

Herman threw a reproachful glance at him. "Shhh," he whispered. "Not so loud. Somebody's coming this way, can't you hear? I bet they heard us, 'cause we talked so loud. I—I just hope they miss our cave."

The footsteps came closer and two or three voices were audible now, conferring in a whisper. The boys lat flat on their stomachs, peering out through the peep-hole. They hardly dared to breathe. They were almost choking with tension. Even Jacob held his breath and ducked his head quite low. Suddenly he was very much concerned about the whole thing and found himself wishing, almost praying, that whoever was approaching might miss the cave and go past it. The footsteps were quite close now, and the leaves on the bushes rustled and swished as they were being brushed aside by a vigorous pair of hands.

"Somebody's coming right at us," Bernhardt whispered sadly. "They've found the cave."

Herman was almost in tears. "Let's fight them," he said, clenching his teeth.

"It's no use," said Bernhardt. "I bet they're stronger than we are. Let's make a pact with them."

"No," Herman said firmly. "Le's fight them."

The boys stood up, and Jacob stood up with them. Together they prepared to face the intruder.

Now the last screen of protecting leafage gave way, and the figure of a lad of about sixteen appeared and stared down at them. He was very tall and tough-looking. His shirt was torn and his trousers were ripped and had holes in them. He put his hands into his pockets, and his right, stockingless foot beat the ground. He leaned his head a little to the side and puckered up his mouth into a contemptuous grimace. For a while he peered at them in silence. Instinctively Jacob put his arms around Herman and Bernhardt and drew them closer to him.

"Go away," Jacob said. "What do you want here?"

The lad paid no attention to him. Suddenly he began to laugh. "Eh, fellers!" he shouted, turning his head a little, "Look what's in here! Chris', look what's in here! Eh, fellers, where the hell are y'? Come' ere. There's two little shrimps in 'ere, an' a ol' man. And the ol' man's got a white suit. I bet you never seen a guy wit' a white suit. First time I ever seen a feller wit' one."

Again the breaking of boughs and twigs, and the rustling noise of parting leaves. Then three little boys scrambled up. None of them looked older than thirteen. The big lad was evidently their leader. Silently, and obviously in great wonderment, they gazed down at Jacob. For the moment Herman and Bernhardt did not seem to interest them.

Jacob felt uncomfortable under the scrutiny of their hungry eyes. "Go away," he said again, moving his hands as if he were chasing flies, "go away."

They did not budge an inch. The big chap asked, "You ever seen a guy wit' a white suit, fellers? Bet a suit like that gets dirty faster'n hell."

"Eh, Ferdl, look," said one of them, addressing the leader of the bunch, "he's got white shoes, too, an' a white shirt. Chris', he's white all over!"

Herman sensed that they were very much impressed, and freeing himself from Jacob's arm, he stepped forward a little.

"Now scram!" he said firmly. "Scram, I tell you, or else my uncle's going to beat you up. You know what? He's just come all the way from Canada, and that's way, way over the ocean, and he lives in Toronto, and that's right next to Chicago, and he c'n beat you up. So scram! My brother an' I were just showing him our cave."

"Ahhhhh!" said the big chap ironically. "Is that so? You was just showing him your cave? Who says it's your cave in the first place?"

"I say. My brother an' I discovered it an' it's secret. So there."

The big lad said, sing-songing the words, "Well, it ain't secret no more, so there. We discovered it too, an' now it's ours."

"It is not," shouted Herman.

"All right, then. Wait'll we get you alone. When the ol' man ain't there." He leered down at them, his eyes squinting. Then a contemptuous and derisive smile spread slowly over his face. "Hey, fellers!" He spoke without moving his head at all. "You know what's in this cave? Two little Jew-boys and a old Jew." He spat.

Jacob's eyes grew large. He drew the children back. All the air seemed to have been cut off. It was almost like being in a small, windowless room, pressed against a narrow corner. He felt the pounding of his heart and he was afraid.

"Let's clear 'em out of the cave, fellers."

"You will not!" cried Herman, his face red with anger. "This is our cave." He could hardly control himself. Reaching behind him, he grabbed a stick, and rushed forward. Before the big lad knew what was happening, Herman had hit him twice over the head with the stick, and then jumped back, seeking protection with Jacob.

"You little rat! Eh, fellers, didya see this? The little Jew-rat hit me. Go on, fellers, jump down an' hit him back."

"Whyn't you jump down yourself?" said one of his friends. "Why d'you send us alla time? I know why. 'Cause you're scared. 'Cause you're scared of the little white ol' man."

"Who's scared?" the big lad yelled, grabbing him by the collar and shaking him.

"Lemme go!" he screamed. "Lemme go!"

Jacob stepped forward. "Go away. Go fight somewhere else. Don't show your faces here again. This cave belongs to the two boys. Now go away."

The big chap released the little fellow from his grip and

ooked at Jacob. Jacob glowered back at him, trying to give his face a fierce expression. Then he took one more step towards him and the youth drew back a little. Herman ventured closer and brandished his stick.

"This is our cave," he said. "Isn't it, Bernie? We discovered it, didn't we, Bernie?"

"Yes," said Bernhardt timidly. "We did."

"Like hell," said the big lad. "Wait'll we get you alone. We'll knock the hell outa you."

He turned sharply about and strode away quickly. The three little boys jumped up and followed him obediently. The one who had refused to attack Herman lingered behind, and then hurriedly and with great contempt he spat twice, threw himself down on the ground and crawled away as nimble as a weasel. "Ferdl," he shouted, "Ferdl. I spit at 'em!"

Herman wanted to shout something in reply, but Jacob restrained him. His hands were trembling. Suddenly a stone came flying through the air and hit him on the shoulder. He started, and ran out.

"You, you . . ."

A burst of laughter answered him and the voice of the big bully, shouting hatefully, "Goddam Jews. Wait'll we get you alone."

Then they scurried away rapidly and their footsteps died away in the distance.

Jacob did not go into the cave again. "Come out, boys," he said. "I think we should go now." The incident had visibly shaken him.

"Anyway," Herman said, "we beat 'em off."

"They'll be laying for us now." Bernhardt said softly. "We can't ever come back here now."

"Oh, there are lots of caves around here. We can find another one and hide out there." Herman assumed an air of careless bravado. "Besides, we could've beaten them off even without Uncle Jacob's help."

"No we couldn't," Bernhardt said. "I'm scared."

"Come on, boys," Jacob called again. "I want to get away from here."

"Yes," said Bernhardt, "let's go. There'll be a lot of people in the Prater now."

Jacob breathed easier as soon as they came upon a beaten track, and after that it did not take them long to reach the centre of the Prater. There were great throngs of people around, and they could hardly move. It took Jacob a little while to get used to the noise. The joyous cries of children mingled with the general laughter and merriment. From all sides came the tin-clang of weary Wurlitzers, accompanying the endless circles of merry-go-rounds. In the beer-gardens and in the open-air cafés loudspeakers blared out the latest jazz hits, newly imported from America. It was a mad, whirling, strident cacophony,

The children seemed to have completely forgotten the depressing incident of a few minutes ago, but Jacob could not so easily shake it off. He let himself be dragged along by the boys. Gradually their happy mood infected him too, and he began to work up enthusiasm for the things they were doing. Soon his stocky, droll little figure could be seen swaying to and fro on a merry-go-round horse; he staggered up and down "wiggle-woggle" stairs; he had his hat nearly blown off when they went down a steep on a roller coaster, and he was enjoying himself.

"Le's go now and see *die Dame ohne Unterleib*, and the knife-thrower," said Herman, panting and excited, his face glowing.

"It's over there," said Bernhardt. "We know the clown there."

"He's the funniest clown in the Prater, I think," Herman said.

On a little platform, quickly improvised with a few wooden boards and a rough railing, a man was blowing a bugle, and another kept shouting, *"Kommen Sie näher, kommen Sie alle näher!"* and he clapped his hands to attract the crowd. "Everybody come close! Everybody come close!"

The crowd gathered round the platform, giggling and talking, shuffling impatiently, like a lowing herd of cattle waiting to be led to pasture.

"As soon's there're enough people here, the clown's going to come jumping out," Herman said. "You'll see, Uncle. He's funny." He laughed in anticipation.

"Tra-la-la-la, tra-la-la, tra-la-la-la-la," came a croaking baritone from behind a grimy red curtain that partitioned the barker's platform from the inside.

"That's him," cried Herman. "That's him."

The man who had shouted and clapped his hands disappeared behind the curtain and came back dragging the clown by the ear. The crowd yelled and laughed.

The clown cried, "I'm going to tell my father. I'm going to tell my father." He had a false nose and his face was painted with a thick coat of red and white paint, and he wore a patched, vari-coloured costume. He was a very ordinary clown.

"What's your father?" asked the man with the bugle.

"He's going to say my father's dead," whispered Herman.

"My father's dead," snarled the clown.

"Well, what was he before he was dead?" asked the man with the bugle.

"He's going to say he was alive before that," whispered Herman, laughing.

"He was alive before that," bellowed the clown.

"*Nein, du Dorftrottel.*" The man with the bugle hit him over the head. "You idiot. Doesn't anything ever get into that thick skull of yours? I mean what did he do to earn his daily bread?"

"He ate no bread," the clown cracked. He spoke slowly," drawlingly. "Beer was the staff of his life."

"Oh, you're hopeless. Now listen carefully." The man with the bugle talked to him now with exaggerated patience. "What did he (your father, that is), what did he do to earn the money to buy his beer?"

"That's what my mother always wanted to know too," the clown said.

The crowd roared with laughter. The clown kept on making jokes which were ancient and bad, but he had a receptive and very uncritical audience, ready to laugh at anything, and thankful that they were being entertained free of charge. Herman and Bernhardt had heard the whole routine so often that they knew it by heart, but yet they laughed, and their laughter was as fresh and spontaneous as if they were hearing the jokes for the very first time.

When the routine was finished, the boys pulled Jacob over to the box-office to buy the tickets. The clown was standing there, shouting and trying to make as many people come in as he possibly could before the crowd scattered.

"*Meine Damen und Herren,*" he yelled. "*Eine Weltsensation! Die Dame ohne Unterleib!*"

"Hallo," Bernhardt said to him. "Hallo. You were really funny today."

The clown pushed them inside. Sweat was running down his face and dissolved the paint, and the red and white merged and trickled down in ugly streaks, and he kept wiping his face with his sleeve.

Inside there were a few rows of wooden benches, and a small, crude stage made of rough boards. Then the show began. To the accompaniment of an untuned piano a man threw knives at a girl, narrowly missing her. A youth ate flames and spewed them forth again, and an old and tired magician performed tricks as old and tired as he. But yet the children were fascinated, and Jacob was fascinated, because they were.

And then at last the star of the show—*Die Dame ohne Unterleib*. She was wheeled onto the stage, for she could obviously not be expected to walk on. Great applause greeted her. The fact that the wheelchair was not of the orthodox kind, but looked rather like a big wooden box on wheels, seemed to trouble few of the spectators.

Bernhardt strained forward on the bench. "I saw her," he whispered to Herman. "I saw her a few days ago. I remember her face. She was standing outside, talking to somebody, and she had legs then. I saw her walk inside afterwards."

But Herman, his eyes glued to the stage where the lady was now bowing her head and blowing kisses to the audience, could not so easily be shaken. "It must've been another woman that you saw," he whispered back, "because this one hasn't got any legs. So how could she walk?"

CHAPTER

XI

Lord, what is man, that Thou hast regard for him?
Or the son of man, that Thou takest account of him?
Man is like a breath,
His days are as a fleeting shadow.
In the morning he flourishes and grows up like grass,
In the evening he is cut down and withers.
His body is like unto a leaf
And yet his spirit is crowned with glory.

Jacob's lips formed the words silently. He read them, slowly and haltingly, hardly aware of their meaning. Around the grave of Solomon Grossman stood his widow, his son, and his daughters. They stood in deep solemnity, looking at the little plot of grass and at the simple black marble stone that towered over it. No one spoke. It was peaceful. A great stillness lay spread over this field of final rest. The mother's eyes glistened. She had long hoped for this moment. She knew that the soul of her husband must rejoice now where he sat among the righteous, for his son had travelled thousands of miles to do homage to him, and the homage of a son is a great thing. This act would now be duly recorded and would speak powerfully in favour of Jacob when the time came for him to stand and be judged. The thought of it blotted out all sorrow from her heart. She almost smiled. Jacob said the *Kaddish*, the prayer honouring the memory of the dead. Shaendl slipped her arm through his to steady herself. Manya blew her nose.

They stood over the grave for some time, and then turned away, Jacob and Shaendl walking behind the others.

"For this alone I would have come all the way," he said. "A pity I couldn't see him alive."

She lifted her face to him. The pale colour of her cheeks contrasted sharply with her wonderful, alert black eyes, and combined to give her an appearance of fragility and yet amazing vitality. "You probably won't like what I'm going to say now, Jacob." Her voice was low. "I'm really glad that Papa died when he did. I'm glad he didn't live to see Hitler come to power. At least that was spared him. I think he's better off."

He wasn't shocked to hear her say that because the thought had occurred to him, too. "Perhaps it is better the way it is," he mumbled. He cast a quick glance at the stooped back of his mother. "I hope Mama can live out her years in peace."

"I hope so too, with all my heart," she said fervently. "That, and time for Bernhardt and Herman to become more independent, so they could look after themselves in case anything happens here. And when I say that I'm being optimistic."

"You think like Albert thinks?" he asked softly.

"More or less. I'm not a good prophet, but the sky looks very dark."

"You know what happened yesterday when I went out with your children? They told you?"

She looked puzzled. "They had a wonderful time. They didn't behave badly, did they?"

"No, no." He stood still and faced her. For a long time before he went to sleep last night he had thought about the incident in the cave. The memory was repellent to him, but it kept on forcing itself into his consciousness. She listened quietly as he related it to her now, her eyes gazing past him over the long rows of graves.

"No," she said when he had finished, "they didn't mention it. It's nothing new. They're used to that kind of thing. They've run up against it every since they can remember, in school and out of school. That's the way things have been here for a long time. The Nazis will find the soil fertile here."

They started walking again. He was quite upset, but didn't say anything, just gripped her arm tighter.

"Tell me," she asked, "how is it in the New World? We hear so much about the freedom there, about tolerance, about the rights of the individual. We hear other things, too, but these are the things we like to believe and look at. It's like a light shining in great darkness. Tell me, then—what happened to you and the children yesterday—could it happen there, too?"

He bent his head and stared down at the path. He became aware of the gravel crunching under his shoes. "Yes," he said at last, raising his head, "yes. I wouldn't lie to you. It could happen there, too. Things like that have happened to me." He saw her face fall, and he added quickly, "But I think also, Shaendl, that a man has a better chance there."

"Perhaps it's as much as we can ask," she answered sadly.

"After all, you went there, a poor, inexperienced young man. And you succeeded."

He averted his eyes. For a moment he felt like telling her the truth. What better time than now, after they had just come away from the grave of their father?

"Yes," he murmured half-audibly, "yes. I made a success."

"Albert never had a chance," she said softly, and then an imploring note slipped into her voice. "All we want now is that our children have a chance. I know it's silly to say so, but I feel that Bernhardt will be a fine artist some day, if he is allowed to develop. He's only a child, but somehow I'm sure of it. Don't ask me how I know. I've no proof except that I believe it."

Her eyes blazed and her whole face had become tense. Jacob looked at her in astonishment, and he would have embraced her if they had been alone.

She relaxed, and said with a smile, "Of course, it may only be a mother dreaming."

At the gate the others were waiting, and Jacob and Shaendl joined them. A ragged figure came hobbling up with outstretched hand. "I will say a prayer for you," he muttered. Jacob fumbled about in his pockets and brought out all the loose change he had and gave it to him. The beggar drew back, amazed, and then almost prostrated himself before Jacob, calling down upon him a thousand blessings. Then he shuffled off, still mumbling. The mother was pleased and smiled at Jacob. For this act of charity, too, was even now being recorded in the Book of Life.

"There's a taxi stand not far away," Jacob said. "I saw it when we were coming here."

"Who needs a taxi?" Manya remonstrated. "The streetcar is cheaper."

"Ach!" He waved her objections away. "I can afford a few cents more."

He took Shaendl's arm again. An odour of jasmine and lilac came wafting in on the breeze. He sniffed the air. "What a lovely smell."

"Lilac," she said dreamily. "Albert came with me to visit Papa's grave just after we were engaged. That was in May, too. Afterwards we walked here for an hour. I remember it so clearly. It was in 1921, just a year after Papa died. We had only known each other for a month."

"You made a quick job," Jacob quipped. "Only a month and already engaged."

"We could have done it after a week. We were so sure." She

paused, sunk in recollection. "I don't like to think back over the autumn and the winter that went before. Mama and Manya had picked a man for me, and he kept on calling and sending me presents, and Mama wanted me to accept him. God, I was unhappy. Reuben was the only one I could come to. He seemed to understand. He has always been wonderful to me. We don't see eye to eye on many things, but that never made any difference to him."

"Noo," Jacob asked, "what was wrong with the other man?"

"Nothing was wrong with him. He was nice to me, and I tried to like him at first, but I couldn't. I felt terribly sorry for him, but he wasn't for me. We were poles apart. I don't know what I would have done if I hadn't met Albert just then." A mischievous grin spread over her face. "I'll never forget the day we met. They were giving *La Bohème* at the Staatsoper, and I wanted so much to see it. None of my friends was much interested in that sort of thing and so I had to go alone. I bought myself a standing room ticket because I didn't have much money. The soprano who sang Mimi that night was a big, fat woman. She must have weighed at least three hundred pounds." She threw her head back and laughed. "Do you know *La Bohème*, Jacob?"

"No," he said, "I don't know it."

"It doesn't really matter. There she was, supposed to be a thin and fragile little seamstress wasting away with consumption. I had a pair of opera glasses and I couldn't help laughing every time I looked at her. She was a picture of glowing health. Suddenly a man behind me told me to keep quiet and I turned round, a bit angry. I couldn't see his face clearly, only his thick glasses. And then I had a sudden impulse. I thrust my opera glasses into his hand and told him to take a good look at Mimi. He thanked me and whispered that he'd come to hear the music. I felt badly about it, and when the act was over and the lights went on I spoke to him and said I was sorry if my laughing had irritated him. He laughed, too, and we began talking. We strolled out in the lobby and he bought me a glass of ice water and a chocolate cookie."

"He *bought* you a glass of water?" Jacob interrupted her incredulously.

"Yes," she said. "It's a concession, and so you have to pay for it. The last act was terribly funny. I could hardly control my laughter. I knew I was acting like a silly school girl, but I couldn't help it. Mimi was dying. She lay stretched out on a camp-bed, gasping out her life, her body completely wasted away now. But . . ." Shaendl had to stop because she was laughing so hard, "but there were great masses of flesh hanging down all over. She could have filled three camp-beds, and there would still have been something left over. Her cheeks were full and red, and I just couldn't make myself believe that she was a seamstress dying of consumption. It was silly, I know, but I had a lot of fun. And then, when I was getting my coat, there was Albert again standing behind me. He said I had spoiled the evening for him, and more, I had spoiled *La Bohème* for him for ever, and he thought the least he could do was to take me home. I didn't see the logic of this, but he insisted, and so we walked home together, talking all the way. It was wonderful the way he talked to me. I liked him almost at once, and I was hoping and hoping that he wouldn't just leave me at the door and go away without asking to see me again. He didn't. And we've always been happy that the soprano that evening was so awfully fat."

"T-t-t-t-t. Such a romance!" Jacob said, wagging his finger. "And it is still such a romance between you now?"

"More than ever," she said seriously, "because he needs me more now than ever before."

"Tell me, how is he making out in his store?"

She hesitated a bit. "Times are bad and we've had a lot of tough luck. When you have nothing better to do one afternoon, why don't you drop in to see Albert? The shop isn't far from Mama's place."

"Sure," he said. "I'll go see him."

She didn't tell him that they had decided to approach him for a substantial loan of money so they could pay their most pressing debts.

CHAPTER

XII

———————

ALBERT'S bookshop was wedged in between a grocery on one side and a butcher shop on the other, and while there was a lot of coming and going between the two, Albert's shop was generally neglected. It had a small front, and there was a painted sign over the door which read:

ALBERT REICH—BUCHHANDLUNG

A few books, very tastefully arranged, were displayed in the two small windows on either side of the door. The shop itself was quite narrow, but made up for it in length. Jacob was surprised to see the long book-shelves well stocked. He had rather expected to find a small, musty, disorganized shop with heaps of books lying about, gathering dust.

Albert was at the far end of the shop, talking to a man who stood with his back turned to the door so that Jacob could not see his face when he entered. Albert looked up, and for a moment it seemed as if he did not recognize Jacob, but then he smiled.

"Oh, Jacob," he said, coming towards him. "How are you? Very nice of you to come." They shook hands. "I'm sorry I wasn't home two days ago when you came to see us."

The man with whom Albert had been talking turned his head without turning his body. His face was youthful though there were deep furrows in it which showed that he was older than he seemed. His eyes were very large, so large that even when he contracted his brows, a motion which had grown to a habit with him, they still remained large. A thin, filmy layer seemed to veil them, spanned across the pupils like a protecting screen, as if to prevent people from dectecting everything that went on in them. He was a middle-sized broad-shouldered man. His collar was open at the throat, the first button of his shirt was missing, and a few chest hairs showed and curled lightly around the edge of the shirt.

"This is Herr Grossman, my brother-in-law," said Albert to his friend, who had now half turned and was leaning against the counter. "And this is Robert Koch," he said to Jacob, "a very good friend of mine."

"I am glad to know you," said Koch. He had a deep, slightly dragging voice.

Jacob smiled and shook hands with him.

"Well, I think I'd better get going," said Koch. "I'll drop in tomorrow, Albert. You'll want to talk to your brother-in-law now."

"No, no, stay," said Albert quickly. "You've got nothing to do now. It's not three-thirty yet, and you don't start work until five. You can stay a while."

"Sure," said Jacob jovially, "stay, Herr Koch. I like to be with a lot of people."

Albert drew up a chair for Jacob, and then he went behind the counter and sat down. Koch remained standing, leaning his body against the counter.

"Phew," Jacob said. "It's hot."

"This is an unusually hot spring," said Albert.

"It should do something for the tourist trade," said Koch. "You'll be proud to know, Albert, that the tourist business is up ten per cent over last year. I read it in the paper yesterday."

"I'm happy to hear that something is prospering," said Albert.

"I saw a funny thing the other day," Koch said. "I was passing by the Rathaus when one of those sight-seeing buses stopped and a group of people piled out and started—er—sight-seeing. Along came two young fellows in *Lederhosen* and *Bauernjanker* and little sugar-loaf hats. Suddenly two hefty, middle-aged women with hats like pudding basins detached themselves from the sight-seeing group and pounced on the boys. God, I thought, they're going to attack them. I went nearer. But it was quite innocent. All they wanted apparently was for the two fellows to keep still a second so they could snap their picture. The two women, all excited, kept on pointing at their cameras and then at the boys, gabbling in English all the while. You should have seen the expression on the faces of those two fellows. They didn't know what was going on. Then one of the matrons grabbed them and led them off under a tree. By this time, I think, they had fairly well grasped the idea, but the expression on their faces hadn't changed. I can't quite describe it. They looked utterly lost and bewildered. The ladies clicked their cameras, and then walked off happily. Two natives caught in action and immortalized! I thought. They kept on standing under that tree for some time, but finally they must have come to the conclusion that it was safe to go, because they moved on again. I wish I could get hold of that picture. It must be priceless."

They laughed.

"A pity I didn't bring a camera," Jacob said.

The door opened and a few boys came in. Albert got up to serve them. Koch let his eyes glide over Jacob.

"How long have you been here now, Herr Grossman?" he asked.

"It will be two weeks next Thursday."

"How long are you going to stay?"

"Another three weeks, I think."

"I hope you're enjoying yourself." Koch's voice, slow and drawlingly Viennese, seemed curiously familiar to Jacob. He thought that he had heard it before, but he didn't know where. "Have you seen all the things worth seeing here?"

"In the last few days I have gone around all over. Schönbrunn I liked best of all. The flowers and the trees cut so straight they look like a regiment of soldiers. And the palace! I went inside with my mother. A guide explained to us everything. When I was a little boy in a village far away, who would have thought that one day I would be walking around in the great Kaiser's palace with my own feet?" He smiled. "Napoleon lived in the palace too. The guide showed us the bed where he slept. It is a tremendous bed, gilded, and with beautiful curtains and everything. I always hear Napoleon was a little man. So I stood by the bed and I thought to myself: a bigger man than Napoleon could get lost in this bed."

Koch burst into laughter. "I must remember that."

Albert came back and joined them. "Good old Caesar," he said. "He keeps me alive. Where would I be if students didn't have to read De Bello Gallico? They started a new book yesterday, and the boys have been in here all day buying cribs ... What's the joke?"

"Napoleon's bed in the palace of Schönbrunn. Your brother-in-law saw it. It's a huge four-poster, and he thinks Napoleon got lost in it. I must go and see it sometime. For some reason I've never been inside the palace. I never felt like spending the schilling. The only way to see all the attractions of a great city is to be a tourist, a foreigner. Then you can follow your Baedeker, never look to the right or the left, always straight ahead. This enables you to see the palaces, but spares you the sight of the hovels."

Jacob thought of his mother's dingy little flat. "I have seen other things besides palaces," he said.

"Oh, but you have relatives here," Koch said, "and they are not among the aristocrats. That's a terrible disadvantage, for they are sure to tell you things. No, to enjoy himself thoroughly, a man should come alone and have a great deal of money. What goes on in the world must not concern him. He must be selfish—definitely not his brother's keeper." He furrowed his forehead. "Personally, I think I am a man who has been cursed with two much conscience. Things that would leave most people completely unmoved bother me." He leaned his elbows on the counter. "To counteract this, I sometimes play a little game. I imagine myself to be extremely wealthy, arriving in Vienna (it's always Vienna) to have a good time. I come from far away. I never specify the country. This would be unfair, I feel, because I frankly don't pretend to be the kind of specimen a country would choose as its representative abroad. I'm a man, say, engaged in the white slave trade. That's a good, old trade. A suite in the Bristol is always reserved for me. As soon as I get there, bellboys, doormen, chambermaids, all pander to me, for I'm well known, and very free with money. With my business connections it is of course only a matter of two hours or so before I'm provided with a slim and raven-haired—"

"No, no, no," Albert interrupted. "Surely you can imagine yourself as the twin brother of Apollo?"

"No trouble at all."

"Then I think it's shameful that you should have to rely on professionals. With all that money and all that charm."

"Ha! A wonderful idea. Well, then, we have a delicious meal first. Then I take her to the Prater. We pass a side-show. On a platform a man is blowing a bugle and we stop to watch. The man disappears behind a grimy curtain, and comes out again, dragging a clown by the ear. Now he starts pushing and pulling me, I mean the clown, about. I have a crude sense of humour, and I think that's very funny. Tears are rolling down my cheeks. My little girl laughs, too, and we have a wonderful time. And then, ah! then back to the Bristol. A warm bath, a soft bed, low lights, sweet music. Ah!"

"Do you always choose to be a white slave trader?" Albert asked with a twinkle.

Jacob glanced from Koch to Albert and back. He was losing track of the conversation.

"No," Koch said, "not always. Why do you ask?"

"Because I think you've chosen the ideal trade. A slave trader would hardly be concerned about the cynicism and the amorality which is everywhere in the world, since he has already degraded himself to the subhuman level. He must always have regarded human beings as things deprived of all humanity, or he would never have become what he is. Until recently there was at least one consolation. The law at any rate condemned him. He could bribe his way out, but in principle he stood condemned. But now men commit atrocities and change the laws to sanction their crimes, and so all mankind degrades itself. Man falls in full consciousness, and therefore falls below the level of the wildest beast."

Koch listened quietly, slowly rolling himself a cigarette. "It is also true," he said after a short pause, "that man raises himself in full consciousness, and then he soars. He has cast out the tyrants that oppress him before, and he can do it again."

"Ah! Echoes of *Wilhelm Tell*. You've always been fond of Schiller. I would like nothing more than the downfall of dictators, but this will not in itself solve the world crisis."

"I'd sleep much better if the newspapers carried banner headlines tonight, announcing that downfall."

"That goes without saying," Albert waved him aside impatiently. "The load that would drop off my heart would probably be greater than yours. If the worst happened here, you could even put on the swastika to save your life."

"I resent that," Koch cried. "If all I wanted was to live and be successful no matter what the price, I could have paid it long ago."

Albert got up from his chair and laid his hand lightly on Koch's shoulder. "I'm sorry I ever said that. You know I didn't mean it."

They paid no attention to Jacob. He sat there, listening, trying to understand.

"Let me get back to my subject," Albert continued. "I see man involved in a moral crisis which goes to the deepest roots of his being. Hitler is only the worst symptom of a disease which is spread throughout the world. Everywhere there is a decay of human and spiritual values, of all the things that have made Western civilization great, and the tragic thing is that few people really care."

Koch kept on rolling the cigarette between his fingers without wetting the paper.

"One evening last year I was walking home and bought a paper on the corner," Albert went on, his voice low. "And there, on the front page, was a report of the burning of the books in a public square in Berlin. The print blurred before my eyes. For a moment I refused to believe what I had just read. I couldn't believe that such desecration was possible. And then I thought this could happen only because people are not vitally concerned. They don't care. And I think it could happen anywhere in the world, once you allow a ruthless band of demagogues to pander to human bestiality and corruption. The recipe is universal."

"Every book should be supplied with a bomb," Koch said, crushing the unfinished cigarette in his hand and throwing it away. "For use in self-defence only, of course. Barbarism isn't new in the world. The cult of violence and brutality isn't new. And yet I feel that out of all the agony, out of all the suffering, a new state of mind, a new world-spirit will eventually be born, even though I will probably not survive the holocaust."

Albert shook his head. "You know, Koch, I've tremendous admiration for you. After all you've experienced, and in face of all that's happening, you can still say that. You can still dream."

"In the long run dreams are the only reality," Koch said. "Your cool and sober heads, the men who have both feet firmly planted on the ground, but their dull eyes steadfastly turned backwards, have always led the world into dead end streets. And the people have always finally turned to the visionaries. I must believe that, or else how could I go on making a fool of myself day after day?" He turned suddenly and faced Jacob. "I am a clown, Herr Grossman." He was tense and uttered the words sharply and with something approaching a fierce pride.

Jacob jerked his head and stared at Koch. Now he remembered where he had seen him. Only then his face had been covered with a thick coat of make-up, and he had jumped about on a little platform, and the man with the bugle had pulled his ear all the time.

"Yes," Jacob stammered. "I—I think I saw you. I was with my nephews in the Prater." He stopped abruptly. It must be a joke, he thought. He must be making a joke.

Koch's face relaxed and he smiled. "Ah! A new admirer! My reputation is now international." He pushed himself away from the counter and stood up straight. "Time I go. They'll be waiting for me. *Auf Wiedersehen.*" He held out his hand and Jacob took it. "Perhaps I'll see you again before you leave."

"I hope so."

Koch waved his hand to Albert and strode out of the shop. The two men looked after him.

"Who—who is he?" Jacob asked softly, as if he were afraid that Koch might hear him.

"A friend of mine."

"I know that. But—but is he really a clown? I didn't make a mistake?"

"No, you didn't make a mistake. He is a clown."

"A clown should talk like that! Often I couldn't understand what he was saying."

"He is not an ordinary clown," Albert said with a bitter smile.

"Why should a man who can talk like that be a clown? He can't find something better to do?"

"He had something better to do—until last year," Albert said. "He was a journalist. A very good journalist. Fearless and outspoken. In 1931 he exposed the illegal arms traffic between Austria and Italy, and created a great sensation. Mussolini had sent in fifty thousand rifles and two hundred machine guns. That was a first instalment, but it was also a violation of the peace treaty, and it put the Dollfuss government in a very tough spot. There were embarrassing questions in Parliament. Czechoslovakia brought it up before the League of Nations, and England and France, after trying to hush up the affair, finally sent notes to Dollfuss, and asked him to ship the arms back to Italy. But they were never returned because on the way back, in Innsbruck, the trucks were held up in the middle of the night and the arms were stolen. And after all, you can't accuse the government if there are thieves in the country. It is very inconvenient to have a Parliament and a free press. You always have to be afraid that dirty dealings will come into the open, and if you have free elections, too, why, the people may even vote you out of power." He picked up a book that lay on the counter and began to flip its pages absent mindedly. "The arms were put to wonderful use last year in February," he said bitterly. "I hadn't seen Robert for about six months before that. When the smashing-up process began, the paper for which he had written was among the very first to be wrecked. I was sure that he had been arrested. And then towards the end of that terrible week, I went into a little café across the street one afternoon, and he was sitting there, drinking coffee. He looked pale and haggard. By chance he had been out of town when it started. He came back, but he couldn't go to his flat. He couldn't get any money from his bank. He might just as well have walked into a police station. He told me that during the past three nights he had helped to bring food to the besieged defenders of the *Gemeinde Häuser* and to smuggle out the wounded through the sewers so they could get medical attention. In the daytime he wandered about the city, trying to catch some sleep in a dark cinema or in a steam-bath. All the money he had was spent. The fighting was over. Everything was finished. I asked him what he was going to do. He didn't know. He must have been desperate, but I think I was more excited than he. I'll never forget the way he sat there, drinking his coffee and smoking a cigarette, calmly, as if nothing at all had happened. I said it would be a good thing for him to hide until things had settled, and he said that all the people who could help him were either dead or arrested or trying to find a hiding-place themselves."

"Noo," Jacob asked excitedly, "what happened? Did he find a place?"

Albert nodded.

"Where?"

Albert's voice sank to a whisper. "There is a little room in the back of the shop. I keep a few odds and ends there. It's too small for a store-room, and it has no windows. An old couch is in there, too. The former owner left it, and I never had it taken out. I told him to come here after dark, about five o'clock. He stayed over three months. I brought him food every day. Nobody knew. Only Shaendl."

"A dangerous thing," Jacob said, shaking his head. "What would have happened if the police had come . . . and found him here?"

Albert shrugged his shoulders. "A man's life was in danger. The life of a friend, after he had fought a good fight and lost. I didn't think about the police when I saw him sitting there, not knowing what to do next. Nothing happened. Fortunately nobody ever came to look for him here. Early in June he thought it was safe enough to come out. By then the fury of the police had died down a bit. He changed his name. He called himself Koch, and rented a little room just around the corner. Then he heard that one of the side-shows in the Prater needed a clown. He had no money at all, and this was the only thing he could take. It's the kind of job that requires no labour permit and nobody asks you any questions. And what's more, you can disguise your face."

Jacob sat quietly and nodded his head, slowly and rhythmically, as if he were beating time with it to a sad and solemn chanting melody. The sun, streaming in through the two small windows, reflected slanting panes of yellow light upon the first few rows of books.

Albert's hands twitched nervously. His eyes were fixed on Jacob. How should he go about asking for the money? Should he say, "Jacob, I need five thousand schillings. It's very urgent, Jacob. We're in debt and I don't know what to do. Creditors keep asking for the money, and I keep putting them off, but I don't know how long I can do it. You could help us, Jacob." No, it couldn't be done that way. It was too direct an appeal, too abrupt. His hands began to sweat and he took out his handkerchief and wiped them. "We find ourselves in financial difficulties." Perhaps that was a better way to start. More formal, more . . . God, it was hateful to have to come hat in hand, like a beggar. "Times have been bad, and I was laid up for almost a year. And now with another baby coming, we don't know what to do. We didn't want this baby, Jacob. We . . . No, it sounded like a sob-story, embarrassing and dreadful.

A woman entered the shop and browsed around among the books. Albert gave a sigh of relief, and hurried over to her. He could have hugged her for coming in just then. He hoped she would stay a long time.

Jacob got up and looked about himself, his eyes searching for the door that led to the little room in the back. There it was. He took a few paces forward and opened it. The room was not much bigger than a closet, just big enough to hold a small, tattered couch. The air was stale and musty. How could a man stand it in there for three months without going crazy? He shrunk away and closed the door quickly.

"I'll wrap it up for you." Albert put paper round the currently popular romantic novel, and handed it to the woman. Then he came back to Jacob.

"Tell me, Albert," Jacob said, his voice somewhat shaky, "how—how could a man live in that hole there? I couldn't even stay in there for an hour."

"You're not afraid of the police," Albert said.

"God should never punish me so hard," Jacob mumbled. "What—what did he do in there?"

"Most of the time he read. And he wrote a good deal, too. He had enough to do to occupy his time."

"And you—you wasn't scared, ever?"

"Sometimes. I didn't think too much about it. . . . Forget I told you, Jacob. Don't say anything to Reuben or to your mother. They don't know, and it's better that way. Tell your friends in Toronto. But say nothing here."

"Sure not," Jacob said. "I understand."

For a while they didn't say anything. Albert thought, now I

could ask him. The words played around his tongue. He hesitated. And then suddenly, as if coming to the rescue, another thought flashed through his mind, and he said quickly, "I meant to tell you, Jacob. Your friend Tassigny held his first exhibition in Paris last week. I read about it in the Journal of Art."

Jacob's little eyes danced excitedly. "Messiey Tassigny! Oh, I am glad to hear that. What a gentleman! And he could play the piano! I am telling you, I have never in my whole life heard such a beautiful piano."

"He didn't play the piano in Paris," said Albert, smiling. "I have the Journal here somewhere." He bent down to look for it. "Here it is."

There was an article of about two pages, and three of Tassigny's paintings were reproduced in black and white. Jacob looked carefully at them, and he was proud of Tassigny. Again he felt, as on that first evening when he had sat listening to him play the piano, as though he had something to do with Tassigny's artistic expression.

"He paints good, Messiey Tassigny, eh?" he said.

"Some critics liked his work, others didn't," said Albert. "I can't tell. I haven't seen enough of it."

"Oh, look!" cried Jacob. "This picture. It says here it is a sunset. He showed it to me in his cabin. It must be the same picture." He got up abruptly and began to re-enact the scene for Albert. "The picture was standing here," he said, "and I was standing there, and Messiey Tassigny was holding me by my arm like this. A beautiful picture, no? Only it makes a whole difference if you see it painted with colours."

It was impossible for Albert to ignore the admiration which mirrored itself in Jacob's eyes, and he found himself envying the Frenchman. He felt suddenly small and insignificant, and the very idea of asking Jacob for money just then became repulsive to him.

Jacob closed the Journal and put it down on the counter. Albert picked it up and threw it into a drawer where he kept various periodicals and magazines.

"I didn't know you was a painter, too," said Jacob. "Bernhardt told me."

"Oh, no," said Albert, raising his brows behind the walls of his glasses, "I a painter?" He chuckled. "I play around with paints a bit, but that doesn't make me a painter. No, I'm not an artist. Perhaps Bernhardt will be some day. Maybe he has what it takes. IF! There are almost too many ifs when you start thinking. Who can tell what's going to happen in this crazy world tomorrow? It's impossible to make any plans. I just wish the children were older. I often worry about Bernhardt. I worry about him more than about Herman. He's too sensitive, too easily hurt. It takes a lot to get Herman down, I think. Even now he can take a lot and come back fighting. And you have to be like that if you want to get on in the world. Bernhardt takes too much after me. I only hope he will have some of Shaendl's driving force. That's what I lacked. You know, Jacob, your sister Shaendl is really an extraordinary woman. I often wonder how it happened. She is so different from all the others in your family. Of course, I didn't know your father. Perhaps she takes after him. If I had some of her force and determination, I might have gone further. I could always go so far and then somehow my energy gave out and I cracked." Albert's eyes wandered along the bookshelves and he did not look at Jacob.

Jacob thought about Shaendl and his father. Did she take after their father? What did Albert mean when he talked about her force and her determination? Was she a good business woman? Could she make a lot of money? It didn't seem like it. Then how was she strong? And his father? He remembered him shutting himself off in a small room after he came home from his work, and poring over the Holy Books by the light of a flickering candle till late into the night. He remembered, too, the heavy tread of his black boots, and his deep, commanding voice. He had been a typical patriarch of the old school, and he had expected his family to obey his commands without questioning. In his dealings with outsiders, however, he had been less successful, and he had always been a poor and unimportant man in the eyes of the world. And for a moment Jacob thought about himself, Jacob Grossman, toiling in the steam and in the sweat of a factory for thirty-three years, always the underling, always bossed, always obeying. He threw the thought away as though it were a dirty, stinking rag. He threw it into a little cranny of his brain and hid it there that he might not see it.

But his voice was unusually harsh and rasping when he asked, "How is Shaendl strong, Albert?"

Albert moved his head slowly until he faced Jacob again. "Shaendl?" he said. He pronounced the name softly and it sounded very lovely the way he said it. "I don't know that I can sum it up in a sentence. She is a great fighter. When I first met her, she seemed to me a bundle of energy. I could hardly keep up with her. She was trying furiously to find out about things. She was rebelling against the petty and meaningless life she was forced to lead. I admired the courage and the determination with which she tried to fight against hopeless odds. There she was, a poor dressmaker's helper with a village school education, reading books on history and economics that were often way over her head, but once she sank her teeth into something she wouldn't let go. It was pathetic and wonderful, and that's why I loved her. She fell in love with me, I suppose, because I seemed to know the answers to some of the problems she was grappling with."

Was this his sister Albert was talking about? Jacob found himself thinking. The pig-tailed girl, the sweet, innocent child who used to love riding pick-a-back? His little sister reading such books?

"I took her to lectures in the evening and we studied together," Albert said. "And then one day she came to me with an idea. She thought that if we worked hard and saved our money, we could get enough together for me to go to the university. It sounded crazy to me at first, but she persuaded me. I was making a fair amount of money, she said, and she would go back to work, and in three years we'd have enough money to cover expenses for the first two years. And, by God, things seemed to work out the way she said they would. We didn't have quite as much as we had counted on, but enough for one year, anyway. It was the happiest year of my life. Just when the term finished Bernhardt was born. We were very happy even though it meant that I would have to stay out a year. It didn't worry us. A year or two didn't make so much difference. But the times were against us. Suddenly I had to take a cut in my salary. Only a temporary setback, everybody was saying. It wasn't. It was a rehearsal for the real thing. And all the beautiful plans fading away. Then I lost my job and the dreams blew up in our faces. It nearly finished me. For months after that I was like a paralysed man. I dragged myself around, half-dead, looking for a job. Nothing for weeks. And then something at last, paying half of what I earned before. I worked there for some years, hating every minute, and finally I just couldn't go on any longer. I don't know what I would have done without Shaendl. With two children to look after, and everything gone to pieces, she seemed to me like a rock, growing stronger as I grew weaker. All the old tenacity and toughness was there again, and she could be gentle and sweet at the same time. Sometimes I think I let her down. She expected so much of me. . . . You don't mind a steep road as long as you know there's something waiting for you at the end, and a bit of light and hope to guide you on. But when the road is endless and dark . . ." He broke off and his voice trailed away. Now perhaps I could ask him, he thought. Now that I've prepared the way.

"Your family couldn't help you out to go to school?" Jacob asked.

Albert shook his head. "No. My father died when I was sixteen. I barely managed to finish the *gymnasium*, and then I had to go to work. My mother died soon after."

"And when you went to the university later on, you wanted to become a doctor maybe?"

"No," Albert said, "I'm not interested in medicine. I'm interested in literature and in history. That's what I wanted to study."

"What?" Jacob cried, curling his lower lip down, and half-closing his eyes. "Lit'ritshure? History?" He was baffled. What did a man do after he had studied these things? How did he make a living? A doctor looked after you when you were sick, a lawyer defended you when you were in trouble, an engineer built roads and bridges, but a man who spent his time studying literature, of what use was he? "Lit'ritshure?" he repeated. "History? What kind of a study is that?"

Albert tried to explain, but he didn't seem to have much success for Jacob looked just as puzzled as before.

"Noo," he said, "and to learn about books you have to go to a university? You have to spend good money for that? I can read a book, too. Did I have to go to a university, and spend good money? You should have picked out something practical. A man goes to a university so he will learn a good profession and make for himself a good living afterwards. They teach him there how he should be a doctor, or a dentist, or a lawyer, or a engineer. But lit'ritshure! Foolishness! Anyway, I don't think you should be so sorry you couldn't go on. You only saved yourself a lot of money." He meant it kindly, and he was not aware how much he irritated Albert. "God forbid I should say anything against books." He laid his hand over his heart to show that he was sincere. "If a man wants to read books," he proclaimed, "he can go to the public library and for a few cents a year he can read books till he is blind. He doesn't have to go to a university. Now my David . . ." There it was again, the pride in the voice, and the sense of achievement as he held forth lovingly on the accomplishments of his son.

Albert tried not to listen. He was sorry he had ever told Jacob of his hopes and of the crack-up. In any case, that was all past, and now he found himself wishing that Jacob would go away so he wouldn't have to think about asking him for the money. He couldn't do it. Not now, at any rate, and never without feeling an acute sense of shame. Yet Shaendl was right. Nobody else could help them. But this wasn't the right atmosphere. Shaendl can do it better than I, he thought. After all, she is his sister. He heard Jacob say, "All afternoon only two customers came in here. How you making out in this business?" He couldn't have asked for a more perfect opening. He could take it from here. Nothing was easier. All he had to do was tell the truth. But the words stuck in his throat. His eyes began to water and everything blurred and swam before them. He muttered something about this being the slack season in the book business. Coward, he thought. Pride and shame, hell! Why should everything always roll onto Shaendl's shoulders? He would swallow his damned pride and ask, but she should be there, too. She wouldn't have to say a word. And Jacob should be approached after a good meal when he was in a jovial mood. Better ask him right now to come for dinner on Sunday. Jacob said he would come with pleasure. The matter was settled, then. Albert felt relieved, even though he realized that nothing had been solved. The problem had merely been postponed for a few days. He removed his thick, horn-rimmed glasses and wiped some of the moisture off them. Then he rubbed his eyes with his handkerchief and looked at his wristwatch. It was about twenty minutes to six. His throat was parched. He couldn't think of anything nicer just now than a cup of hot coffee.

"I'm going to close up," he said. "There won't be any more business today. How about a cup of coffee?"

"Sure," said Jacob, "sure. I would like a cup of coffee."

It had cooled down outside and the sky was overcast with grey, lazily moving clouds. While Albert was pulling down the *Rollbalken*, the iron shutters, and securing them, Jacob watched four boys playing a peculiar kind of game with a tennis ball, knocking it about with hands, feet, and heads, using the curbstone as a goal. They were completely absorbed in the game, only stopping now and then to let a car pass. A band of street singers came round the corner and struck up a tune. There were three instruments, an accordion, a piccolo, and a violin. While the three musicians played, their two helpers went about collecting the tribute of the passers-by which came to them in periodic dribbles of copper pennies.

The one who played the accordion now started to sing in a husky, guttural voice.

> *Ich bin ja nur ein armer Strassensänger,*
> *Ich such' mir irgendwo ein Stückerl Glück.*

This was the hit tune of the moment and Jacob had heard it often. He hummed the refrain, his foot beating time on the pavement. "I am only a poor street singer, searching somewhere for a bit of luck."

"Well, shall we go?" said Albert.

"In a minute," Jacob said. "I want to listen to the music. They play good, eh?" He beckoned to one of the men, and he came running over, cap in hand. Jacob dropped a silver piece into the cap.

"Ach, danke sehr, danke vielmals, gnädiger Herr."

"Tell me," Jacob asked, "can your men play the Blue Danube?"

"Aber sofort, gnädiger Herr. Sofort spielen sie's für Sie."

"Tell them," Jacob said, "to play it soft and slow." He turned to Albert. "I love to hear a waltz. Especially the Blue Danube."

"Even now, after you've seen that the Danube isn't really blue at all?"

"It doesn't make no difference to the waltz."

The musicians broke off the piece they had been playing and started the waltz. They were trying to make up the harmony as they went along, and the piccolo was always just a little ahead of the others.

"Tam tarum tam tam, pom pom, pom pom," Jacob hummed.

Albert stood there, feeling uncomfortable. He was sorry for the three men. They were not even pretending to play in harmony any more. Each man played the tune himself, as if he were playing a slow solo, but all three were obviously keeping Jacob's order in mind for they were trying to outdo each other in slowness.

God, Albert thought, it sounds like a funeral march. What are they trying to do, bury the Danube?

"Too slow," Jacob complained. "A waltz you have to play just right. Not too slow and not too fast."

"You didn't give them enough time to practise," Albert said, subduing the fury in his voice. "Come on, let's go."

As soon as the street singers saw Jacob walking away they stopped torturing the waltz and laid into a tango. There was music in the street, but no one danced.

CHAPTER

XIII

FRIDAY came again, and with it the bustling preparations for the Sabbath. Jacob could hear his mother's bed creak as she got out of it, though he was still half asleep. It must be early, he thought drowsily, and turned over on his side.

The mother shuffled out into the kitchen and left the door open. Soon the noise of clanking pots and water about to boil penetrated the semi-consciousness of his half-sleep, and seemed much more booming to him than it actually was. Then he heard the shuffling footsteps once more, and was dimly aware that she was standing by his bed.

"Here," she said, "here. I have brought you tea, Yankel. Afterwards you can sleep again. First drink the tea."

She had done this every morning since his arrival. It made him feel uncomfortable to have his old mother pamper and serve him as though he were a sick child, but when he voiced a protest her thin lips came together into a pained smile over her toothless gums. Why do you want to take this little pleasure away from me? she seemed to say. And so he had finally given in to her, and now he accepted her attentions as a matter of course.

He sat up and rubbed a bit of sleep from his eyes. "It must be early," he said. "Why do you get up so early, Mama?"

"It is not so early," she said. "It is half-past seven, and I have a lot of work to do. I wanted to get up earlier, but I overslept. You can sleep for another hour, and then you will go to the bath with Reuben."

"Mhm," he said and yawned. He finished his tea, and she took the empty cup and pottered out into the kitchen.

He stretched himself and rolled over. Two weeks already, he thought, and they have gone by so quickly. It seemed to him as if he had only come yesterday. Another three weeks, and he would be going back to the same dreary life he had led for thirty-three years. He wished it were possible to stop time and ban the fleeting moment into permanence. Then he dozed off again.

He was awakened by a loud, clamouring voice, speaking in

obvious agitation. He roused himself with a start. The voice came from the kitchen, and the words were at first only an incoherent mass of sounds, but then he heard his mother give a short cry, and he was suddenly wide awake, filled with a great uneasiness.

"Yankel," he heard his mother cry, "Yankel, come quick." She came running into the room, followed by a husky woman who was wearing a dirty white apron and a pair of old, men's shoes, several sizes too large for her.

"Herr Grossman," she shouted, "Herr Grossman, come quick. Frau Reich is sick."

Frau Reich? Frau Reich? Who is Frau Reich? What do you want me for? He stared in consternation.

"Yankel," the mother cried. "Get up, get up! Shaendl! They are taking her to the hospital."

His head was spinning, and he was not conscious of what he was doing. For a second he glared at the woman. He did not even think of asking what had happened. He acted completely on instinct. He jumped out of bed, disregarding the fact that the two women were standing there. He was dressed within a minute. One would never have thought that his limbs could be so flexible. And now for the first time since he had heard the excited voices from the kitchen he was aware that he was consciously thinking.

"What happened?" he asked the woman while he tried to fasten his shirt collar with nervous, twitching fingers.

"I don't know," she said, "I don't know. I'm Frau Reich's neighbour. They told me to run here and get you fast. I don't know exactly what happened. The doctor just came and he sent somebody down right away to telephone for the ambulance. I think she fell, Frau Reich did, and she hurt herself."

He did not wait for the women but ran out and panted down the flight of stairs into the street. People stopped and stared at him. They had always seen him strolling along slowly, lingering over his walk, taking his time. But now Jacob Grossman, who had always appeared in the street immaculately, painstakingly dressed, was running, and his tie was fluttering about his collar untied, and he carried his jacket in his hand.

The door of Shaendl's flat was open and he walked straight into the bedroom. Shaendl was lying quietly, her head sunk deep into the pillows, and her hands stretched out before her on top of the yellowish-brown blanket that covered her. She lay with her eyes closed, and her thin face, usually pale, was paler still, as if all the blood had been drained from it. Her hair was dishevelled and untidy, and a few locks had fallen loosely over her forehead and the perspiration had clammed them to it.

Jacob remained standing on the threshold, because he was afraid to venture further. A woman was leaning over the bed, and now and then she applied a cold towel to Shaendl's head. A little fattish man, dressed in a grey business suit, was standing by the window, looking out into the street. After a few moments he turned and saw Jacob.

"Who are you?" he asked.

"My name is Grossman," Jacob said. "I am Frau Reich's brother."

"Oh," said the little man, "I am glad you came. I am Dr Hoffmeister." He came quickly over to Jacob and drew him aside, out into the hall. "The ambulance will be here any minute now," he said, "and—"

"What happened to my sister?" Jacob asked, interrupting him.

"She suffered an accidental haemorrhage," the doctor said. "They will have to perform a Caesarean section immediately."

"Oh." Jacob could hardly speak. "Will she be all right?" he breathed.

"I hope so. There is nothing I can do right now. I was just waiting for you to come. I've sent someone out to telephone her husband and tell him to come to the hospital. I've got one more important call to make and then I'll try and get there myself as quickly as possible."

The mother came in just as the doctor was about to leave, and she stopped him. "Dr Hoffmeister," she cried, all out of breath, "what happened to my daughter? Oh, God, God, what happened to my daughter?"

"Your son will tell you," he said quickly and pushed out of the door.

Jacob told her haltingly, but she hardly listened to him, and what she heard she could only dimly comprehend. Forgotten now were the clashes she had had with Shaendl. Forgotten now was that uneasy and intangible feeling that Shaendl was drifting away from her and becoming a stranger whom she could no longer understand. In the face of the grave crisis the differences dwindled away, and there was left only the basic relationship of a mother and her child.

They went softly up to the bed. Shaendl opened her eyes, and a smile glided down over her face and buried itself around the corners of her mouth.

"*Tochterle*," said the mother, "*Tochterle*. What happened to you?"

Shaendl did not say anything. She reached out her hand and grasped her mother's. The mother pushed aside the neighbour who had come in to help Shaendl, and she gave way immediately, recognizing the rights of the shrivelled old woman. The mother took the wet towel and kept on applying it to Shaendl's forehead, and the mere fact that she was actively doing something which seemed to help her daughter eased her heavy heart.

"How are you, Jacob?" said Shaendl weakly. "You were supposed to come for dinner on Sunday."

"Shhhh," he said, "don't worry about me. Lie quiet, Shaendl."

"I'm all right," she said. She stopped, and the muscles of her face contracted. Then the pain subsided, and she said, "Somebody must phone Albert."

"Shaendl," Jacob broke in, "don't talk so much. Albert knows. He will come."

"The children . . ."

"We will look after everything."

The minutes trickled away slowly, like drops of water dripping from a faucet. Jacob kept looking at his watch impatiently, almost counting the seconds. At last, after a long, long five minutes, they could hear the shrill, long-drawn sound of the ambulance siren, and then the sudden shriek of the brakes as the ambulance came to a stop in front of the house. Jacob felt a chill running down his spine and his body stiffened imperceptibly.

An interne and two attendants, coldly official in their white uniforms and white caps, came in with a stretcher. Slowly and with great care they lifted Shaendl from the bed onto the stretcher, folded heavy blankets over her and strapped them fast.

It was a quarter past nine, exactly ten minutes since Jacob had come.

"Mama, you will go home now," Jacob said. "I will go to the hospital with Shaendl."

"No, I want to go too," said the mother.

"We can only take one person," the interne said.

The mother, weak and distressed, gave in.

Outside a crowd had gathered, staring busily to see who was being taken away.

"*Da kommen sie*," someone cried.

"Make room for the stretcher now," the interne said sharply. "This isn't a circus."

The crowd pressed closer to the big doorway.

"Who is it they're taking away?"

"I can't recognize the face."

"It looks like it's Frau Reich."

"Who d'you say?"

"Frau Reich."

"No, no, it can't be. I only saw her yesterday."

"My God, it is at that. Two days ago I talked to her, and I said to her, I said . . ."

"*Ach, die arme Frau.* She's so pale.'

Jacob climbed into the ambulance. The voices of the crowd died away behind him. He sat down on a little chrome-coloured stool. The interne, who was sitting next to Jacob, facing Shaendl, asked him a few particulars, and entered them on a chart.

The jolting of the car caused Shaendl some pain, but she did not utter a sound. Only her face showed that she suffered. Her big black eyes, always so restless, were still. Why does this child hurt me so much? she thought. And then it suddenly occurred to her that the child might not live, but strangely enough this thought did not shock her, nor did the feeling that perhaps she did not want the child to live, because it might be luckier for the child to die. But these thoughts only fleeted through her mind and were gone again, and she did not ponder over them.

Jacob, looking out through the window, saw the column of the Tegetthoff monument rising against the clear, blue sky, and soon they had reached it. The ambulance circled the square and went past it, speeding on through streets already baking under a hot morning sun.

Albert had arrived at the hospital a few minutes before the ambulance got there, and was waiting in a terrible state of agitation. He was far more excited and upset than Shaendl. They carried her up the stairs, and Albert walked beside the stretcher. He was almost in tears when he saw how much she suffered, and finally it was she who calmed and soothed him, and she tried to seem unconcerned, and forced a smile to make him believe her.

Then Jacob and Albert were left alone in the wide corridor. Albert's face was pallid, and his eyes twitched nervously. Jacob suddenly remembered that his tie was still hanging down unied, and he knotted it quickly, glad that he had something to do with his hands.

"How could it have happened?" Albert kept repeating. "God, how could it have happened?"

Jacob said, "Everything will be all right, Albert. These things happen. Don't drive yourself crazy. She is in good hands."

Albert didn't hear what Jacob said. He felt feverish. Drops of sweat appeared continually on his brow, and he kept wiping them away with his handkerchief in quick, nervous motions. His shirt stuck to his body, but he was shivering in spite of the heat. His hands were moist and cold. He kept on staring at the door behind which they must be working on Shaendl now, his eyes bulging wide as if they hoped to pierce the wood. He turned his head away hastily, trying to find another object to distract his attention because he was afraid he might make a dash for the door and burst into the room.

Then that hateful door suddenly opened and a nurse came out, calm and efficient, and asked if Jacob and Albert were relatives of Frau Reich. Albert grew visibly paler because he thought that it was all over. He could not utter a sound. Frau Reich, the nurse said, would need some blood transfusions, and would they step in here, please, and have their blood tested.

Albert sighed deeply. It was a sigh of relief. "Of course," he mumbled. At least he would be allowed to do something for her. But he asked immediately, "Is it that bad with her?"

"She's lost a lot of blood," the nurse said.

They went in. Albert had hoped to see Shaendl, but she was not there. Jacob's blood was the right type. but Albert's was not.

"Go into the next room, please," a doctor said to Jacob.

There were two tables in that room, and Shaendl was lying on one, pale, her eyes closed.

"Lie down there and bare you arm," the doctor said. He disinfected a small area and applied a tourniquet, and immediately afterwards Jacob felt the sharp prick of a needle. Then the blood began to flow out of his veins, slowly and smoothly, into the veins of his sister.

"That's all now," the doctor said. "You can go and rest up a bit in the other room."

Jacob got up, feeling a bit groggy, and rolled down his shirt-sleeve. Shaendl smiled weakly at him. He bent over her and said, "Don't worry, Shaendl, everything will turn out fine."

He went out, pulling the door shut behind him. Albert

149

pounced on him and asked what had happened. Jacob told him, and he drank the words in greedily, asking the same questions over and over again and getting the same answers.

After Jacob had rested for a while and smoked a cigarette, they went out into the corridor again. They spoke very little, just waited. Albert paced up and down, and Jacob smoked one cigarette after another. Every time a nurse or a doctor walked along the corridor, Albert stopped and his heart almost stopped beating because he was afraid they were coming to tell him that Shaendl was dead. He asked a few times, but nobody could give him any information. The mere thought that she might die was unfathomable. Life without her seemed impossible and hardly worth living. He tried not to let himself think of it, but the idea kept recurring to him again and again, as if it were whispered by somebody who was standing at his elbow and whom he could not silence. He felt like screaming, I am responsible. And once this feeling of guilt had taken hold of his mind, he could not shake it off, and it was the more agonizing because it remained vague and undefined, a monster without a head, lurking on the fringes of his consciousness. He recalled every harsh word he had even spoken to her. Trifles assumed magnitude, and he blew them up into things of immense importance. The agony became unbearable. He saw her again, pale on the stretcher, and the beautiful eyes, the restless, sparkling eyes so still and bottomless as if they were already gazing on something beyond life, annihilating time and space. No, no, why think of that? Why not think of her laughter, why not of her thrusting out a pair of opera glasses, saying, "Take a good look at her three chins, and then tell me if you can really make yourself believe that she's consumptive." Red circles flashed before his eyes. He stopped pacing up and down and tried to steady himself against the wall. Jacob drew him to a bench and made him sit down. He tried to calm him, but his words fell flat.

And then at long last the wait was over. The same nurse who had spoken to them before came out again and told them. Shaendl's condition, she said, was serious. The child, though weak, was alive. It was a boy. It was by no means certain, however, if he would live.

Albert wiped the sweat from his brow. He hardly thought about his child. At the moment he was only concerned about Shaendl. "Can I see my wife?" he asked hoarsely.

"There's no point now," the nurse said. "She is still under the anaesthetic. And I don't think she'll be allowed to see anyone today. She is much too weak. There is nothing you can do for her."

"Let me have a look at her for only one moment," said Albert. "Please."

She smiled and gave in to him. They tiptoed into the ward. Shaendl's face was very white. She was sleeping quietly. After a few minutes they went out again.

Jacob felt a heavy load fall off his chest. It was a wonderful, instantaneous relief. He was suddenly very hungry and his throat was dry.

"Thank God," he said. "Thank God it is over. Come, Albert, let us go home and tell my mother and the others. They will be waiting to hear. It is almost one o'clock now."

"I'm going to wait here until she wakes up," said Albert.

"But you can't go into the ward. Not today. The nurse told you. Shaendl is too weak."

"I'll go in," Albert said sharply. "I don't care what the nurse said. I've got to see her. The nurse said her condition is serious. So it's not all over yet. What—what if she should . . . well, what if something happens and I'm not here? You go home and I'll stay here."

"Nothing will happen. Don't be a fool. You come with me. You are as white as a sheet. Come with me. You need to eat and to drink something. You can come back immediately. Besides, the children will come home from school, and you should be there."

In the end Albert let himself be persuaded. He did not speak a word on the way home, though he seemed outwardly more composed.

Reuben and Manya were waiting at the mother's flat. Bernhardt and Herman had come home from school. Finding no one at home, they had gone to their grandmother. She had told them that Shaendl was sick and had gone to see a doctor. She had given them something to eat, and then they had gone with their friends to a nearby park to play football.

Reuben said to Jacob, "Four times I have telephoned to the hospital, but they could tell me nothing. I was just going to go there."

They were concerned only about Shaendl. Nobody seemed to think about the child, and it came almost as a surprise, even to Albert, when Manya suddenly asked, "And the child? And what about the child?"

"It's a boy," said Albert slowly. "He's still alive."

"Sit down and eat something," said the mother.

"No, no I couldn't eat anything."

She brought him a cup of tea and a sandwich. He pushed the plate away. "I'd only be sick."

"Drink the tea, at least."

"No, nothing, thanks," he said wearily.

"A glass of schnapps?"

"All right."

She poured him a drink and he drained it in one gulp. He sat hunched up holding his aching head, and gnawing his cold lips. The room seemed to be moving and everything danced before his eyes. And then a nameless fear gripped him and he jumped up suddenly. "I'm going now," he said. "I'm going back to the hospital."

"Wait a while," said Jacob. "I'll go with you."

"No. I'm too nervous. I'm going. You can come down afterwards. Take your time."

He walked out of the room. His head began to spin, slowly at first, round and round, in large circles, and then faster and faster, with the circles narrowing until his head seemed to revolve around a tiny axis at fantastic speed. He slammed the door behind him.

"How did Shaendl look?" the mother asked for the tenth time.

"She will be all right," Jacob said. They sipped their tea slowly.

Suddenly there was a terrific commotion outside in the hall-way, and then came a sharp, loud knock on the door. It was the caretaker, a Czech who spoke a broken German and rolled his r's.

"Frrrrau Grrrrossman," he shouted. "Yourrrr son-in-law I saw him rrron out of house, and he rrron straight in big trrrrock, as if he is blind."

And for the second time Jacob jumped up and rushed down the stairs into the street. A mass of people were clustered about the spot where it had happened. Nothing was to be seen there. A few men had picked up Albert's dead body and had carried it into the back room of a grocery store. They let Jacob come in. He stood there, shattered, and he could not believe that it had happened. He lifted the handkerchief which someone had placed over Albert's face and looked at him. His glasses were broken, and a thin trickle of blood oozed slowly from the corners of his mouth.

"You say he is—he is dead?"

The men who stood about him nodded.

When Albert's body had been taken away, about half an hour

later, the family went back to the mother's flat, benumbed by the impact of the tragedy, and unable to grasp fully what had happened.

Jacob locked the door and tiptoed softly into the room. He was worried about the mother. She sat in her favourite chair, close by the window, and looked out into the yard. Her face was haggard and sunken. When Jacob came over to her and put his arm round her shoulders, she sobbed a little and was still again. Jacob saw that her lips were moving, and he realized that she was silently praying. She possessed fully the wonderful gift of her race, a gift acquired in centuries of persecution. It was the gift to endure an almost unbearable burden of suffering and to grow even stronger in the face of it.

Strangely enough, it was Manya who broke down completely. Manya, whose dislike for Albert had bordered almost on hatred. She cried hysterically, and Reuben, patient Reuben, consoled her and talked to her soothingly as if she were a child.

Then he said, "Somebody will have to tell the children. Yankel, I think it would be good if you tell them. They like you best of all."

Jacob's heart was heavy. He did not cherish the task. "Well," he said, "if it has to be. I will tell them when they come."

"No," said Reuben. "Go and get them. Otherwise somebody else will tell them. And it is better if they hear it from you."

"But I don't know where they are."

"Come with me into the street, and I will find somebody to show you the way. I will stay here with Manya and your mother."

There was still a great deal of commotion in the street. Two policemen were interrogating the eyewitnesses and making notes with dull pencil-stubs which they kept wetting from time to time. The Czech caretaker was re-enacting the accident with large gestures and deep, rolling r's. A group of people was gathered around him, listening gravely, asking the same questions over and over again.

Reuben looked about to find somebody who could lead the way for Jacob. Little Holzinger was standing there with a bunch of boys. Reuben had often seen him with Herman. He went up to him and tapped him on the shoulder, and Holzinger turned round.

"Little boy," said Reuben, "do you know where the Rotunden-park is?"

Holzinger knew.

"Herman is there. Go and show this gentleman where it is."

Holzinger rubbed his nose. "Sure," he said, "sure, I c'n take him." He was happy that he had an opportunity of walking with Herman's rich uncle, who had come all the way across the ocean from the land of cowboys and Red Indians.

"My name's Holzinger," he said. "I saw you once on a Sunday. But I was hoarse then. I'm not hoarse any more."

Jacob was wondering how he should prepare the children before he told them. Holzinger, in a quick gesture of intimacy, slipped his hand into Jacob's. Jacob was not aware of it. He kept looking straight ahead and walked very quickly so that Holzinger had difficulty keeping pace with him.

"D'you think Herman will cry when he hears it?" Holzinger asked. "My father died last year, and I didn't cry hardly at all. Only the first day. But I felt sad for a long time. I saw how it happened. I saw how Herr Reich ran out of the house, and there was a big brown truck coming fast, and—"

"Shut up," snapped Jacob. "Don't say a word. I don't want to hear about it. Keep quiet."

Holzinger looked at Jacob. He did not know why Jacob should be offended. He was not conscious of having done anything wrong.

"We're almost there," said Holzinger suddenly. "I can see them playing football now. Can you see them? There." He pointed his finger.

Jacob's knees threatened to give way under him. He felt a sudden weakness. He was afraid to go on and shatter the blue sky of the children by a piercing flash of lightning. He slackened his pace. But even as he was beating his brain to find the right beginning, Holzinger let go of his hand and ran ahead, shouting, "Herman, your father was killed by a brown truck."

The children stopped their game instantly. They gathered around Bernhardt and Herman. Jacob was terribly angry at Holzinger, but at the same time he could not help feeling that he had saved him at least something of his task. Bernhardt and Herman stared at Jacob, and then they ran to him and clung to his coat, their eyes seeking confirmation in his.

And Jacob, because he did not know what to say, shouted at Holzinger, "Go away, you . . . you . . . you . . . go away, I don't want to see you."

Holzinger scratched his red hair, and rubbed his little snub-nose. He was confused. He slunk away like a dog that has been beaten without knowing why.

Bernhardt stammered, "Is it—is it true what Holzinger said, Uncle Jacob?"

Jacob took the boys by the hand. He went up to a bench with them and sat down. Then he put his arms round them and drew them to him. He did not say a word. Suddenly a tremor went through Herman's body as if a peal of thunder had shaken it. And it was Bernhardt then who consoled him, Bernhardt, the older one, the less aggressive of the two. But neither of them could really comprehend what had happened, and it was as yet impossible for them to picture a life in which Albert had no part.

Jacob tried to smile. "After all," he said, "we are confederates. Confederates have to be strong, eh? Now come. We'll go home now."

"Is Mama at home?" asked Bernhardt.

"No," said Jacob. "Your mother had to stay in the hospital. You will be able to see her in a few days." And then he suddenly remembered. "You have a new brother, children," he said.

Rivka was there when Jacob came in with the children. The eyes of the women were red from crying. But now they were remarkably quiet. Rivka took the children with her. They would stay with her until Shaendl was back again.

As soon as dusk had gathered and the room was almost dark, the mother went over to the table and lighted the candles to welcome the Sabbath. She spoke the blessing as she had always done. The candles threw a friendly gleam over the room, and it was almost as if they were bidding the people in it to come and seat themselves around the table. No one came. No one ate that night. They sat silently, resigned. The silence weighed heavy upon the room.

At last Jacob got up. "I'm going to telephone to the hospital," he said.

He felt better when he was outside and saw people walking about the streets. It helped him to regain something of his balance.

He telephoned the hospital and was informed that Shaendl's condition was unchanged. The child was still alive.

He did not want to go back home right away. The fresh air did him good, and he decided to stroll about for half an hour. And suddenly, as he walked, alone and unable to escape from his own thoughts, he felt the desire to mingle with a large crowd of people, to disappear in it, and thus perhaps to escape from himself. He was walking towards the Prater, though he did not know it. If this had to happen, he thought sadly, then why did it have to happen while I was here? He was now selfishly bitter. Thirty-three years I have been away and I come back once, and am here only two weeks and this happens. *Shlimazl* that I am. So many years, so many weeks from which to choose, and I come now. But then he checked the flow of his thoughts, and was deeply ashamed that he had been capable of thinking in such terms on a night like this.

The crowd grew thicker now and surged about him in a great mass, and he had to walk slowly. The beer-gardens were packed with people. Jacob watched them drink their beer, he heard their laughter, and he envied them. He walked by a café, its terrace ivy-covered. A few people were standing outside, peering through the thickly clinging leaves on to the terrace. Jacob stopped. He looked through a slit in the leafage. A band was playing soft music, and couples were crowding the floor, dancing intimately, close-pressed, their bodies almost merging into one.

God, what will Shaendl do now? It flashed through his head. How will she bring up her children? Three children. The mere thought threw him into a state of panic. He couldn't bear to dwell on it. Oh, if he could only talk to someone now. He felt a great longing to speak and be spoken to. Yet, who would want to listen to him? What was he to these people? He could die on the spot and none of them would care. He shuddered. He knew the cruelty and the indifference of a great city. He knew how utterly alone a man can be even among a million other men. The crowd pushed and pulled about him, hundreds of men and women, out to amuse themselves and have a good time, but he was not a part of them. That was the way he had felt, walking the hot pavements of New York and Detroit and Toronto with Sam Silver.

"Wanna buy a balloon, a nice big balloon? Got 'em in all colours. Buy a balloon for the kiddies."

Jacob looked up. A tattered old man, his face wrinkled and his nose red from drink, held out a shaking hand which gripped the strings of several balloons.

Jacob was thankful that someone had spoken to him, and he searched his pockets for a coin and bought a balloon. Suddenly it occurred to him that he might go and find Koch. But how could he find him? He did not remember the way. Then something clicked in his mind.

"Oh," he said to the old man who had sold him the balloon,

"perhaps, my good man, you can tell me where I can see *die Dame ohne Unterleib?*"

The old man leaned forward a little and peered into Jacob's face. "You sure you're all right?" he said. "You sure you didn' have a li'l bit too much t' drink?"

Jacob said, "No, no, no. She is a lady who—who . . . I want to know . . ."

"No hard feelings. Happens to all good men. Happens to me practic'ly every day. Y' don' need to apologize . . . Balloons, balloons! Nice, big balloons! Buy a balloon for the kiddies. Got 'em in all colours!"

Jacob pushed on, cursing under his breath. It must be around here somewhere, he thought. He recognized the roller coaster on which he had gone with the children. And then they had led him—yes, he knew now. He turned a corner, and there it was. He could see the little improvised platform. Nothing was happening. and he realized that a performance must be going on inside. He came closer, and he could see Robert Koch immediately, grotesque in his clown's costume, leaning against a post, smoking a cigarette.

"Herr Koch!" Jacob called out. "Herr Koch!"

Koch raised his head. When he recognized Jacob, he began to laugh. Jacob glared at him. He could not understand why Koch was laughing.

"Pardon me for laughing," said Koch, "but you looked awfully funny running up to me with this great big balloon in your hand."

Jacob looked at his hand. He had completely forgotten about the balloon. He opened his palm, thus releasing the string. The balloon, like a dove suddenly set free, rose steeply and floated towards the sky.

"Did you come here all alone?" asked Koch.

"Yes," said Jacob. "You do not know yet?"

"Know? What?"

"Shaendl is in the hospital," said Jacob very slowly, "and my brother-in-law—Albert. He—he was killed."

Koch straightened his body with a jerk. "What are you talking about?" he gasped.

Jacob nodded his head slowly. "Yes."

"When did all this happen?" Koch thrust his body forward. His voice was suddenly hoarse.

"Shaendl was taken to the hospital this morning," said Jacob. "And Albert—this afternoon. A few hours ago."

"How?" Koch's face was pale behind the mask of red and

white make-up. He passed his hands over it, and the cheap paint came off on his fingers.

Jacob told him as quickly as he could, expressing himself more by gestures than by words. Then he stopped abruptly and let his hands sink down slowly.

The two men looked at each other in silence. They were now an island within themselves, isolated and far away, and the noise which raged all about them came to them, muffled and indistinct, like the sound of little waves lapping and breaking themselves against a desolated shore when the sea is calm.

At last Koch said, "Could you give me a cigarette, Herr Grossman, please?"

"Yes," said Jacob, "of course. Here."

Koch lit the cigarette and inhaled deeply.

"Eh, Koch! *Wo bist du?*" came a sharp, rasping voice from behind. "How many times do I have to call? What the hell do you think this is? Come on, the show's almost over inside."

Koch roused himself and shook his body like a man who has been rudely disturbed in his sleep. "All right," he said without turning round. "All right. I'll be with you in a minute. Listen, Herr Grossman. Where do you live?"

"Hillergasse 4."

"Koch!"

"I'll come over to see you tomorrow morning."

"Come on, Koch! Hurry up. I want to start blowing my bugle."

"I'm coming, I'm coming. Go on, start blowing the bugle. I'm just going to put some more paint on my face. The damned stuff keeps coming off all the time."

"Come on. Get behind the curtain."

Jacob was very close to the little platform and he could hear the boards creak as the man climbed onto it. He put the bugle to his lips and tore the air with a few loud, cracked blasts. Another man kept shouting, "*Kommen Sie näher, kommen Sie alle näher!*" and he clapped his hands to attract the crowd. "Everybody come close! Everybody come close!"

Jacob stared up at the man with the bugle. He envied him his apparent carelessness and serenity. He seemed so completely carefree, with not a worry in the world save blowing his bugle.

Suddenly Robert Koch's croaking baritone came from behind the curtain. "Tra-la-la, tra-la-la, tra-la-la-la-la." The man who had shouted and clapped his hands disappeared behind the curtain, and came back, dragging Koch by the ear. The crowd yelled and laughed.

Koch cried, "I'm going to tell my father! I'm going to tell my father!"

"What's your father?" asked the man with the bugle.

"My father's dead," snarled Koch.

Jacob could not stand it any longer. He pushed his way through the crowd. A few people scowled at him, annoyed at the disturbance he was causing.

"Well, what was he before he was dead?" asked the man with the bugle.

"He was alive before that," bellowed Koch.

The crowd roared with laughter.

Jacob was out of it now, but the laughter of the crowd followed him long after he could hear the jokes of the men on the little platform. He wondered how it was possible for Koch to get up there immediately after he had heard the news and sing and jump about as if nothing had happened.

He walked very quickly and it did not take him very long to get back. He opened the door quietly and went into the room. They were still sitting as he had left them, statuesque, stiff, silent. The mother in her chair close by the window, Reuben on the sofa, with his elbow propped against the hard cushion, Manya near the door.

The room was almost dark. The candles were burned low, two tongues of flame, flickering up and down.

Reuben lifted his head. "Yankel?" he asked, peering towards the door.

"Yes," said Jacob, "it's me."

"Did you telephone?" asked Reuben.

"Yes. She—she is a bit better."

"Thank God," sighed Manya.

"And the child?" the mother asked.

"He's alive."

"How come you took so long?" asked Reuben.

"Nothing. I just walked a little bit." He went over to the sofa and sat down beside Reuben.

The candles flickered high in a last effort, and then sank down, two yellowish-blue tips, and went out completely. If someone had walked into the room, he would have thought that people were asleep in it.

After a long time Reuben got up. "Manya," he said, speaking into the darkness, "let us go home."

"Yes," said Manya.

When they had gone, Jacob said, "Go to bed, Mama. You must be tired."

"No," she said, "I'm not tired. I'll sit like this. It's a soft chair. In bed I would only turn and turn, but I couldn't sleep this night, I know."

He did not say any more. He was exhausted, and yet he felt that he would not be able to sleep, either. He stretched out on the sofa, though he did not undress. After a while he fell into an unruly and restless slumber, and he roused himself often with a sudden shudder, as if a shrill voice had called him.

He was glad when day broke. He looked over at his mother. She had dozed off in the chair. He got up softly, trying not to disturb her, and tiptoed out into the kitchen. There he poured cold water into a wash-bowl, and then splashed it over his hands and face. He felt refreshed. Then he went back into the room.

Koch came at eleven. He looked haggard, as though he, too, had not slept well that night. He was not shaved. He took Jacob's hand and held it for a few moments.

"Come in, Herr Koch," said Jacob.

"I hope I'm not disturbing you."

"No, no. Nobody is here except my mother."

They went into the room.

"Mama," said Jacob, "this is Herr Koch, Albert's friend."

Koch took her hand. "I'm very sorry," he said softly.

"Sit down, Herr Koch," the mother said.

"Thank you." He drew up a chair. "Does Shaendl know already?"

Jacob shook his head. "I spoke with the doctor this morning on the telephone and told him what happened. He said we couldn't tell her for a day or two. The shock would be too great, he said. In the meantime they wouldn't let us in to see her. I don't know how it's going to be when she hears." He passed his hands over his face. "I'm afraid to think about it even. Such a terrible thing should happen. It's—it's . . ." He threw his hands up in despair. "I don't know." Then he added, "The doctor told me the child will live."

"*Na, wenigstens das,*" Koch said lamely. "At least that." There was no conviction in his voice, but he felt he had to make some sort of remark. What he really wanted to say was, I don't know whether that's something to be happy about.

The mother rose. "I will leave you here now to talk alone," she said. "Manya hasn't come down yet, so I will go upstairs to see how she is feeling." She said "*Guten Tag*" to Koch and went out of the room.

"Who's Manya?" Koch asked.

"My sister. She has a flat on the second floor."

"Oh."

Koch had noticed Tassigny's painting as soon as he came in, but he had paid little attention to it at first. Now his eyes were drawn to it as by a magnet. How the hell did this get here? he wondered. The garish, bald colours held his eyes and would not let them go. Slowly he began to single out the elements in the painting, the legs out of all proportion to the body, the megaphone-like contraption where the head should have been, the tortured face staring at him from behind the right leg. He felt a strange and morbid fascination which grew more irresistible the longer he looked at the picture.

"How—how on earth did this ever get here?" he asked at last without taking his eyes off the picture.

"I—I bought it," Jacob said awkwardly. "On the ship. It's a man without a face. I bought it from a Frenchman. Funny. I hung it up there the first night I came, and I haven't even noticed it any more since then."

"I think I better go and sit over there," Koch said, "so I won't have to keep looking at it." He changed his seat, but even though he couldn't see the picture, he was still conscious of it and felt its stark colours glaring down at his back.

"When I saw you last Tuesday," he said, "I didn't think we would meet again the way we did last night. I saw you pushing your way through the crowd as soon as I started my song and dance. You must have thought I am a man wholly without feelings."

Jacob's face grew red. "No, no, no," he said, "I—I understand."

"There've been many times when I lit a cigarette and held the burning match in my hand and thought, 'All you have to do now is to take one or two steps and hold the match to that grimy red curtain and the whole goddam place would go up in flames and you could stand there and laugh and watch it burn.' But then I think, 'Why bite your own nose?' and I always blow out the match and throw it away. A man must eat, and at the moment that's the only way I can earn my bread. The man I work for is not very sentimental. The death of a friend means nothing to him."

"I know," said Jacob, "I know."

"Do you know what I thought as I came out from behind

161

the curtain? I wished it had happened to me instead of Albert Reich."

Jacob leaned across the table. "It is not right that you should talk like that. Not a young man like you."

Koch smiled. "Why not? Look at the matter objectively. Two men about the same age. Many years ago they went to the same school. One has two children, and his wife has just given birth to a third and is having a very tough time. The other is all alone. He has no wife, no children. Perhaps he isn't altogether useless, but the work he does could be done by another. Which of the two can better afford to die?"

"Herr Koch," Jacob said uneasily. "Please, why should you say these things?"

"There is another point. Once, in a very ticklish and dangerous situation he who was killed took a great personal risk and helped the other." He checked himself. "You're right, Herr Grossman, all this is idle speculation. Tell me, who's to blame for the accident?"

"All the people who saw it, about six–seven people, they all say it was his fault. They all say the driver couldn't help it. They say Albert ran straight into the truck, like a blind man."

"No chance of compensation, then?"

"No, I don't think so. I—I blame myself, Herr Koch. I wanted to go back to the hospital with him, but he wouldn't wait. I shouldn't never have made him come here in the first place. He didn't want to come, and if he had stayed in the hospital, this wouldn't have happened maybe."

"That's nonsense," Koch retorted sharply. "It was nobody's fault, least of all yours. It wasn't the driver's fault, and it wasn't even Albert's fault. His mind must have been miles and miles away when he ran into that truck. Who can blame him? Who could have foreseen it?" He lowered his voice. "In some ways I envy Albert," he said quietly, "because he is out of the turmoil. He's past all worries. It is more important to think about the living. Shaendl and the children. What are they going to do now?"

Jacob cringed. He didn't want to think about that now. "Shaendl and the children," he muttered in a toneless voice, repeating Koch's words almost mechanically. "What are they going to do?" Wasn't his heart heavy enough without thinking about that? Why did Koch have to bring it up?

"The best thing of course would be for her to get out of here, if this were possible. But how?" He paused and rubbed his chin with his hand. "I often marvel when I look about me and see that men and women still have the courage to bring children into the world. Is it just a natural instinct, I wonder, or is it a real and conscious affirmation of life? Maybe one of these days I'll get married and try to find the answer." There was a slight, hardly perceptible overtone of irony in his voice. "Too bad the little victims have no say in the matter. I know if I were asked whether I wanted to be born now, I'd say, not now, please. In a few years perhaps. Let me first see what the world is going to look like. The little fellow who was cut out of Shaendl's body yesterday—he wasn't born at the right time, and he wasn't born in the right place."

Jacob shifted about uncomfortably in his chair. He wished Koch wouldn't talk like that. "You think things will get better here maybe?" he asked.

Koch nodded his head slowly. "I think so. Some day. But I'm a realist as well as a dreamer, and I know they will get a lot worse before they get better. Those who feel that they must swim against the stream will probably get swallowed up before the bright day dawns. Your people have of course no choice in the matter. They must swim against the Fascist stream because even if they wanted to, they wouldn't be allowed to swim with it. The best thing therefore, for those who can, is to get out of the water and wait on the bank."

"And you?" Jacob asked. "You, Herr Koch, are you going to stay here?"

"Yes. Perhaps I'd like to get out, but there are many reasons which make me stay. I have a lot of work to do."

"What?" Jacob asked. "To be a clown?"

"*Vielleicht*," Koch said, and his eyes twinkled. "Maybe to be a clown." He spoke the words slowly. An ironic smile played round his lips. "After all, isn't it something to entertain people, to make them forget their worries for a while? Eh, Herr Grossman?"

Jacob was uneasy. He didn't know how Koch meant what he said, and he tried not to look him in the face.

"This is really none of my business, Herr Grossman," Koch said, switching his tone, and very serious now. "Albert told me once that you are a man of some means. Well, couldn't you do something for Shaendl?"

Jacob averted his eyes quickly. He felt the blood rushing to his face, and his heart beating against his ribs. "I'll try what I can do," he muttered, his voice hardly audible. Oh, why did I come here? he thought helplessly. Why did I come?

He turned his head slowly back to Koch. "Herr Koch," he

said hoarsely, "when the time comes to tell Shaendl, will you tell her?"

"Why should it be me? After all, there is the family. One of you should tell her."

"We're all afraid, Herr Koch. I know if I had to tell her, I wouldn't be able to open my lips. I—I couldn't do it, Herr Koch. I had to tell the children, and my heart nearly broke inside. You—you was a good friend of his . . ."

"It seems that in the past few years I've had to bring nothing but bad news," Koch said sadly.

"How—how you think she will take it?"

Koch contracted his brows. "She loved him very much," he said. Then, after a pause, "When is the funeral?"

"Tomorrow morning at eleven. On the Zentralfriedhof."

"I'll be there." He rose heavily. "I couldn't sleep last night. Maybe I can snatch a few hours now."

They shook hands. Koch turned. There was the picture again, staring at him from the wall. He took a long, long look at it. "All the agony and the torture," he mumbled enigmatically. "God damn it."

CHAPTER

XIV

Six men carried him from the hall, Jacob and Reuben, Manfred and Koch, and two other men. The long, wooden coffin rested heavily upon their shoulders, and they walked very slowly. When they came to the open grave, they lowered the coffin carefully, and set it down in the grass beside the grave. And then they spoke prayers for him, though he had never laid great store by them while he was alive, and had long since drifted from the old faith.

And they said, "The Rock, His work is perfect, for all His ways are judgement: a God of faithfulness and without iniquity, just and right is He. The Rock, perfect in every way, who can say unto Him, What workest Thou? He ruleth below and above. He killeth and maketh alive. He bringeth down to the grave, and bringeth up again."

And they said, "If a man live one year or a thousand years, what profiteth it to him? When his days are done, it shall be as if he had never been."

And they said, "The Lord hath given, and the Lord hath taken away. Blessed be the name of the Lord."

Then the coffin was lowered into the grave, and came to rest on the ground. And they went up to the grave, one by one, and looked down into it, and threw a handful of brown earth onto the coffin, and said, "May he come to his place in peace." Then they bent down, and plucked grass, and threw it behind them, and said, "They of the city shall flourish like the grass of the earth. He remembereth that we are dust." And Robert Koch, though he was not a Jew, did as he saw the others do.

And when they had done all these things, they went back to the hall, and poured water over their hands from a pitcher, and said, "He will destroy death for ever. And the Lord God will wipe away tears from off all faces. And the rebuke of His people shall He take away from off all the earth. For the Lord hath spoken it."

CHAPTER

XV

WHEN Jacob and Manya came into the ward on Monday afternoon, Shaendl knew already. Robert Koch was standing at the foot of the bed, his hands gripping the steel rail. He had asked them to come half an hour later so that he might be able to speak to her alone. Koch was sweating and his breath came fast. He had tried to get the painful task over as quickly as possible, sparing her as much agony as he could. And now she knew, and lay perfectly still, with her arms stretched out to the side, her hands balled into fists and her lower lip curled up inside her mouth. Her black, restless eyes were directly on Jacob, but there was no sign in them that they recognized him. They lay in their sockets, burningly dry.

Jacob went up quite close to her and stroked her pale cheek with his hand. "Hello, Shaendl, my dear," he said. "How are you?" There was nothing more he could think of saying, and he sank into silence, withdrew his hand from her face, and laid it over her fist.

The ward was filled with laughter and gladness. This was a happy ward, where people came and listened to the rapturous voices of new mothers.

After a long time, Shaendl asked softly, "Where are my children?" Her lower lip was white, and the marks of her teeth could plainly be seen where she had bitten it.

"They are at Rivka's place," said Jacob. "They will be there until you can come home again."

"Do they—do they know?" she asked.

"Yes," said Jacob, "I told them. You have two wonderful children, Shaendl."

"Three," she said. "Poor little ones." And after a pause. "Why didn't you bring them?"

"Your brother wanted to," Koch said. "But I thought it would be better if they didn't come today. I thought it might be better if your mother didn't come today, either."

"They showed me my child for the first time today," she said. "He's an awfully tiny baby. But he's going to live." She was grateful now that the child would live. She wanted it to ive. She desired it passionately. And for a moment a feeling of happiness and hope drowned out her pain and her despair and the consciousness that Albert was no more. She was silent again, and lay almost motionless.

Manya edged her way closer and bent over the bed until she almost touched Shaendl. She kissed her quickly and with great tenderness. Her lips quivered and her hands twitched on the blanket. And then she could not control herself any longer, and began to sob bitterly.

Koch came over to her and tried to soothe her. The laughter and the talk ceased abruptly in the ward, and people turned and stared.

"Why don't you cry, Shaendl?" Manya sobbed. "Why don't you cry? Cry a little, Shaendl dear. Cry."

Shaendl closed her eyes and passed her hands over her face. "I think you'd better go now," she managed to say. "Please leave me now."

"I think that would be best," Koch said, leading Manya away gently.

Shaendl turned her eyes towards Jacob. "Bring the children tomorrow, Jacob."

Jacob patted her hand. "I'll bring the children. Sure, sure. I'll bring the children."

The whole family was there next day. They surrounded the bed, talking to her. But Shaendl hardly listened to them. She was too absorbed in her children. Herman and Bernhardt were standing on either side of the bed, looking curiously at their mother. She put her arms round them and drew them down to her, deriving more strength and consolation from one touch of their cheeks than from a million kind words.

Herman asked, "Where does it hurt you?"

She smiled at him. "It doesn't hurt at all now," she said.

"Then why don't you come home with us now?" asked Herman.

"I can't come home yet, darling," she said. "But I'll come home with you soon. I have to stay here for a while. I have to rest up."

"Why can't you rest at home?" said Herman.

"I can't at home, darling."

"Why did it hurt you at all, Mama?" asked Bernhardt.

"Because I brought you a new brother, children."

"Oh!" said Herman, and he puckered up his lips, and furrowed his forehead. "Oh! He is a bad brother then. We won't like him, because he hurt you, will we, Bernie?"

"Oh, no, you mustn't say that." She tried to sit up in bed, but she was still too weak. "You must love him very, very much. You must take good care of him because he is so much younger than you. Every child hurts its mother when it comes into the world."

"Did I hurt you, too?" asked Herman.

She nodded her head lightly.

"Oh!" he said, and opened his eyes wide in wonderment.

"It doesn't matter," she said. "I love you all the more for it. You'll understand some day."

"All right, then," said Herman. "We'll love him, then. What's his name going to be, Mama?"

"We're—we're going to call him Albert," she said, speaking very slowly. "We're going to give him Papa's name. So we'll always remember Papa."

"But Papa isn't going to come home any more, is he, Mama?" said Bernhardt, his voice low and sad. "Ever."

And when she heard him say that, the tears, long wished for, came at last. She let them flow gladly, because they dissolved some of the tension within her and made her feel better. Herman, infected by her tears, began to cry too.

"Don't cry, Mama," said Bernhardt. "Don't cry, Mama. We're going to take care of you, aren't we, Herman?"

"Sure we are," said Herman, sobbing and nodding his head violently. "Sure we're going to look after you."

Manya said suddenly, in a vain effort to console Shaendl, "You are still so young, Shaendl, and you are pretty, too. There will come a nice man, and—"

"Manya, Manya," said Reuben from the other side of the bed, "for once talk a little less. It would be better if you keep quiet for a while."

And for once, whether she realized her mistake, or whether she was cowed by Reuben's unusually firm tone, she did not say any more.

Shaendl stretched out her hand and ruffled Herman's hair. "You need to have your hair cut, Herman dear," she said, smiling through her tears. "It's getting awfully long. We'll ask Uncle Jacob to take you to a barber. Jacob will you go with Herman and see that he gets his hair cut?"

"We'll go right away," said Jacob, "eh, Herman?"

"I don't need a haircut yet, do I, Mama?" asked Bernhardt.

"No," she said, passing her hand through his hair. "You can wait a while. You can wait until I come home again."

Jacob came to see her every day. One day, when no one else was there yet, and they had been talking for about five minutes, Shaendl said suddenly, "Manya is already trying to marry me off again. But she is such a simple woman, and she really does mean well, and so I always find it hard to be angry with her."

Jacob fidgeted about, not knowing what to say. "But Reuben is nice," he said at last.

"Oh, he's lovely," she said. "I've never known a man so kind as he. He was the only one who was not against Albert when I first met him. I've never forgotten that. And he's always been so nice to my children. They love him, though ever since you came they've neglected him a bit." She smiled.

"But I will go in two weeks," Jacob said, "and then they will have Reuben again."

"Two weeks? Is it that soon?" She seemed surprised. "I hadn't thought about it, really. It seems as if you've been with us always. We'll miss you. There'll be a gap somewhere when you're gone. I'm only sorry things didn't turn out the way you must have expected them. You should have had a pleasant and gay time. But instead . . ."

"I didn't come to have a gay time," he said. "I came to see you all."

"We appreciated it. It—it made all these terrible things a bit easier to bear."

"Soon you will have forgotten about me," he said.

"That's not true. It's more likely that you should forget us than that we should forget you."

"I wish I could do something to help you," he said. "I will feel terrible when I am on the ship and will know all the time what is happening here. I—I wish I could stay with you until things are a little brighter."

She looked at him. Her eyes penetrated deep within him and gripped him like claws. He found it impossible to evade them. Then she looked away, smiling a bitter smile. "I'm afraid you'd have to stay a long, long time," she said.

"If only I could do something," he mumbled.

"Perhaps you could do something."

"What can I do?"

She didn't answer immediately. Then she shook her head and said quietly, "I don't know."

He felt uncomfortable because there was something else, unsaid, but nonetheless clearly implied, in the way she spoke the words. He was glad when she changed the subject and asked, "Did you really tell me the truth when you said that Mama didn't come today because she is too tired? Is she feeling all right?"

"Oh, yes, yes," he said quickly. "On my word. But it is so hot out, and I told her to stay at home."

"Poor Mama," said Shaendl. "She's had to take so much in her life. It was really wonderful of you to visit her. She always used to talk about you coming to see her. It was her greatest dream. And when Papa died, she hardly lived for anything else, especially after I disappointed her and married Albert."

Jacob shifted uneasily. "Shhhh," he said, "why do you remember these things now? What is the use if you are angry about all that? It is now so many years ago. Better not to think about it."

"Oh, but I'm not angry, Jacob. I'm not angry at all. And I do like to think about it. I'll always want to think about Albert, and how we met, and about our life together." She paused for a moment and looked him full in the face. "Did Mama tell you about us?" she asked then.

And when he did not answer, she said, "I'm sure she did. She must have. Poor Mama! She probably told you Albert and I were so very unhappy. Did she tell you that, Jacob? Tell me, Jacob, did Mama say that?"

Jacob's round, pudgy face grew red with embarrassment. He hoped somebody would come so he wouldn't have to answer her question. Shaendl held him with her eyes.

"She—she didn't say that, Shaendl," he said. "She said that sometimes you was very happy, and that sometimes you was very unhappy, but that she wished she knew why you was unhappy, because then perhaps she could help you."

Her eyes released him. "Mama could never understand us," she said. "We were never unhappy for the reasons she thought we were. We were unhappy because—well, because we wanted so much out of life, and every time we thought we were at last close to what we wanted and hoped for, the thing just seemed to melt and slip away. But when I told that to Mama, she thought I was lying in order to calm her fears. She couldn't understand, and then she always tried to explain it in more conventional terms. Once she even thought Albert was unfaithful to me. Or she thought I was unhappy because we didn't have enough money, and then she always talked about the beautiful match I could have made. As if all I ever wanted from life were diamond rings and mink coats."

"So Mama was telling me the truth when she said you was unhappy sometimes," he ventured to say.

"Yes," she said, and her eyes filled with tears, "but not because I loved Albert less, but because I loved him more and more. I was unhappy because Albert had given up all hope. All his old courage was gone. He didn't trust himself any longer. He was afraid to do things, because he was convinced that whatever he did would turn out to be a failure. Then of course there was the political situation, getting worse from day to day. His nerves were raw. It got so that he couldn't even read any more, he, a born student. But he couldn't concentrate. And I tried so hard to help him, but there was nothing I could do. Something had died within him. That's what made me unhappy. But now . . ." She broke off the sentence.

Jacob didn't say anything, just put his hand over hers and stroked it gently.

"Ach!" she exclaimed suddenly. "Look who's here."

Jacob turned his eyes towards the door. There was Koch coming up to the bed, holding a bunch of spring flowers awkwardly in his hand. Jacob was glad to see him. They shook hands.

"How are you, Shaendl?" Koch asked, looking at her critically. "Are you feeling better?"

"Oh, much, much better, physically," she said, brushing her hair back with her hand. "It's relatively easy to restore the body. I managed to get up today for the first time. I think they'll get rid of me early next week."

"That's wonderful."

"Thank you for the lovely flowers."

"Oh, just a trifle."

"And what about you?" she asked. "You're quite a stranger. Last time you were here you said you'd come the next day. It's three days now."

"I know, and I apologize. But I couldn't help it. Even today I wasn't sure whether I'd be able to make it. I've been very busy."

"Important business?"

"Vital." He cocked his eyebrow and lowered his voice to a mock whisper. "From now on I am giving my days and nights to a serious study of clowning, and I'm about to develop a revolutionary technique. I think the world nearly lost a great clown in me." He turned to Jacob. "You have seen me perform, Herr Grossman. What do you think?"

Jacob looked at him, bewildered. "S—sure," he stammered, "s—sure, Herr Koch. Who knows? You can earn perhaps a lot of money like that."

"*Sie haben recht,*" Koch said. "It might well pay off."

Shaendl smiled a mischievous smile. From the other side of the ward came the tinkling sound of a little bell, marking the end of the visiting hour.

"You see," said Koch. "It seems I just barely made it in time today."

"Well, perhaps you can do better tomorrow," she said.

"Perhaps," he said. "If clowning leaves me time."

They brought her home on Wednesday. The mother and Manya had tidied up her flat, and Jacob had bought flowers to decorate her room.

At three o'clock Jacob took the boys with him to the hospital. He ordered a taxi, and then they went upstairs.

Shaendl was dressed already, and her eyes lit up when she saw them coming into the ward. The boys ran up to her, and nearly overwhelmed her in their eagerness to embrace her. Jacob stopped a few feet away from them and did not interfere, but his eyes smiled, and grew moist a little.

"Are you going to come home with us right now?" asked Herman.

"Yes," she said, "right now."

"And you're not going away again, ever?"

"No, I'm always going to stay with you."

"Promise?" Herman's eyes glistened.

"Promise," she said.

Bernhardt asked, his voice filled with grave concern, "Doesn't it hurt you at all now, Mama?"

"No," she said, "not a bit."

A nurse came into the ward. "Are you ready to go, Frau Reich?" she asked.

"Yes," said Shaendl. "These are my two little boys."

The nurse smiled. "We're going to give you the third to take home," she said.

Shaendl got up, and Jacob stepped forward to help her. She took his arm and supported herself on it.

"You told me it didn't hurt you at all, Mama," Bernhardt said. "That's what you told me. Then why can't you walk straight?"

"I'm all right, darling. Really I am. It doesn't hurt a bit. In a few days I'll be able to walk as straight as ever."

"I better help you on the other side," said Bernhardt. He took her arm. "Lean on me, Mama," he said.

"I want to help you too," Herman said, looking jealously at Bernhardt.

"You're too small," said Bernhardt.

"No, I'm not. Can I take your arm a little bit, Mama? Just a little bit?"

"All right," she said, laughing. "You go over and help Uncle Jacob."

And then they were in the taxi. The children peered at the little blue bundle which Shaendl was holding in her arms. From it there protruded a little pink face, and that face was asleep.

"Is that him?" asked Herman.

"Yes," said Shaendl. "That's your little brother."

"He's ever so tiny," said Bernhardt.

"Oh, he'll grow," said Shaendl.

"You know what?" said Herman to Bernhardt. "When he's eight, I'll be sixteen." He scratched his head. "I'll—I'll almost be a man then, won't I, Bernie?"

"Sure you will," said Bernhardt. "And I'll be—I'll be nineteen. I'll be a real grown up man then. Almost." He pronounced the words slowly and solemnly as if he could hardly believe them.

"This is a nice taxi," said Herman. "Nicer'n the one we rode in when Uncle came here. This one rides smoother'n the other one."

"No, it doesn't," said Bernhardt. "It rides the same."

"No, it rides smoother. I can tell . . . Oh, Mama, look what Uncle Jacob bought for me. I didn't show you yet." He reached into his pocket. "He bought me a fountain pen, too, just like the one he brought for Bernie. Now the soldiers belong to both of us, because I got a fountain pen, too, like Bernie. I had a pencil, too, but I broke it."

"That was awfully nice of Uncle, wasn't it?" she said.

Jacob leaned back into the cushions and smiled. He said nothing, because he did not want to disturb the intimacy of a mother and her children. They chattered on, and Shaendl seemed quite gay. But as Jacob looked at her, he could see a big tear stealing out of the corner of her eye, and he watched it roll down her cheek, and she lifted her hand quickly and wiped it away.

"It will be hard for Shaendle now," said Reuben. "I am telling you I cannot fall asleep because I think about her all the time. A young woman with three little children in a time like this."

No one answered him. They had just left Shaendl's flat— Manya, Rivka, Reuben and Jacob. The mother had stayed behind to be with Shaendl and look after the children.

"We'll walk with you to the streetcar, Rivka," Jacob said.

"I don't know what will happen now," Reuben mused. "I don't know. I don't know."

"The best thing for Shaendl will be to find a man," said Manya. "A nice, respectable man. Maybe a man who is a little older. A man who will look after the children and after her. She is still a young woman, and a pretty woman, too."

"You are talking like a big child, Manya," said Reuben, slowing his pace. "You think the men are waiting around the corner? A man needs another man's three little children like I need a broken leg. If a man can afford to bring up three children, he wants at least to make them himself."

"Manya is right," said Rivka emphatically. "It doesn't have to be a young man. What does Shaendl want, a film star? Albert wasn't such a beauty either. There are plenty men who would take Shaendl, even with three children. Perhaps, like Manya said, an older man, a man fifty, fifty-five maybe."

"Bla-bla-bla," mocked Reuben. "After so many years you still don't know your sister Shaendl."

Rivka threw her head back in a gesture of defiance. "I am only saying a sensible word. If I know Shaendl or if I don't know Shaendl makes no difference."

"Shhhh," Reuben said. "Don't talk so loud. We are walking in the street."

"How will she bring up the children, then?" Manya asked. "How will she get money to buy food and pay the rent?"

Reuben shrugged his shoulders.

They had come to the streetcar stop, and after a few minutes Rivka's car came along and she got in.

"I don't know how long Mama will have to stay with

Shaendl," Manya said to Jacob as they walked homewards, "but in the meantime I think it will be better if you will come and eat with Reuben and me. It will be easier for Mama."

"It isn't so important, anyway," he said. "It's only a matter of a week or so. Eight days and then I will be gone."

They kept on talking. Reuben didn't join in at all. He walked a few paces ahead, his hands crossed behind his back, his body stooped forward. It was not until they were inside the house and Jacob was about to say good night that Reuben asked, "Are you very tired now, Yankel?" His voice sounded strange, not at all the way it usually did.

"No," Jacob said, quickly glancing at Reuben. "Why do you ask me that?"

"I would want to talk with you," Reuben said. "It's something very important."

"What is it?" Jacob asked apprehensively.

"It is better if we go in the flat and sit down." He turned to Manya. "You go upstairs. I want to talk to Yankel alone."

She nodded briefly. Jacob unlocked the door.

"I—I don't know how I should begin to tell you," Reuben said awkwardly. He passed his hand over his large, shiny, bald pate.

"Noo, what is it?"

"We knew all the time that Albert had debts," Reuben said slowly. "How much he owed we didn't know. He didn't say, and we didn't ask. Yesterday when Shaendl came home from the hospital, she took me aside and she told me." He paused and stared down at his hands. "Yankel, you must help Shaendl. Already she has had letters from the lawyers. The creditors want the money. Yankel, we have to pay up Albert's debts. The name of a dead man must be honoured. A good reputation is more than silver and gold . . . Yankel, you must help Shaendl."

Jacob nodded his head. He wasn't even surprised. Somehow he had know that this would happen, though he had hoped that it wouldn't.

"What does she need?"

"She hasn't got a groschen left," Reuben said. "She needs money."

Jacob closed his eyes. His head was turning. She needs money . . . She needs money . . . She needs money . . . She needs money. Endlessly revolving like the needle of a gramophone caught in the spiral groove of a record.

"How much money does she need exactly?" he found himself asking.

Reuben hesitated. "It is quite a bit of money." He dropped his voice. "She needs altogether five thousand schillings . . . With five thousand schillings she could pay up all the debts."

Jacob grew hot and flustered. He wanted to speak, but the words stuck in his throat. Five thousand schillings, he thought. One thousand dollars. Where am I going to take the money from? What shall I say now, God, what shall I say?

"This morning," Reuben went on, "I went to see Rivka and to find out what she could do. Manfred is away travelling and he will not come back until a week or later. But she said she thinks they can give six or seven hundred schillings . . . I have already given to Shaendl everything I have saved up. I gave her three hundred schillings this morning . . . So now she only needs four thousand schillings."

Four thousand or five thousand, Jacob thought despairingly, what's the difference? If I could give her four thousand, I could give five thousand, too. But how can I give what I haven't got? He was afraid to look at Reuben.

Reuben waited for him to say something, but he kept quiet. Then Reuben bent forward, very close to Jacob, until his chin almost touched Jacob's coat. "Yankel," he said softly, imploringly, "help Shaendl. To you four thousand schillings must be like nothing. If you give it to Shaendl, you will still have plenty left for yourself, and you will do one of the greatest things a man can do in this world, to help a widow and her children . . . Yankel, for the sake of your father (may he rest in peace) and for the sake of your mother, help your sister Shaendl."

What shall I tell him? God, what shall I tell him? What will he say when he knows the truth? What will Manya say? How will they look at me when I tell them? And my mother, and Shaendl, what will they say? Will they believe me? Will they believe me when I tell them?

But not now, not now. He couldn't tell Reuben now. He wanted time to think about the matter. Perhaps there was a way out—somehow. Perhaps.

"I—I will talk with Shaendl tomorrow," he said at last, "and —and I will try to fix things up."

Reuben grasped Jacob's hands and squeezed them. "I feel better now that I have told you," he said.

He left after a few minutes. Jacob was glad when he had gone. He was grateful that his mother wasn't there, that he was alone, that for some hours at least he wouldn't have to talk to anybody. He went out into the kitchen and searched about for the bottle of schnapps and found it. It was a small bottle, about a quarter full, and he took it back into the room.

Eight hundred dollars. A thousand dollars. It wasn't really very much money, but it was a tremendous amount for a man who didn't have it. If he could only borrow the money. He dismissed the idea immediately. Oh, God, if only his son were in practice already, it would be nothing, then. Wouldn't it? He was not so sure. David had never been very generous with money. There had been times . . . What was the use pondering about that? Right now he certainly didn't have that much money, so there was no point even approaching him.

He kept drinking, pouring himself one glass after another. Rosie, he thought. What will she say when I tell her? Would she gloat? No, no, she would never know, he would never tell her about it. But what was he to say to the people here?

Why didn't I tell them the truth right away when I came? He was ashamed of himself. You are a designer, eh? he castigated himself. You come to your office at ten, ten-thirty? You work a little bit, not too much any more? Hah, it's a good joke.

He cringed and squirmed as he recalled all this. The illusion, the wonderful illusion of the past few weeks had now suddenly come to a shattering, painful, ugly end. He was an insignificant, poor presser again, No. 1003, pushing his way into crowded streetcars every morning hurrying to punch the time clock, and all the grandiloquence, all the splendour, all his luxurious pretensions had now quite fallen away, and from the recesses of the past mocked at his pitiable nakedness.

The bottle was empty, and he shoved it aside. His head was reeling. He couldn't think coherently any more. The bed beckoned him. He staggered to his feet, struggled to get his clothes off, and crawled wearily into bed. He had left the light burning, but he did not have the strength to get up again and switch it off.

He woke early, but stayed in bed until well past ten, trying to sleep, trying not to face the thing he had to do. He wished it were possible for him to pack his suitcases and sneak away during the night, like a thief.

He got out of bed eventually, dressed, and went upstairs to Manya's flat. There he ate and then lingered for about two hours, afraid to go and see Shaendl. Finally Reuben reminded him delicately that he had not yet seen his mother and Shaendl today, and he left hurriedly. On the way over he thought frantically about how he should explain things to Shaendl, but when he got there and saw his mother, he grew confused, and said nothing. He couldn't talk to Shaendl in his mother's presence. He would have to see her alone. He could not face his mother, too.

The boys came home from school and got into a fight, and Jacob settled the dispute. Then Bernhardt asked him if he would go out with them, and Jacob seized the opportunity immediately. He was grateful to the children for having asked him.

"You know what we will do?" he said. "We will eat supper in a restaurant afterwards."

They were delighted and ran to tell their mother.

It was dark when they returned. Shaendl heard them and called to Jacob to come into the bedroom immediately. He felt dizzy for a moment. Now! he thought. He braced himself and went in to her.

She was sitting up in bed, her face tense. "Jacob, do you know what happened?"

"What—what is it?" he said, fear rising in his voice.

"Robert Koch has been arrested."

The words hit him with tremendous force. He was too stunned to speak. "Arrested?" he said at last. He sat down on the edge of the bed. "How—how do you know?"

"It was in tonight's paper," she said. "The police raided a house and found him and three others. They were printing an underground newspaper. Somebody must have informed."

"How you know it's him?" Jacob asked. "Maybe it's somebody else by the same name?"

"No," she said. "There's no doubt about it." The newspaper was on a chair beside the bed. She picked it up and gave it to him.

"You read it to me," he said. "I can't read the German script so good."

"There's not much," she said. Then she read, her voice bitterly ironic. "The journalist Robert Bruckner, who became notorious for his slanderous attacks against the government, and especially our late, sainted Chancellor Englebert Dollfuss, and our faithful ally Benito Mussolini, when such poisonous material was still allowed to be freely published, was arrested last night. The police raided—"

"Wait," Jacob interrupted. "Wait. It's not the same name."

"His real name is Bruckner," she said.

"He is a strange man," Jacob said after a while. "Often he

178

talked so I couldn't understand him. But I liked him. I liked him right away."

"Men like him are becoming rarer and rarer," she said. "They will soon be museum pieces. A type of man that existed once, but there were not enough to stand up against brutality and force. Any idiot can blow out the brain of an Einstein."

"What do you think will happen to him?" Jacob asked. "What will they do to him?"

She shrugged her shoulders. "I don't know. I don't think they'll ever bring him to trial, and if they do, he won't have a chance. He'll probably just rot away in a prison, like so many others, for telling the truth."

What will she say when I tell her? Jacob thought suddenly. But he couldn't tell her now. Not after this. I'll tell her to-morrow, or the day after tomorrow. Maybe I can think of something. Maybe a miracle will happen.

"I'm tired," he said. "I'll come tomorrow." He bent over the bed and kissed Shaendl lightly on the forehead. "Sleep well," he said. Then he went into the other room where his mother was talking to the children, trying to make them go to bed. He stayed for a little while and then left.

Perhaps it was somebody else, after all, he thought suddenly as he came out into the street. Perhaps Koch was still playing the clown in the side-show. It would be wonderful if he could come next morning and tell Shaendl that Koch was all right. The idea cheered him up and he changed his direction and hurried towards the Prater. This time he had no trouble finding the place. He could hear the cracked bugle-blows before he rounded the last corner, and his heart began to beat with excitement. A crowd had already gathered before the platform. Jacob pushed his way to the front, searching eagerly for Koch. He couldn't see him anywhere. He must be behind the curtain, he thought. Sure, that was it. In a minute he would start singing and then the man would drag him out on to the platform. Jacob's hands began to sweat. He waited impatiently.

The curtain parted. A man stepped out from behind, but it wasn't Koch. It was a tired-looking old man with big moustaches, wearing a shiny tuxedo and an ancient top hat. Jacob's heart sank.

"Ladies and gentlemen!" the man with the bugle shouted. "I have the honour to introduce to you now Signor Garibaldi, the greatest living magician. Signor Garibaldi comes to you straight from a sensational appearance in New York. What you are about to witness, ladies and gentlemen, is only the merest indication of the breath-taking performance he will give inside the theatre."

Signor Garibaldi did a few card tricks and conjured up a handkerchief—"out of thin air," the man with the bugle explained.

There was no sign of Koch. Jacob waited until the crowd dispersed and then he walked away slowly. Koch was gone. There had been no mistake. A green-uniformed policeman was coming towards him, idly swinging his night-stick, and Jacob was suddenly afraid. He didn't know how it happened. He had a vision of the policeman laying his hands on him and arresting him for no reason at all, just because it pleased him so. Panicky, he crossed over to the other side of the street. He mopped his brow, and turned to see if the policeman had followed him, but he was out of sight now. Jacob laughed. The whole thing was crazy. But for a moment he had been frightened, really frightened. It was a kind of fear he had never known before.

CHAPTER

XVII

SATURDAY went by, and Sunday, and Jacob said nothing. There were times when he thought Reuben looked at him strangely, as if trying to admonish him, but he kept his peace. Once or twice, when he found himself alone with Shaendl, he was almost ready to burst out with the truth, but his courage failed him. No one said anything to him, and yet he could feel the tension, and he knew they were waiting for him to declare himself. He was like a man treading a narrow ledge over a precipice, not daring to look either to the right or the left.

His departure was now only four days off. He had to get his papers ready, and he went down to the consulate on Monday to have everything arranged. It was a blisteringly hot day, and it took longer to get all the formalities settled than he had expected.

He came back at about five o'clock, tired, his clothes sticking to his body. Nobody was in. He went out into the kitchen, washed, and gulped down a glass of cold water, feeling momentarily refreshed. Then he went into the room, took off his coat and threw it carelessly over a chair, too exhausted to hang it up properly. Something slipped out of the inner pocket and dropped down on the floor. He picked it up. It was his passport. He flipped the pages, looked at his own photograph, soberly staring at him from the page. A passport, he pondered. A piece of paper with a photograph and a few things written in, and with the passport I am somebody and without the passport I am nobody. He shoved it back into the pocket.

Tomorrow, then Wednesday, and then Thursday. Three days. And Thursday, at four o'clock in the afternoon he would be on the train, and he would be gone. No matter what happened, he would be out of here. He felt a sudden intense relief which was immensely gratifying. But yet he knew that his departure could not alter things. Shaendl could not leave, her children could not leave, his mother could not leave. And all the others —they would have to stay and face the cold and hostile reality which confronted them.

He went over to the sofa and stretched himself on it. It was very quiet in the room. A few swallows kept diving past the windows, and a dog barked somewhere in the distance. Jacob shifted uneasily on the sofa. And then he realized suddenly that he could not leave either. He realized that even though he would be two thousand miles away, divided from them by a vast expanse of ocean and a long stretch of land, he would never be able to shake off the experience he had had here. If he had never come, it would have been different. If he had only heard about Albert's death in a letter, he could have forgotten about it. He would have felt sorry for a week or so, and then it would have slipped from his mind. After all, he had not really known Shaendl until five weeks ago; he had not known Albert or the children at all; the image of his mother had grown dim through the passage of the long years. A few weeks ago they were virtually strangers to him. Two months ago the death of the man who worked next to him in the factory would have affected him more. But all that was changed now. He had been too deeply involved in the happenings of the past weeks. It was easy to go away, but it was impossible to forget.

And what should he say to the people back home? To Rosie? Should he say to her, Oh, I have had a wonderful holiday. It was worth every penny I spent. What a beautiful city, this Vienna! He remembered Koch in his clown's costume, and Koch sitting in this room, and Koch arrested. No, he couldn't say that. But if he told her what he had seen and heard, would she believe him? And if she believed him, would she care? What were these people to her? She had other things to worry about. And he could almost hear Sydney Black's raucous voice, greeting him when he came back to the factory. "Well, well, well, Jake's back. How d'ya make out with the women, Jake?"

He tried to sleep, but he couldn't. It was too hot. After a while he looked at his watch. It was past six. He got up and put on his coat, and walked slowly up the stairs to Manya's flat.

Reuben was reading the paper when Jacob came in. He let it drop down on the floor beside his chair, and turned to Jacob.

"I was looking for you everywhere in the afternoon, but I couldn't find you."

"They had to fix up my passport," Jacob said. "It took them longer than I figured."

"You are going away on Thursday?"

Jacob nodded. "The train leaves at four o'clock in the afternoon."

Manya came in from the kitchen. "We will eat in a few minutes," she said. "I am only waiting for the potatoes to get soft."

"I'm not very hungry," said Jacob. "All of a sudden I have a headache."

"It will go away when you have eaten," said Manya. She noticed the paper sprawled out on the floor, disorderly, crumpled. Her brows contracted into an angry frown, and her forehead became furrowed. She stooped down, picked up the paper, and folded it neatly. Then she put it on a chair. She darted a piercing glance at Reuben, and walked out into the kitchen in silent protest.

"Manya's worries!" exclaimed Reuben. "Even if the house were on fire, she would be angry because the newspaper is on the floor."

After a few minutes Manya came back, carrying two plates of steaming hot noodle soup.

"Come to the table," she said, "and eat. The soup will get cold."

She went out again and came back with her own plate. Jacob stirred his soup listlessly, and then he ate a few spoonfuls. The long, slippery noodles hung down over the edge of his spoon, and he watched them dangle. A few slithered back into the plate.

Reuben said, "You have put too much salt into the soup, Manya."

"I couldn't help it," she said. "It's because you came into the kitchen and made me nervous. Every time you come in the kitchen, something goes wrong."

"I had to come into the kitchen then," said Reuben. "I didn't come because I wanted to. It was important."

"What happened?" asked Jacob. "What happened?"

"It was something about Shaendl," Reuben said significantly. He shifted uneasily in his chair, and gulped down a big spoonful of soup. "Ugh," he said, distorting his face. "It's hot."

"Eat slow," said Manya, "so you won't burn yourself."

Jacob could not finish his soup. He threw down his spoon, and pushed the plate away.

"Why don't you finish your soup?" asked Manya.

"I'm not hungry."

She shrugged her shoulders. "Give me your plate, Reuben," she said.

Reuben reached his plate over to her. She got up and went out. Reuben stared down at the tablecloth. He picked up his knife and scraped the breadcrumbs together into a little heap, and then formed them into a circle with the tip of his knife.

Manya brought in the big, white dinner plates, piled high with meat and mashed potatoes and green beans, and placed them before the men. They fell to eating, and did not talk. The meat was tough. Manya was angry at herself for not having cooked it longer. It was a humiliating sight for her to watch Jacob sawing away with his knife. Reuben's eyes were fixed on his plate though he was not at all interested in the food. He poked about with his fork and knife, like a child unwilling to eat, but forced by commanding looks to get on with the meal. He was thinking now how he could best say what he had to say without hurting Jacob's feelings. He ate slowly. Then suddenly he laid aside his fork and knife, and interlocked his fingers.

"What is the matter?" asked Manya. "Come, come, the meat is not that hard. Once I make a mistake, and look what he does."

Reuben disregarded her. "Yankel," he said, lifting his head and staring up at the ceiling. "Yankel, I must ask you."

Manya looked quickly at him, and cautioned him with her eyes. This is not the right time to ask him, she thought. Not in the middle of the meal. Reuben should have done it afterwards, when they were drinking the tea. That would have been the right time, not now.

Reuben laid his hands flat upon the table, pushing his plate away to make room for his hands. "Yankel," he said quietly, looking straight down at his hands, "when I told you a few days ago that Shaendl needed money and asked you if you would help, you said that you would go to see her and you would fix things up. But you are leaving here in three days, and so far you haven't said a word." There was a trace of reproach in his voice. "I didn't want to press you, and so I said nothing. I was waiting for you to come to Shaendl. She wanted to talk to you already, but I said no. If she asked you, it would be like begging. I know how it is. I can ask for somebody else, but for me alone I cannot ask. Soon you will not be here any more, and you must say now once and for all if we can count on you." He leaned back in his chair and mopped his brow with a whitish-grey handkerchief. Then he picked up his fork and knife and began to eat again.

Jacob gulped down a big piece of meat. It almost choked him, and he began to cough violently. The blood shot into his face, and his puffy cheeks and the sagging flesh under his chin vibrated quickly. Manya took the glass which stood in front of him and filled it with water. He drank and stopped his coughing. He wiped his lips and inhaled deeply.

"Yes," he said at last. "Yes." He was very tired, and his headache had grown worse.

"You will help Shaendl?" asked Manya eagerly.

"Shaendl doesn't want you should give her the money," said Reuben. "She wants you to lend it to her. It will take a few years before she will be able to start paying you back. But some day, I know, she will pay you back. If not she, then her children."

Jacob's hands trembled and he gripped his fork and knife firmly, as if he were hanging on to a railing, weakly supporting himself. He felt like shouting, I want to give her the money. I want to, believe me, I want to. I would have given it to her five days ago, ten days ago. But I have no money. I am a poor man. I am poor like you all. But it was too humiliating a confession, and the words would not out.

"You will help Shaendl?" asked Manya again, her voice unusually gentle.

"I will help her," Jacob mumbled.

Manya sighed deeply. "I knew all the time that you would help Shaendl. I said so to Reuben when he came in the kitchen before. I said to him, 'Don't worry, Yankel will help Shaendl,' and I looked at him all the time, and so I didn't see how much salt I was putting in the soup . . . Come on, Yankel, finish off the meat. It's a shame to leave it."

"I can't finish," said Jacob. "I have eaten too much already."

"It's a shame to throw out good meat like that," said Manya. She looked at Reuben, her eyes flashing triumphantly. "You see, I told you. You was afraid Yankel wouldn't help because he didn't come himself and tell Shaendl." She smoothed her hair with her hands, and turned to Jacob. "I said to Reuben, I said, it is almost like God sent you to be here with us just at this time. Like a good angel—"

"All right, all right," said Reuben, holding up his hands in a gesture of restraint. "We don't have to talk about it any more."

"When you bring in the tea, Manya," Jacob said, forcing a note of casualness into his voice, "bring a couple of aspirins for me too, please."

She turned her head quickly, searching his face with her eyes. "What is wrong?" she asked. "What happened?"

"Nothing, nothing," he calmed her. "I told you before I had a little headache. I'll go downstairs soon, and go to bed right away. I will be all right tomorrow." He wanted to rush from the room immediately. He could not bear to look into Reuben's face.

Reuben rose from the table, walked over to his easy chair, and let himself drop into it heavily. Manya brought a box of aspirins and put it on the table in front of Jacob.

"You have no fever, Yankel?" She was very much concerned about him, and felt his forehead with her hand.

He pushed her hand away almost rudely. "No, no," he said harshly, "I am all right."

She looked at him quickly, with a hurt expression, and then left the room.

"I hope you are not angry that I spoke to you like that," said Reuben, his eyes half-closed. "But there was no way out. In a situation that is so difficult and urgent you can't help yourself. And you are the only hope we have." He opened his eyes and turned to Jacob.

Jacob deliberately avoided Reuben's look. "Of course," he said, "why should I be angry?" He let his head drop forward onto his chest. "What would happen if Shaendl didn't have the money?" he asked suddenly in a strained voice.

Reuben straightened his body and stared over at Jacob. "God forbid," he said. "Yankel, why do you ask that question? . . . Shaendl would have to declare a bankruptcy, and people would begin to talk. They would say Shaendl doesn't want to pay off the money. They would say she is trying to cheat and swindle. Albert's name would be dishonoured. No, no, God forbid that this should happen. And what would happen to the children? When they grow up, what will they think about their father?" His voice became insistent, beseeching, full of pleading. "Why do you ask that, Yankel? You are going to help? You said you are going to help. Why do you all of a sudden ask what would happen?"

"Why shouldn't I ask?" snapped Jacob.

Reuben stalked over to the table and sat down opposite Jacob. "You are angry," he said. "Yankel, you are angry."

"No, no, no," cried Jacob, his voice dragging and tired. "Why should I be angry?"

"Open the door! Open the door for me! I have my hands full."

Jacob got up and opened the door for Manya.

"What happened here?" she asked. "Why did you shout so?"

"Nothing," said Jacob. "Who shouted?" He went back to the

186

table. "I will go and see Shaendl right away in the morning," he said, "and I will speak with her."

Reuben said, "All right. And now, please, we will not talk about it any more."

Jacob left as soon as he could. He stumbled down the stairs. A bedraggled-looking, haggard woman, her thin, muddy-grey strands of hair fluttering untidily about her head, passed him on the stairs and stepped aside to let Frau Grossman's rich son pass. A look of envy played about her eyes, but her voice was sweet and insinuating when she said, "Good evening, Herr Grossman. God, it's hot outside. We haven't had so hot a June in years. It's getting so stuffy out, I guess it'll just have to rain before long."

Jacob nodded his head. He was hardly conscious of her presence, and went past her without replying. She took it for haughtiness, and was deeply hurt. Her face set. She started after him with a coldly hostile glare.

He fumbled about nervously to fit the key into the keyhole, and then unlocked the door quickly, bolting it securely behind him. He walked limply into the room, went up to the table, sat down, his body bent forward, his elbows supporting his weight against the table.

It will all come out now, he thought. Tomorrow. But my mother must not know, he thought desperately. Perhaps she would have to know sometime, but he would be gone in three days, and perhaps he could somehow keep it from her. After he was gone, well, she would probably know then. She would have to know because the money would not be there, but at least he would be spared the look in her face when she found out. He would not have to see her skin becoming taut over her face, and her eyes growing filmy with tears when she discovered that her prayers had not found their fulfilment in him after all, that he was poor and insignificant and of no account. He would ask Reuben and Manya and Shaendl to keep it from the mother until he was gone. Surely that was not asking for much. Surely they would do that for him. Perhaps they would even be able to keep it from her for a longer period of time, perhaps . . . perhaps she need never know. Perhaps she need not die with disappointment weighing heavy on her heart. That would be good, he thought, that would be very good. Sure, he thought, sure. They can do it. They are going to do it. I know they are going to do it. After all, why shouldn't they do it?

He sat up straight in his chair.

Why am I afraid? What have I done?

He began to see things a little more clearly now. The thought of confessing his poverty did not seem so terrible and humiliating any more.

What have I done? I have nothing to be ashamed of. I am an honest man. That at least no one can take from me. I have worked all my life. I have worked hard, and I have looked after my family well, and I have educated my children. I have done all this alone, without asking help from anybody. So why am I ashamed? I had a little money, and I came to see my mother. Good. I have done nothing that was wrong.

But still, my mother shouldn't know. Why does she have to know? No, no, no, Reuben will not tell her. He will understand. Shaendl will not tell her. And Manya?

He was afraid of Manya. Her sharp tongue frightened him. But what did she have to do with it? It was none of her business. It only concerned Shaendl and himself.

The room grew dark, but he did not get up to switch on the light. His fingers drummed slowly on the table, and he leaned far back in the chair.

I spent a lot of money for this trip, he thought. Why did I come? It would have been better if I had stayed home. Rosie was right. I shouldn't have come . . . Why? Why shouldn't I have come? Has a son no right to visit his mother, and to see the grave of his father? . . . Then why didn't I tell them the truth right away? Why didn't I tell them in the very beginning that I am a poor man? . . . I longed to come here. I wanted so much to come. For thirty-three years I dreamed about it . . . Why didn't I tell them that I am a poor man? . . . Why should I have told them? What difference would it have made? They will know now . . . They wouldn't have believed me anyway, so why should I have told them? . . . What harm did I do? They need money, and I haven't got any money to give. If I had told them before, it would have been the same. Albert would have died just the same, and Shaendl would have needed the money, and there would have been no money. Everything would have been exactly the same . . . I spent a lot of money for this trip . . . So? It was my money, and I could do with it what I wanted. I was never extravagant in my life. There was only work and worries, always. A few days' holiday once in a while. Many years not even that. Once in a lifetime a man has a right to be a little extravagant . . . Then why shouldn't I have come? My life is almost over. My daughters are married. I helped my son to become a doctor. Malke is dead. I am all alone now, who can say I shouldn't have come to see my family? I wanted to see my mother once more before she dies. I wanted to stand over the grave of my father and pray there . . .

The room was very dark now. His fingers drummed a tattoo on the table, and his chair was tipped far back and he balanced it on two legs. He stopped his drumming suddenly and leaned forward over the table, and the legs of the chair came down on the floor with a sharp thud.

How much money have I left?

He didn't know the exact amount. About seventy dollars, he thought.

I have my bank book somewhere. I think it must be in my coat.

He searched his coat. The bank book wasn't there. Then he remembered that he had put it into his little grey portmanteau. He stumbled to his feet and tapped his way to the wall, groping about for the switch. He turned it on. The electric light swept the room and threw black shadows about the walls. Jacob went out into the hall and switched the light on there. The little grey portmanteau was on top of the suitcases, stowed away against a corner. He opened it and fumbled about in it until he found the bank book. Then he went back into the room, leaving the light burning in the hall.

He had seventy-six dollars and fifty-five cents on his account. The figures danced before his eyes, became unnaturally distorted, as if seen through a trick-mirror, ran together into one large ink blot, then gradually seemed to straighten themselves, and were clearly distinct $76.55.

The clerk's hand had apparently been a little shaky when he made the entry.

There was a light knock on the door. Jacob sat up and listened. The knock came again, slightly louder.

Who could it be? Why can't people leave me alone? He remained in his chair, hoping that whoever it was would go away. The knock came again, harder, more insistent. Jacob rose slowly and threw the bank book on the table. He went to the door and opened it.

It was Reuben.

"Yankel," he said, somewhat apologetically, "I felt after you went away that you was angry with me. It didn't give me peace, and so I decided to come down and see you and ask you. Then I remembered you said you was going to bed right away. But then I came down just the same, and I saw the light burning in the hall. So I knew you must still be up . . . You are not angry, Yankel?"

Jacob twitched his fingers nervously. "No, no, no, Reuben," he said, forcing a laugh. "You shouldn't think that. I wasn't angry at you . . . Come into the room. I want to tell you something."

Reuben followed him and sat down, waiting uneasily.

Jacob was silent for a few moments, and then he said slowly, "Reuben, I must tell you. I—I have no money to give to Shaendl."

The two men stared at each other. A look of utter bewilderment spread over Reuben's face. "But—but," he stammered, "only a short while ago—only before—before when we were eating—only then—you said then—you said you would go to her tomorrow morning—you said to Manya and to me . . ." He stopped abruptly, too stunned, too confused to go on.

"I didn't want to tell you then, Reuben," said Jacob painfully. "I was too excited. I—I wish I had money, Reuben. I would give her the money with all my heart. But what can I do? I haven't got the money to give."

Reuben regained some of his composure. "Yankel, Yankel," he beseeched him, "what are you saying? I can't believe what I have just heard . . . You—you will not help Shaendl? Is that what you said? You are going to forsake your sister now. Why, Yankel, why?"

"Reuben, I would help Shaendl with all my heart. But what can I do if I haven't got the money? You think I would have waited for you to ask me? Reuben, you don't know how I felt in the last few days. I wanted to tell you, and I wanted to tell Shaendl, but I was ashamed, Reuben. I wish I had the money. Believe me I would have given it to her a long time ago."

"You wish you had the money," said Reuben softly, smiling a sad smile, "you wish you had the money . . . I wish I had the money, too . . . You would give her the money with all your heart . . . I would give her the money with all my heart, too. But I haven't got the money." He lowered his voice a little. "And now all of a sudden you haven't got the money." His eyes strayed towards the open windows. "All of a sudden," he repeated.

"Reuben, please believe me," pleaded Jacob, leaning forward and touching Reuben's arm. "Please believe me, Reuben. Reuben, I have no money. All my life I was working for somebody else. I am a poor man, Reuben. I am poor like you all."

Reuben sat immobile and he seemed oblivious to Jacob's hand clutching at his sleeve. "You are poor," he said. He nodded his head slowly, very slowly. "You are poor like all the rich men when a poor man suddenly asks for money." His voice was bitter. "If you are really poor, then why didn't you never tell us? Why didn't you never write it in your letters? How did you come here if you have no money? How can you buy yourself such good clothes? You came here with a new white suit. If a man can buy himself a white suit, he must have money to buy himself a few other suits. Because if a man can only afford to buy a suit every three, four years, he doesn't buy white suits. Jacob, Jacob, I thought you was different from the rest. But now I see, when it comes to the pocket, few men are willing to give. Words and good wishes—sure, sure. Why not? It doesn't cost a groschen, not a groschen."

Jacob said, "Reuben, Reuben, please don't say these things. I didn't never tell you because I didn't want my mother to know. I wanted she should think that I was doing good. All her children are poor. I wanted she should think at least one of her children—her only son . . ." His voice trembled, faltered, and broke.

"Sure," said Reuben, gently rocking his body. "Sure. I have known many men in my life who had money. And it was always the same. Always the same. Perhaps that is how it should be. Who knows? Who am I to talk? I had never more than just my living. Perhaps I would be the same. I don't blame you, Yankel. It is easy for me to sit here and talk." His voice became impatient. "But what is the use talking? Words, words, words. And meanwhile a great thing must be done. A dead man's name must be honoured. His memory must be clean. His children must remember him with pride. So it was always in our family."

"I know, I know." Jacob's voice was rasping and hoarse. "But what can I do? What can I do? I have no money. Reuben, believe me, please believe me, Reuben." His eyes fell on the bank book which was lying open on the table. His hand reached out and grasped it, like a shipwrecked man clutching at a piece of board.

"Here," he said, thrusting the little red book at Reuben, "here. You can look for yourself. This is all the money I have. I was looking at it when you knocked on the door. I have not even a hundred dollars. I had a few hundred dollars saved up, and I spent all to come here. Reuben, please look in the book."

Reuben shook his head. His hands lay on his knees, motionless. "If you say what you say, I must believe you. But I have known rich men in my life, and I know they don't keep all their money in one place."

"Look in the book, Reuben! Please look in the book!"

Reuben gave a short laugh. "You talk like a child, Yankel," he said. "So what will happen if I look in the book? You say you have no money. Good. If I look in the book, will you suddenly be able to give the money to Shaendl? I don't care how much money you have. All I want is that the memory of a dead man should be honoured. That's all . . . And we all thought that you would help us. But now you say that you have no money to give us. I must believe you because you say so." Reuben rose stiffly. "I will go now," he said.

Somebody rattled the front door. Jacob sat up with a start. "What's that?" he said.

"It's probably Manya," said Reuben. "She must be wondering where I am so long."

Jacob jumped to his feet and started towards the door. He was hoping it wouldn't be Manya. He was afraid of her. There was an impatient knock on the door.

"Stay here," said Reuben. "I will go to open the door."

"What happened?" came Manya's voice from the hall. "Why did you stay so long? Yankel wants to go to bed, and you sit here and talk with him."

Reuben came slowly back into the room, and she followed him.

"Yankel, go to bed right away!" she said commandingly.

The two men were quiet.

"What's the matter?" she asked. "Why don't you say a word?" She turned sharply to Reuben. "Reuben, what happened? Why do you look like that?"

"Manya," said Reuben slowly, "Yankel says he has no money to give to Shaendl."

"What?" cried Manya. Her lips came together into a thin, straight line. She drew herself up to her full height, and stood there, hovering over Jacob like an avenging fury.

"Yankel, is it true? Is it true what Reuben just said?"

Jacob rose slowly from his chair. He was a full head shorter than Manya. "Yeh," he said, his voice trembling, "I—I have no money to give Shaendl. I want to give her—with all my heart I want to give her the money. But how can I give it to her, when I have nothing to give? I have no money, Manya. I am a poor man."

She was shocked. Her lips moved, but no words came. At last she found her speech, and burst out, "Your own sister. Your own flesh and blood. What a great shame is this! Suddenly you changed your mind, eh?" Her voice rose and became shriller. "Two hours ago you said you would give her the money. And now suddenly you are a poor man. How did you lose your money so quick? You threw it out of the window, eh? Sure, sure. You threw it out of the window! Ha! Remember!" She raised her hand and waved it accusingly. "Remember! Your own sister, your own flesh and blood, a poor widow with three little children, and she needed money in a time of great sorrow, and you didn't give it to her. Remember!" Her voice rose to a pitched scream, and she seemed unable to control it. "Remember, because perhaps there will come a day when you will be poor and old and sick, and you will need money, but there will be nobody to give it to you." Her breath came in heavy gasps and her hands gripped the back of a chair, and then she stumbled over to the sofa and sat down.

Jacob cowered. After a while he asked timidly, "What will happen now to Shaendl?"

"Don't worry about Shaendl," snapped Manya. "We are still here. Poor people always help most." Her voice was now full of pride. "As long as we have something to eat, she and her children will not go hungry. They will always have a roof over their heads. You go back to your great country, to your Niagara Falls! We will look after Shaendl."

Jacob, like an animal trapped in a snare, implored Reuben with his eyes, but he met only an empty, cold stare, and he shrunk back, beaten and cowed. Then he said slowly, beseechingly, almost verging on tears, "I swear to God, I swear by my children, that I am a poor man, and that I have not more money than is written here in this book. Not even a hundred dollars. By the grave of my father I swear I have no more."

Reuben held up his big hand. "Don't swear, Yankel," he said firmly, "don't swear."

Jacob was exasperated and angry and bitter. "But I have no money!" he screamed. "I have no money!"

"You have no money," scorned Manya. "And what about the picture, eh? What about the picture?" She jumped to her feet and stared hatefully at Tassigny's painting on the wall. "You could pay a hundred and fifty schillings for a little picture like that, eh? You had money then, because it was for your own pleasure. But now—now—now . . ."

"I didn't never want to buy this picture," he said slowly. "I had to buy it. It was on the ship, and I couldn't help myself. I had to buy it."

"You had to!" Manya jeered. "Did you have to have the money, too?"

"No," he cried, "no, no, no, no." He stepped angrily towards the sofa, reached over and tore the painting from the wall. He gazed at it hatefully. "I didn't want to buy it," he roared, and then suddenly dashed it to the floor. The wooden frame cracked and splintered. Jacob wiped the sweat from his brow and passed his hands over his face. Manya and Reuben stared down at the painting, silently and in disgust.

Then Manya said mockingly, "Listen to him. He had to buy it. What did he do, your Frenchman on the ship? He held a revolver to your head and forced you to buy the picture, eh?"

"I didn't like this picture when I bought it," Jacob hissed. "I never liked it. But I couldn't help myself. I was in such a situation that I couldn't help myself. I had to buy it. I had to." His body was shaking, and in sudden fury he brought his foot down on the painting and dug his heel into the canvas. He ripped a hole in it, and then kicked it away. The picture skidded along the floor, and came to rest under the table.

"Come, Manya," said Reuben.

They went out of the room. Manya called back over her shoulder, "Come and lock the door after us. Thieves could come, and maybe they would take away your money."

Jacob paid no attention to her. He sank down on the sofa. From where he lay he could see the picture, one half dipped in the black shadow thrown by the table, the other half lighted up by the yellow glare of the electric bulb, staring at him, grotesquely, mockingly, weird.

He didn't know how long he lay there, but at length he roused himself, his heart beating wildly. It was long past midnight and the light in the hallways was turned off. He groped his way to the staircase in the darkness and began to climb the stairs. Then he tapped his way along the wall until he came to Manya's flat. He knocked loudly, and the hollow sound of his knuckles against the wood of the door echoed through the sleeping house. He waited impatiently. At last he could hear a rustling inside, and dragging footsteps.

"Who is it?"

"It's me," he said, "Jacob. Open the door for me, Manya."

"What do you want so late in the night?" she asked angrily. "You have to wake us up out of the best sleep, eh? Or perhaps you have suddenly found your money?"

"Manya, please," he said. "Open the door for me."

He heard her push back the latch, and then she turned the key in the lock and opened the door. She was standing there in a long flannel nightgown, and her hair was loose and came down over her shoulders. She was in her bare feet, and still she was much taller than Jacob.

"What happened to you in the middle of the night?" she asked him. "Why do you come to wake us up out of the best sleep? What have you come to tell us?"

"Manya," he pleaded, "don't be angry. Please don't be angry. I have only come to ask you for a little favour." He saw her face become stern, and almost hostile, and it hurt him to see his sister looking at him like that. "I had to come to ask you this, because I was lying on the sofa, and I was thinking about it and thinking—"

"So you couldn't have waited until the morning?" she interrupted him rudely. "What are you worried about? Your thoughts will get sour maybe, like milk in the sun?"

He stood pressed against the door, and she stood in front of him as if she were trying to bar his way. He looked tired and untidy. His face seemed gaunt in spite of its pudginess, and the knot of his tie had slipped under his collar.

'Where is Reuben?' he asked.

"Shhhh. He is in bed. He is a good sleeper. He didn't wake up when you knocked. . . . There now, now he woke up, because you speak so loud."

"Come into the room, Manya," said Jacob. "Please come into the room. I want Reuben to hear, too. I will not stay long, and then I will go away again, and you can go back to your sleep." He laughed bitterly. "Only two more days, and I will not be here any more and you won't never see me again in your life."

She turned quickly and walked away, and he followed her. When she switched on the light in the bedroom, Reuben sat up drowsily and rubbed his eyes.

"What is the matter?" he grumbled. "Who's here? What happened?"

"Yankel is here," said Manya.

Reuben shook himself. "Yankel?" he said. "Yankel? So late in the night?" He sat up and opened his eyes fully.

Manya climbed back into bed, and Jacob drew up a chair close to the bed and sat down.

"I have only come to ask you one little thing," he said. He paused for a moment. "Does my mother know how much money Shaendl needs, and that you have come to me for the money?"

"We haven't told her yet," Reuben said. "But she will have to know soon."

"I—I have come to beg you," Jacob said haltingly, "that—

that you should not tell my mother what has happened here this evening. Please do me this one favour. If my mother must know, then let her at least not know until I have gone away that I am a poor man and that I have no money to give to Shaendl."

"Ha!" cried Manya, outraged. "Now we shouldn't tell Mama! You don't want to give money to Shaendl, and we should keep quiet. A widow with three little children, the youngest not a month old yet, your own sister and she needs the money like a piece of bread, and we shouldn't tell Mama. Why shouldn't we tell Mama? You think she will not know? You think when Shaendl has to declare a bankruptcy, Mama will not know? You will be on the ship again and buy pictures for your own pleasure, and then you say we can tell her. But not before, eh? Not so long as you are here, eh?"

"Manya," he said, "I know that you don't believe what I have told you tonight, but I swear to God that I have told you the truth. I didn't never write to you in my letters because Mama and Papa didn't feel so happy when I went away from home, and so I wrote all the time that I was doing good, so that they should not feel bad about me. But I wasn't never lucky. Not like some of the other people who went over with me. As soon as I came there, I found a job in a factory, and I have worked there all the time since then. I wrote to you that I had a job in a factory, but I was ashamed to tell you what I was doing there. I was never more there than a little presser, and I earned just enough money to make a living, and save up a few cents now and again." He swallowed hard. "When I told you that I was a designer, I was telling a lie. Don't ask me why I told it. I work hard, every day from eight o'clock in the morning until six o'clock at night and I don't earn only a little money. Often I wanted to open up a business like other people, but I didn't have the courage, never. And now my children are grown up, and Malke is dead, and so I wanted to come here to see you all once again. I wanted to see our mother once more in my life, and I wanted to see the grave of our father—may he rest in peace."

"Amen," said Manya. "He was so proud of you, Yankel. Not a day went by that he shouldn't talk about you, and he used to tell people what a fine son he had, and how you had worked yourself up from nothing and had become a big and important man. And meanwhile you was never telling the truth to us in your letters. But how did you have enough money to come here? And how could you spend so much money for a little picture like that? And you came here dressed up like a king. Who gave you money so you could do all these things?"

Jacob's face grew red. "Nobody gave me money. I had a little saved up. But now I don't want you should believe me. I don't care any more. You can think I am a rich man, and you can think I am a man without a heart. God knows I have told you the truth. But I don't care. All I want is that you should not tell it to my mother as long as I am still here. Afterwards you can say what you want. It is all the same to me. Only what good will it do? If you make me out to be a bad man, and a heart-less man, will you make things better for my mother?"

"But she will have to know soon," said Reuben. "What difference does it make if she knows now or in six days' time?"

"Reuben," said Jacob, "Reuben, you was always my good friend. Help me now. Perhaps she needn't never know. Perhaps you can keep it from her altogether."

"No," said Reuben, and he shook his head. "A thing like that you cannot keep from her. If it is the truth what you have told us, then perhaps you shouldn't never have come. A poor man has to think long before he spends a lot of money for a pleasure. How many times have I stood and watched the big ships go by on the Danube, and often I have wanted to go on them far away. And there were times when I could have done it. When times were good and we had a little money. And yet I didn't never do it, because I was afraid of bad times. Not for myself only was I afraid, but also for the family. If something should happen like now, and I would know that I spent a lot of money for a luxury once, how would I feel? And times like that did come when we had to help out. It is written in the *Gemarah* that when a man sees a stranger in the wintertime and the stranger has no coat, he should tear his own coat and give half to the stranger. How much more should a man help when a sister is in trouble and calls to him for help. A man cannot always be thinking of himself."

"I wasn't only thinking of myself," mumbled Jacob. "I was thinking of my mother also. In every letter she wrote to me how she wanted to see me once again before she died. That is why I came above all."

He rose slowly and pushed his chair back against the wall. "And now I will go," he said quietly, and almost in tears, "and will leave you to go back to your sleep, and I am sorry that I have waked you up so late in the night. Tell my mother or don't tell my mother, it is now all the same to me. But to her— to her it is not the same."

CHAPTER

XVIII

JACOB did not come for breakfast the next morning. He went to the nearest café and bought himself something to eat there. Afterwards he walked slowly round the block, and then went back to the flat. He would wait until he was sure that his mother was out, and then he would tell Shaendl. He tried to write a letter to his son, but he found it hard to concentrate.

He wanted to call his son to be his witness. Let him write to Manya, and tell her that what his father had said was the truth. Let his son tell how hard he and Malke had worked that his life might be easier than theirs had been. Let him bear testimony to the many days Jacob had worked overtime so they could pay his tuition.

All these things he wanted to say, speaking from a full heart, but the words were cold once he put them on the paper, and when he read over what he had written, he was dissatisfied and tore up the letter, stuffing the pieces into his pocket. He could not express in writing what he wanted to say. He would have to see the boy and talk to him, man to man, heart to heart. Or perhaps it would be better not to say anything to anybody. They did not have to know at home what had happened here last night, what Manya had said to him. It could do no good.

He looked round the room. I could start packing my things, he thought. Now is a good time to start packing up my things.

He went out into the hall and brought two of his suitcases into the room, put them down on the floor and opened them. He threw open the clothes-cupboard and took out all his suits, except the brown one in which he intended to travel and, taking them from the hangers, laid them on the sofa. Then he emptied the chest of drawers of his shirts and underwear. These, too, he piled on the sofa. He searched the pockets of the suits, and threw everything he found there on the table. Bits of paper, an odd groschen, an odd penny. He folded the jackets carefully, turning them outwards and laying sleeve against sleeve, so that they would not get too badly crumpled. When he came to put the white alpaca suit away, he hesitated for a moment. He held the jacket up and looked at it. Perhaps Malke and his daughters had been right after all when they protested every time he expressed his desire to buy a white suit. Perhaps it was gaudy and loud and unbecoming. Perhaps white suits were only for rich men, men who could afford to have a lot of suits, like Reuben said, for men like Mr Duncan. But then, he had wanted it so much. A crazy idea. Maybe just a crazy idea. He put it away quickly, and soon it was buried under a mass of other things.

When he had finished his packing he took the suitcases back into the hall and stacked them against the wall where they had been before. Then he went out for lunch.

It was terribly hot outside. A sultry heat that pressed down hard upon the pavement and seemed to melt the asphalt beneath the shoes of the pedestrians. Now and then a weak breeze rose seemingly from nowhere and fanned the heat, but was itself absorbed and burned in the attempt, and the air was still again.

Jacob ate a bit of cold meat and drank some beer.

"Too hot to eat, sir, eh?"

Jacob nodded his head.

"It can't go on being this hot. Never does. There's got to be rain soon. I think we'll get some rain before the night comes on. Maybe sooner. I saw clouds gathering east over the Danube. . . . Say, you're Frau Grossman's son, aren't you, living down in Number 4?"

Jacob looked at the man. "Yes," he said. "How do you know?"

"Oh, well. Everybody knows you around the neighbourhood. It isn't often we have rich visitors from faraway countries around here. How is it you're eating out? Your mother not well or something?"

"Oh, no, no, no. I just . . ." The rest of the sentence was lost in a gulp of beer.

"I'm glad you came in. Next week you wouldn't have been able to any more."

"Why not?"

"I'm going to close down this place. Can't make a go of it. Doesn't even pay for expenses no more. Twelve years I've had the place, but now I can't even pay expenses no more. Times are bad around here. People has no money. I'm telling you one thing, sir. This country's going to the dogs. When people has no money to come in a café, that's a bad sign. That's the end, sir. They tell me great things is going on across the border. They say prosperity come back there. They sat Hitler is doing great things. Of course, it's bad for the Jews there. But still, he's bringing prosperity for the other people. Now I myself, I wouldn't like to see nothing happen to the Jews. Why, my best customers was always Jews, and so are some of my best friends. But still, you got to admit one thing, sir. The Jews still has the money, and I got to close down my place."

Jacob glared at the man. "How much do I owe you?" he asked.

He paid and left. He had not been back for half an hour when his mother came in, carrying a little basket.

"Yankel," she cried. "Why didn't you come to see me? Not last night, not today. What is the matter?" she looked round. He had forgotten to close the cupboard, and she could see that it was empty. "Yankel," she said tremblingly, "you have taken away your suits."

"I have packed them away," he said, "so I will not have so much to do later on."

Her eyes filled with tears. "I wish you could stay longer. Only two more days. I don't think I will ever see you again."

He put his arm round her shoulders. "You shouldn't think about that, Mama," he said.

"I am thankful for everything," she said, sighing. "I will be happy always, as long as I live, because you came to me, even if it was only for a few weeks. As soon as you are gone, I will move in with Shaendl."

He looked quickly at her. "Why?" he asked. "You always said you wanted to be independent and to live by yourself."

"Yes," she said. "But now things are different. Shaendl needs me now. . . . What is this here on the floor?" She stooped down and picked up the painting which was still lying on the floor. "It's the picture," she said. "How did it get there?"

"It—it fell on the floor," he said hurriedly, "when I took it down from the wall."

"The frame is broken, and the picture is torn here."

"I know," he said, "I know." He wished he had remembered to put the thing away. "It was on the floor and I—I stepped on it by accident . . . Put it away Mama."

"I never liked this picture," she said. "I must go out shopping now. Shaendl is all alone. You go to her and wait there till I come back. See, maybe she needs something."

Shaendl, wearing a long, blue dressing-gown, was sewing when he came in. Her black hair, brushed straight back from her forehead, was gathered up in a loose bun. She turned round and motioned him to be quiet, because the baby was sleeping in his crib. Jacob drew up a chair and sat down beside her.

"Where were you last night?" she asked. "Mama was so worried about you, she almost went down to look for you."

"Ach," he mumbled. "I—I was talking with Reuben and it got late before I knew it." He gazed at the floor. He didn't know what to say to her, and yet he knew he must talk to her now, while his mother was out. He was afraid that Shaendl would not believe him either, and the thought was painful to him.

He sprang to his feet abruptly, and walked over to the window. Big, dark clouds had suddenly gathered, darkening the sky. From all sides the wind massed them and drove them together. There was a flash of lightning. Then a peal of thunder rolled across the sky and was lost in the distance.

"Is it raining?" she asked.

"Not yet."

I hope Mama won't get caught in the storm," she said. "Where are the boys?"

"They're over at a friend's place." She got up and went over to the crib where the baby was sleeping and put another blanket over him.

Jacob stood by the window, trying to deliberate, but his thoughts were an incoherent jumble. Then he turned suddenly and, without uttering a sound, sat down again beside her and grasped her hand in a gesture of pleading. Surprised, she dropped her sewing into her lap and looked at him. There was an expression so pitiful and helpless in his eyes that it frightened her.

"Jacob," she said uneasily. "What is it? What happened? Why do you look at me like that?"

He withdrew his hand from hers and turned his head away. "Shaendl," he said, his voice trembling and weak. "I know that you have waited for me to come to you. Reuben told me and he asked me to help you, but I didn't say a word, because Shaendl—Shaendl . . ."

She waited uneasily, not knowing what he was going to say.

His heart throbbed and sank. He turned his face to her and whispered, "I said nothing because, Shaendl, because I can't help you. I have no money to give you, Shaendl . . . Shaendl, please believe me . . . I am a poor man. I—I have no money to give to you."

Stunned, she drew a little away from him, and her face grew paler and paler.

He searched her face, trying to read there whether she believed him or not, and then bent towards her and laid his hand timidly over hers. "Reuben and Manya didn't believe me. They thought I was telling a lie. They thought I didn't want to help you. Shaendl, if it is not true what I say, then let me not get up from this chair again."

"No, no, no, Jacob," she cried. "Don't talk like that."

"You must believe me," he begged her. "Shaendl, you must believe me."

A shudder passed over her. She had counted on his help, and she saw it crumbling away before her.

When she said nothing, fear came over him. "You don't believe me," he cried. "You are like Manya and Reuben. You don't believe me. I know you don't believe me." He tightened his grip around her hand, and she gave a little shriek of pain. "I don't know what I can do so you will believe me," he said hopelessly, withdrawing his hand. "I can only tell you what is the truth. For thirty-three years, Shaendl, I have been working in a factory. But I am only a little worker there. A nobody. Every day. Every day for thirty-three years. I live now with my daughter Rosie. I have to get up early every morning. In the wintertime it is dark yet when I get up. I don't come to work at ten, like I told you. It was a lie, Shaendl. I press suits in a factory, Shaendl. For thirty-three years I have done the same thing, always the same thing." His voice was flat and he spoke helplessly, hardly knowing what he said, uttering short and jerky sentences.

She knew he was telling the truth, but it was unendurable for her to listen to him. She got up, softly, and stood over him, not taking her eyes off him, and a feeling of great pity welled up in her.

"Oh, Shaendl," he said, "I wish I had money. I would have given to you as much as you needed. Everything I would have given to you." He hid his face in his hands and bowed his head.

"Say you believe me, Shaendl," he begged her. "Say you believe I have told you the truth."

"I believe you," she said softly. "I believe you, Jacob."

"Really?" he insisted. "You really believe me, Shaendl?"

"I do," she said, "I do."

But he was not yet convinced. "I—I know you think like Manya and Reuben," he said desperately. "I know you don't believe me."

She lifted his face gently, and his eyes met hers, and her eyes were so infinitely merciful and so full of compassion, and he knew then that she believed him.

"Oh, Shaendl," he said, "my little Shaendl, why are you so

202

good to me?" He felt great love for her, and he wanted to humble himself before her. He grasped her hands and covered them with kisses, and drew her down on the chair beside him. "If you can, Shaendl, I beg you not to tell my mother as long as I am here. I thought that—that perhaps she needn't never know, but Reuben says you cannot keep a thing like this a secret. Perhaps not. Only don't tell her until I have gone away. Only two more days. Keep it a secret for two days. And then— then tell her if there is no way out."

"She won't know while you're here," Shaendl said. "I promise you."

"I begged Reuben and Manya, too," he said. "Only they didn't promise me. You think—you think they will tell her?"

She shook her head. "Reuben won't tell her, and I don't think Manya will, either. You don't have to be afraid."

"I wish I could be sure," he said. "I couldn't look in Mama's face and know all the time that she thinks I am a liar. She thought that I had made a great success, and that I am an important man. Perhaps twenty times since I am here she has asked me if they could go on working there in the factory without me. What will she say when she knows the truth? But I am not a liar, Shaendl, I only . . ." His voice trailed off and he slumped down in his chair and buried his face in his hands.

Suddenly the door flew open and Bernhardt came storming into the room. He was dripping wet. His face was red and the water was coursing down his cheeks.

"I was standing outside in the rain," he panted. "It was real nice after the heat. I feel nice and cool now. . . . I didn't know Uncle Jacob was here."

"Never mind, now," Shaendl said, frowning. "Go out and dry yourself. Where's Herman?"

"He's out in the street, trying to catch the rain in his mouth."

"Oh, my God!" she exclaimed. "All I need now is to have one of you fall sick."

She went to the window and leaned out. Herman was standing in the middle of the road, with his head thrown far back, and his mouth wide open.

"Herman!" she called. "Herman!"

Herman looked up.

"Come in immediately."

Jacob was sitting there, his eyes closed, paying no attention to what was going on.

Herman came in, his clothes clinging to his body as tightly

as an acrobat's costume. "Here I am," he announced. "It's raining hard outside."

"I can see that," said Shaendl. "Are you out of your mind, standing in the middle of the road, and trying to catch a few drops of rain?"

"I was thirsty," he said, "but all the drops fell on the side. Only a few fell into my mouth, and I'm still thirsty now . . . Hello, Uncle Jacob."

"Go and dry yourself and put on fresh clothes," Shaendl said.

"Uncle Jacob, will you come out and watch while I dry myself?"

"Go out now," Shaendl said. "Your uncle and I have important things to talk about." She closed the door.

Jacob was silent for a long time. Then he said, "Shaendl, Reuben said yesterday, that—that perhaps I shouldn't have come. And before I came my daughter Rosie said the same. She said a man like me can't afford to go on pleasure trips. To me this wasn't a pleasure trip, Shaendl. But now—now all of a sudden I don't know. Tell me, Shaendl, what do you think? Was it right that I should have come?"

"Yes," she said immediately, "it was more than right."

A smile passed over his face. "I am happy you said that. It makes me feel better." But then immediately his face became clouded again, and he asked softly, "What will you do now—about the debts?"

"What can I do?"

"But how will you make a living, how will you bring up you children?"

"I'll work," she said, and there was immense strength in her voice. "I'm a dressmaker. Times are bad, but I'll work hard and long. My children will always have enough to eat."

"Albert and Koch," he said, voicing a great fear, "they told me that things will get worse here. And you said so, too, when we were walking away from our father's grave. . . . If Hitler should come here, Shaendl, what will happen? What will you do?"

Her eyes wandered away from him, over to the crib where the baby slept. "Then—then we'll be like millions of other people, caught and helpless. We'll do what we can do. I will fight for my children as long as I can stand up, as long as there is a breath left in my body."

"Shaendl," he blurted out suddenly and sprang to his feet. "I have a little bit of money left. Seventy-six dollars. Take the money, Shaendl, please. It is only a little bit, but when I come home and I work again, I can send a little money now and then. It isn't much, but all I can do." He saw that she was going to say something, and he held up his hand. "Say nothing, Shaendl," he cried, "please don't thank me. In all my life I have never wanted to help a person the way I want to help you. But I feel like a helpless little child. My eyes have been opened, but I can't do a thing. You called to me to help you and I have come to put out a big fire with one pail of water."

CHAPTER

XIX

Jacob Grossman stood at the open window of the train, dressed in his brown, double-breasted suit, slowly waving his hand. His mother, supporting herself on Manya's arm, waved back, and the tears ran down her cheeks. Reuben, tall and heavy, took his hat from his bald head and moved it up and down in his hand. And now Manya, too, raised her arm, and her small white handkerchief fluttered in the air.

Jacob remained standing at the window long after they had disappeared from his sight. The wind was strong, and he turned his head away from the smoke and the sparks which came flying from the locomotive. They were now passing through the industrial section of the city, and the factory chimneys rose steep and high.

The outline of the city became more and more like a black, blurred mass, framed against the sky. The spire of St Stephen's towered long above the rest of the buildings, but then it, too, faded and could no longer be seen.

Fields stretched wide on both sides, and the mountains rose in the far distance. Cows grazed passively in green, hedged-in meadows and lifted their heads and stared stupidly at the train. Peasants stopped their work in the fields when the train passed by them, and sometimes they waved.

After a while Jacob closed the window and sat down. The day passed quickly. Lights went on in the villages and in the hamlets, and the train raced by them, and they dropped back into the night.

Jacob was tired and hot. From the rack above his seat he took down his little grey portmanteau to get his soap and towel. And when he opened it, he saw Tassigny's painting right on top. He passed his hand over his face because he could not believe that it was there. How did it get there? He had not seen it again after he told his mother to put it away. She must have put it in this morning, he thought, after he had finished his last minute packing.

He took the painting into his hands and looked at it through hazy eyes. He could not distinguish the colours. It seemed all one patch of colour now, a yellowish-green patch of colour.

Did his mother perhaps suspect anything? Did she believe him when he told her that it had fallen down from the wall and that he had accidentally stepped on it? Had she perhaps told Manya about it, and heard from Manya what really happened? No, he thought, no. He was certain that his mother had not known anything while he was still there. She had come to him yesterday and had thanked him for the money he had given to Shaendl. She didn't know then, he was sure about that.

Perhaps my mother knows now already, he thought suddenly, and a cold shiver ran down his spine. Perhaps Manya has told her when they were going home from the station. Perhaps Manya has said to her, "Yankel was lying to you for all these years. He was never a rich man. Never. And he was never an important man. He told a lie when he said he is a designer. He pressed suits in a factory, and he is only a poor man. He is poor like us all."

He slid open the window to let some air in. His hand moved along the frame of the painting where it was broken and splintered. He remembered the first evening, and the way he had shown off the picture, trying to impress them, trying to seem like an important man.

Perhaps, he thought, Manya has said to her, "Yankel didn't want to give money to Shaendl. He is like all the rich men. When it comes to giving money, they are all poor." Perhaps my mother is going to bed now, and her heart is heavy because she knows.

His hand passed over the canvas, felt the spot where his heel had ripped a hole in it, and he thought of Manya gloating and mocking, "What did he do, your Frenchman? He held a revolver to your head?" He stared at the picture, hating it. He thought of Shaendl and the children. He thought of Albert and Koch, and a deep anguish rose in his breast.

"Noo?" he said in bitter exasperation, glaring at the picture. And in final despair, "Noo?"

A tremor went through his body, and then quickly, and with a sharp twist of his hand, he flung the torn painting out of the window into the darkness of the night.

THE NEW CANADIAN LIBRARY